SOVEREIGN HEARTS

RAVEN FONTAINE

Indie Pen Press

TURNING DREAMS INTO BESTSELLERS

Indie Pen Press
Gig Harbor WA 98332
IndiePenPress.com

Second Edition: October 2024

The characters and events portrayed in this book are fictitious. Any similarity to real persons, living or dead, is coincidental and not intended by the author.

Paperback ISBN 979-8-9916530-9-1

 Created with Vellum

ONE
THE WEIGHT OF POWER

Seraphina Blackwood's footsteps echoed through the marble halls of the Council chambers; each click of her heels was a reminder of the power she wielded. The air hung heavy with the scent of polished wood and ancient parchment, starkly contrasting the acrid smog of the outskirts where she had grown up.

As she approached the towering doors of the main chamber, a young male servant scurried past, eyes downcast, arms laden with piles of documents. Seraphina paused to watch him disappear around a corner. His hunched shoulders and quick, nervous movements stirred something in her - a memory, perhaps, or a twinge of some emotion she couldn't quite name.

She shook it off and straightened her immaculately tailored suit, her fingers brushing the small scar on her left forearm. The rough texture beneath her fingertips transported her momentarily to another time, another life - one of dirt and struggle, of hopes whispered in dark alleys and dreams that seemed impossible.

"You're late, Councilwoman Blackwood," a silky voice came from behind her, shattering the moment.

Seraphina turned, her green eyes meeting Lady Meridia Frost's icy blue gaze. The older woman stood like a statue; her silver hair pulled back in a tight knot, her face a mask of cold authority. The Council's pendant —a stylized fist clutching a lightning bolt—glowed at her throat, a constant reminder of the power she wielded.

"My apologies, Lady Meridia," Seraphina said, tilting her head slightly. "There was an incident in the outskirts that required my attention."

Meridia's lips curled into a thin smile. "Ah yes, your... pet project. Tell me, Seraphina, do you really think you can bring order to those chaos-ridden slums?"

Seraphina's jaw tightened, but she kept her voice level. "Every part of Elyria deserves our attention, my lady. Even the outlying districts."

"Indeed," Meridia murmured, her eyes narrowing. "Well, shall we? The Council awaits."

As they approached the doors, two male guards snapped to attention, their faces impassive masks. With a wave of Meridia's hand, they opened the heavy doors, revealing the large circular room beyond.

Twelve women sat around a crescent-shaped table; their faces turned expectantly toward the entrance. Seraphina felt their eyes on her as she walked to her seat, a heady mixture of respect, envy, and suspicion. The air in the room crackled with an almost palpable energy- the collective power of Elyria's ruling elite.

Seraphina's eyes were drawn to the massive window behind the High Matriarch's chair as she sat. Beyond the gleaming spires of the inner city, she could see the hazy outline of the outer districts, a patchwork of crumbling buildings and belching smokestacks. The stark contrast always unsettled her.

To her left, Alderwoman Elena Darkwater leaned forward, her voice a low whisper. "Rough night in the slums, Seraphina? You look... distracted."

Seraphina turned to meet Elena's sharp gaze. The woman's dark eyes glittered with barely concealed curiosity - or was it suspicion?

"Nothing I can't handle," Seraphina replied coolly. "Though I wonder how long it's been since you've set foot outside the inner city, Elena. Perhaps you'd like to join me next time? See for yourself the realities faced by our less fortunate sisters?"

Elena's smile tightened, a flash of something - disgust? Fear? - crossing her face before she could hide it. "Some of us prefer to focus on more... productive endeavors, Councilwoman Blackwood. But by all means, continue your charity work if it pleases you."

Before Seraphina could reply, High Matriarch Evelyn Stormbringer's voice cut through the murmur of the assembled councilwomen. "Let us begin. Lady Meridia, your report on the recent... disturbances?"

Meridia rose, her voice carrying easily over the chamber. "Thank you, High Matriarch. As you all know, there have been increasing incidents of unrest in the outer districts. Factory sabotage, resource theft, and most alarmingly, whispers of organized resistance."

A wave of unease swept through the room. Seraphina leaned forward, her mind racing. She had heard rumors, of course, but to listen to them confirmed in the Council chambers...

"What proof do we have of this organized resistance?" Seraphina asked, her voice breaking the tension.

Meridia's eyes snapped to hers, cold and calculating. "Patterns in the attacks, Councilwoman Blackwood. Coordinated attacks on key infrastructure. And this."

With a flick of her wrist, Meridia activated the holographic display in the center of the room. A symbol appeared, slowly rotating: a fist breaking free from chains.

"This mark has been appearing throughout the outer districts," Meridia continued. "Our intelligence suggests it is the symbol of a group calling themselves the Sovereign Hearts."

Seraphina's breath caught in her throat. The name stirred something in her, a memory of whispered conversations in dark alleys, of desperate eyes pleading for change.

High Matriarch Evelyn leaned forward, her weathered face wrinkled with worry. The cybernetic implant in her temple glowed faintly, a reminder of the advanced technology that kept Elyria's elite in power. "What do they want?"

"To destroy everything we've built," Meridia said, her voice harsh. "They speak of equality, of dismantling the natural order. They would see men given the same rights as women, would see us throw away centuries of progress and stability."

Murmurs of outrage filled the room. Seraphina remained silent, her mind racing. She thought of the men she'd seen in the outlying districts, bent and broken from hard labor. Of the boys torn from their mother's arms to be sorted and categorized like cattle.

Councilwoman Vera Ironheart pounded her fist on the table. "This is unacceptable! We must put down this rebellion before it spreads. Increase surveillance in the outlying districts, double the Guardian patrols-"

"And risk further inflaming the situation?" Seraphina interjected, her voice sharp. "Brute force isn't always the answer, Councilwoman Ironheart. We must understand the root of this discontent before we can address it."

Vera's eyes flashed dangerously. "Careful, Blackwood. One might think you sympathize with these... rebels."

The air in the chamber grew thick with tension. Seraphina could feel the weight of every gaze upon her, judging, assessing. She forced her face into a mask of calm indifference, even as her heart raced.

"I sympathize with the stability and prosperity of Elyria," she said coolly. "Which is why I believe a more measured approach is necessary."

High Matriarch Evelyn raised a hand, silencing the brewing argument. "Enough. Lady Meridia, what do you suggest we do about this threat?"

Meridia's lips curled into a cold smile. "I'm glad you asked, High Matriarch. Given Councilwoman Blackwood's... unique background and familiarity with the outer districts, I believe she's the perfect person to lead our response."

Seraphina's heart raced. This was a test, she realized. A chance to prove her loyalty to the Council to solidify her position among the elite. But at what cost?

"You want me to root out this resistance?" she asked, already knowing the answer.

"Not just root them out," Meridia said, her eyes glittering. "I want you to crush them. Make such a terrible example of them that no one will dare challenge us again."

The room fell silent, all eyes on Seraphina. She could feel the weight of their expectations pressing down on her, suffocating her. She thought of her childhood in the outskirts, of the friends and family she'd left behind in her rise to power. And she thought of the oath she'd taken when she joined the Council to protect and serve all of Elyria.

Seraphina stood, her decision made. "I accept this task, Lady Meridia. I will do whatever is necessary to maintain order in our city."

Meridia nodded, satisfaction shining in her eyes. "Excellent. You will have the full resources of the Department of Order at your disposal. I suggest you start with the slave markets. Our intelligence suggests that the Resistance has targeted them for recruitment."

"The slave markets?" Seraphina asked, a shiver running down her spine. She hadn't set foot in one since her ascension to the Council.

"Yes," Meridia said. "As a matter of fact, there's an auction scheduled for tomorrow. A new batch of men from the breeding programs. It would be the perfect opportunity to observe and gather information."

Seraphina nodded, her mouth dry. "Of course. I'll attend in person."

As the meeting was adjourned and the councilwomen filed out, Seraphina remained in her seat, staring out at the hazy skyline of the outer districts. The weight of her task settled over her like a shroud.

A hand on her shoulder jolted her from her thoughts. She looked up to see Lady Meridia standing over her, a predatory smile on her face.

"I have high hopes for you, Seraphina," Meridia said softly. "Do not disappoint me."

As Meridia's footsteps faded, Seraphina turned back to the window. In the distance, a plume of black smoke rose from the city's outskirts, a stark reminder of the unrest bubbling beneath Elyria's pristine surface.

She stood, smoothed her suit, and made her way out of the chambers. The corridors were quieter now; the day's business concluded. As she walked, her mind raced with plans and contingencies.

A muffled sob caught her attention. Seraphina stopped and looked down a side corridor. Huddled in a corner was a young woman - one of the cleaning staff, judging by her uniform. Her shoulders trembled with soft sobs.

For a moment, Seraphina hesitated. Then, against her better judgment, she approached.

"Are you all right?" she asked, keeping her voice low.

The woman's head snapped up, her eyes widening in horror as she recognized Seraphina. She scrambled to her feet, wiping away tears. "I'm so sorry, Councilwoman. I didn't mean to... I'll get right back to work."

"Wait," Seraphina said, holding up a hand. "What's wrong? Why are you crying?"

The woman's lower lip quivered. "It's... it's my brother, Councilwoman. He's being sent to the slave markets tomorrow. I thought... I hoped to buy his contract and keep him safe, but..." She trailed off, fresh tears streaming down her cheeks.

Seraphina's chest tightened. She thought of the auction the next day and the task Meridia had given her. "What's your name?"

"Lyra, Councilwoman."

Seraphina nodded, making a mental note. "Go home, Lyra. Take care of yourself. And... don't lose hope."

Lyra's eyes widened, a flicker of something - gratitude? Suspicion? - crossing her face. She bowed deeply and hurried away, leaving Seraphina alone in the corridor.

As she exited the Council building, Seraphina's mind swirled with conflicting thoughts and emotions. The gleaming downtown towers loomed above her, a testament to the power and wealth of Elyria's elite. But now, more than ever, she could see the shadows they cast.

Tomorrow, she would descend into those shadows. Tomorrow, she would face the very system she'd fought so hard to escape.

And tomorrow, she would have to decide where her true loyalties lay.

As Seraphina stepped out into the fading light of day, a cool breeze carried the distant sounds of the city hum of hovercrafts, the chatter of women going about their business, and the dull clang and buzz of the factories in the outer districts. The familiar cacophony of Elyria washed over her, but for the first time in years, it filled her not with pride but with a deep, gnawing unease.

She took a deep breath and squared her shoulders. Whatever challenges tomorrow might bring, she would face them head-on. She had fought too hard and climbed too high to falter now.

With a final glance at the darkening sky, Seraphina made her way to her quarters, each step bringing her closer to a future that suddenly seemed far less confident than it had this morning.

TWO
THE AUCTION BLOCK

The stench hit Seraphina first - a nauseating mix of sweat, fear and desperation. She stood at the entrance to the slave market, her face an impassive mask even as her stomach churned. The cavernous space before her was buzzing with activity, a stark contrast to the sterile corridors of the Council chambers.

Women of varying social status milled about, their chattering a discordant symphony. Some wore the crisp uniforms of factory supervisors, others the fine silks of the elite. All shared the same predatory gleam in their eyes as they surveyed the merchandise.

And the merchandise... Seraphina's eyes swept over the rows of men and boys, stripped to the waist and chained to long metal bars. Their eyes were downcast, their shoulders slumped in defeat. She remembered standing among them once, a lifetime ago.

"Councilwoman Blackwood," a clipped voice cut through her thoughts. "What an... unexpected pleasure."

Seraphina turned to face Madame Corvus, the overseer of the market. The woman's pinched face and beady eyes reminded Seraphina of the carrion birds that circled the outskirts.

"Madame Corvus," Seraphina nodded, keeping her voice neutral. "I trust you have received word of my visit?"

"Of course, of course," Corvus smiled, though her eyes remained cold. "We are honored to have you here. Though I must admit it's unusual for a councilwoman to grace us with her presence. Is there something in particular you're looking for?"

Seraphina met the woman's gaze. "I am here on official business. The Council has concerns about... irregularities in recent shipments."

Corvus's smile faltered for a moment before snapping back into place. "Irregularities? I assure you, Councillor, every-thing here is in perfect order. But please, allow me to give you a tour. You can see for yourself how smoothly we operate."

As they walked, Corvus prattled on about efficiency rates and profit margins. Seraphina tuned her out, focusing instead on the faces around her. She was looking for signs of defiance, any hint of the resistance Meridia had spoken of.

They passed a group of boys, no more than twelve or thirteen, huddled together in a pen. One looked up to meet Seraphina's gaze. The raw fear in his eyes made her gasp.

"Ah yes, our latest batch from the breeding programs,"

Corvus said, following Seraphina's gaze. "Fine specimens, don't you think? They'll fetch a good price."

Seraphina swallowed hard, forcing her voice to remain calm. "And their mothers?"

Corvus waved his hand dismissively. "Reassigned, of course. Can't have them forming attachments. Bad for productivity."

Before Seraphina could respond, a commotion erupted from the other end of the market. Shouts and the sound of breaking glass echoed through the cavernous space.

"What's going on?" Seraphina demanded, already moving toward the commotion.

Corvus hurried after her, nervous. "I'm sure it's nothing, Councillor. Probably a disagreement over the bidding..."

But as they rounded a corner, Seraphina saw that it was far more than a simple disagreement. A group of slaves had broken free of their bonds and were fighting the guards. At the center of the chaos stood a man, tall and powerfully built, his dark hair wild and his eyes blazing with defiance.

"Freedom for Elyria!" he shouted, his voice carrying over the marketplace. "Down with the Council!"

The symbol Meridia had shown them - a fist breaking free of chains - was crudely tattooed on his shoulder.

"Seize them!" Corvus shouted, her composure shattered. "Call for reinforcements!"

The guards swarmed toward the rebellious slaves. Seraphina watched as the leader fought with a ferocity she'd never seen before. He moved with purpose, not just lashing out blindly, but strategically disabling his opponents.

Their eyes locked across the chaos, and for a moment, time seemed to stand still. Seraphina saw in his gaze not only anger, but intelligence, determination... hope.

Then a guard's shock baton connected with his side and he crumpled to the floor.

"Take them to isolation!" Corvus barked as the guards subdued the last of the rebels. She turned to Seraphina and smoothed her crumpled clothes. "My deepest apologies, Councillor. I assure you, this is most unusual."

SERAPHINA BARELY HEARD HER. Her eyes were glued to the fallen rebel leader as the guards dragged him away. "Who is he?"

Corvus consulted a datapad. "Let's see... Ah, here we are. Niko Stormwind. Troublemaker. He's been here before, always causing trouble. I'll make sure he's properly disciplined this time."

"No," Seraphina said, surprising herself with the strength in her voice. "I want to question him myself."

Corvus blinked, surprised. "I... of course, Councillor. But surely you don't want to get your hands dirty with such riffraff?"

Seraphina fixed her with a cold stare. "Are you questioning a direct order from a member of the Council, Madame Corvus?"

"N-no, of course not," Corvus stammered. "I will have him prepared for interrogation immediately."

As Corvus scurried off, Seraphina took a deep breath and centered herself. This was it - the trail Meridia had sent her to find. But as she thought of the fire in Niko's eyes, the conviction in his voice, she couldn't shake the feeling that she was standing on the edge of something much bigger and more dangerous than she'd anticipated.

THE INTERROGATION ROOM was small and stark, its white walls almost glowing under the harsh fluorescent lights. Seraphina sat at a metal table, her back straight, her face a careful mask of neutrality. Across from her, bound to his chair, sat Niko Stormwind.

Up close, she could see the scars that crisscrossed his arms and torso-marks of a life spent in rebellion. His dark eyes watched her warily, but there was no fear in them. Only defiance.

"Do you know who I am?" Seraphina asked, her voice cool and measured.

Niko's lips curled into a sardonic smile. "Oh, I know exactly who you are, Councilwoman Blackwood. The Council's attack dog, sent to sniff out trouble in the lower ranks."

Seraphina didn't take the bait. "You caused quite a scene out there. 'Freedom for Elyria,' was it? Bold words for a slave."

"We're all slaves in Elyria," Niko shot back. "Some of us are lucky enough to have a longer chain, but a cage is still a cage, no matter how gilded."

His words struck a chord in Seraphina, echoing thoughts she'd buried long ago. She pushed the feeling aside and focused on the task at hand. "The symbol on your arm - the Sovereign Hearts. Tell me about them."

Niko's eyes narrowed. "Why? So you can hunt them down? Crush them like you do everything else that threatens your precious order?"

"I'm trying to understand," Seraphina said, leaning forward slightly. "What do you hope to accomplish? The Council's power is absolute. Any rebellion is doomed to failure."

"Is it?" Niko challenged. "Then why are you here, Councilwoman? Why would they send one of their own to investigate if they're not worried?"

Seraphina paused, carefully considering her next words. "The Council believes in maintaining peace and stability. If there are... issues that need to be addressed, it's in everyone's best interest to resolve them peacefully."

Niko laughed, a harsh, bitter sound. "Peace? Stability? Is that what you call this?" He rattled his chains for emphasis. "You live in your towers, Councilwoman, playing politics while the rest of us suffer. But change is coming, whether you like it or not."

"Is that a threat?" Seraphina asked, her voice hardening.

"It's a promise," Niko replied, his gaze intense. "The Sovereign Hearts aren't just a group. We are an idea. And ideas, Councilwoman, are bulletproof."

Seraphina stood, her chair scraping the floor. "Bold words, Mr. Stormwind. But ideas won't protect you from what's coming. The Council will not tolerate dissent."

She turned to leave, but Niko's voice stopped her at the door.

"You're one of us, you know," he said quietly. "Or you were, once. I've heard the whispers, Councilwoman. The girl from the outskirts who climbed her way to the top. Tell me, do you ever look down from your tower and remember where you came from?"

Seraphina's hand froze on the doorknob. For a moment, the mask slipped and she turned to face him. "You don't know anything about me."

Niko's eyes softened, just a fraction. "Don't I? I see it in your eyes, Councillor. The doubts. The questions. You're not as convinced of the Council's justice as you pretend to be."

"You are wrong," Seraphina said, but the words rang hollow even to her own ears.

"Am I?" Niko pressed. "Then prove it. Look me in the eye and tell me you believe in what the Council is doing. Tell me you believe this system is just."

Seraphina opened her mouth, denial on the tip of her tongue. But when she met Niko's gaze, the words died in her throat. In that moment, all her carefully constructed walls crumbled, and she saw herself reflected in his eyes - the frightened little girl from the outskirts, the woman who had risen to power on the backs of others, the council-woman who, deep down, still questioned everything.

"I thought so," Niko said quietly.

Seraphina straightened, rebuilding her walls brick by brick. "You will be held here until the Council decides what to do with you. I suggest you use this time to reconsider your position, Mr. Stormwind. Cooperation may be your only chance for leniency."

With that, she left the room, her heart pounding. As the door closed behind her, she leaned against the wall and took deep breaths to calm herself.

"Councilwoman?" a tentative voice broke through her thoughts.

Seraphina looked up to see Lyra, the cleaning woman from the Council building, standing in front of her. The young woman's eyes were red, and her hands were twisted nervously in front of her.

"Lyra?" Seraphina frowned. "What are you doing here?"

"I... I came to bid on my brother's contract," Lyra said, her voice shaking. "But I don't have enough credits. Please, Councilor, isn't there anything you can do?"

Seraphina's mind raced. She thought of the boys she'd seen earlier, of Niko's words about change coming to Elyria. She thought of her own rise from the outskirts, of the compromises she'd made along the way.

"What's your brother's name?" she asked.

"Theo," Lyra replied, hope lighting her face. "Theo Marsh."

Seraphina nodded, making a decision she knew could change everything. "Wait here."

She walked back into the main auction area, her presence causing a ripple of whispers in the crowd. She found Madame Corvus overseeing the bidding of a group of strong, young men.

"Madame Corvus," Seraphina called, her voice carrying over the din. "I need you to remove a slave from the auction. Theo Marsh."

Corvus blinked in surprise. "Pull him? But Councilor, the bidding has already..."

"Did I stutter?" Seraphina cut her off, her voice sharp. "Consider it impounded for Council business. I'll take full responsibility."

Corvus nodded, chastened. "Of course, Councilor. Right away."

As Corvus hurried off to make the arrangements, Seraphina felt the weight of dozens of eyes on her. She turned to survey the crowd, and for the first time, she truly saw them. The desperate hope in the slaves' eyes. The mixture of curiosity and suspicion from the buyers. And in the shadows, a few faces watching her with something like recognition.

She made her way back to where Lyra was waiting, her heart pounding with the magnitude of what she was about to do.

"Your brother will be released into your care," Seraphina said softly. "I've made the arrangements."

Lyra's eyes widened and filled with tears. "Councilwoman, I... I don't know how to thank you."

"Don't," Seraphina said sharply. Then, softening her tone, she added, "Take care of him, Lyra. And... be careful. Both of you."

As Lyra hurried off to collect her brother, Seraphina stood alone in the corridor, the sounds of the auction echoing around her. She thought of Niko, still chained in the interrogation room. Of Meridia, waiting for her report. Of the Council, with its intrigues and politics.

For the first time in years, Seraphina questioned everything she had become. And as she left the slave market, she couldn't shake the feeling that she had just taken the first step down a path from which there was no turning back.

The sun was setting as Seraphina stepped out into the street, casting long shadows across the pristine walkways of downtown. In the distance, the smokestacks of the outer districts belched black smoke into the darkening sky. She paused, gazing out over the city she had sworn to serve and protect.

But as the last rays of sunlight glinted off the towers of the Council building, Seraphina couldn't help but wonder: who was she really protecting? And at what cost?

Taking a deep breath, she straightened her shoulders and made her way to her quarters. Tomorrow she would face Meridia and the Council. Tomorrow she would have to decide where her loyalties truly lay.

But tonight... tonight the carefully constructed world of Councilwoman Seraphina Blackwood began to crumble.

THREE
SHADOWS OF DOUBT

The early morning light barely penetrated the thick smog that hung over Elyria as Seraphina made her way to the Council chambers. Her steps echoed through the empty corridors, each click of her heels a reminder of the weight she carried. The events of the slave market replayed in her mind, a constant loop of faces and voices she couldn't shake.

As she approached the towering doors of the main chamber, a figure emerged from the shadows. Lady Meridia stood waiting, her silver hair gleaming in the dim light, her eyes sharp and calculating.

"Councilwoman Blackwood," Meridia's voice was soft as silk, but with an edge that could cut. "You're early. Eager to share your findings?"

Seraphina met her gaze steadily. "I have my report ready, Lady Meridia."

"Excellent," Meridia smiled, though it didn't reach her eyes. "Walk with me."

They moved down the corridor, their steps synchronized in an uneasy rhythm. Seraphina could feel Meridia studying her, looking for weaknesses.

"I trust your visit to the slave markets was... enlightening?" Meridia asked.

Seraphina chose her words carefully. "It was certainly enlightening. The situation in the outer districts is more volatile than we realized."

Meridia's eyes narrowed. "Oh? Tell me."

"There was an incident," Seraphina began, keeping her voice neutral. "A group of slaves tried to revolt. They were quickly put down, but their leader... he spoke of a movement. The Sovereign Hearts."

"Ah," Meridia nodded, unsurprised. "And did that leader have anything useful to say?"

Seraphina's mind flashed back to Niko's intense gaze, his words echoing in her ears. She pushed the memory aside. "He was uncooperative. But his actions speak for themselves. The unrest is spreading, Lady Meridia. If we don't address it soon, we may have a full-scale rebellion on our hands."

They reached a large window overlooking the city. Meridia paused, her gaze sweeping over the sprawling metropolis below. "And what do you suggest, Seraphina? How do we... address this unrest?"

This was a test, Seraphina realized. Her answer now could determine everything. She thought of Lyra and her brother, of the fear in the eyes of the boys at the slave market. And she thought of Niko, his defiance in the face of over-whelming odds.

"We have to understand," Seraphina said slowly. "These people, they are desperate. Crushing them will only fuel their rage. We need to address the root causes-"

"Root causes?" Meridia interrupted, her voice sharp. "The root cause is their inability to accept their place in society. We've given them order, stability. What more could they want?"

"Freedom," Seraphina said before she could stop herself.

Meridia turned to her, eyes flashing. "Freedom? A dangerous word, Councilwoman Blackwood. One might think you sympathize with these rebels."

Seraphina's heart raced, but her face remained impassive. "I sympathize with the stability of Elyria, Lady Meridia. But we cannot ignore the reality of the situation. If we do not address their grievances, we will face a much larger problem."

For a long moment, Meridia studied her, her gaze penetrating. Then she nodded slowly. "Perhaps you're right. We need more information. I want you to continue your research, Seraphina. Infiltrate this Sovereign Hearts movement. Find out who their leaders are, what they're up to. And when you have all the information we need..."

She leaned closer, her voice dropping to a whisper. "We'll crush them. Completely."

Seraphina stifled a shudder. "Of course, Lady Meridia. I'll begin immediately."

"Good," Meridia smiled, cold and predatory. "Oh, and Seraphina? Be careful. It would be a shame if you got too... close to your subjects. We wouldn't want your judgment clouded by misplaced sympathies."

The threat in her words was clear. Seraphina nodded, her mouth dry. "I understand."

As Meridia glided away, Seraphina remained at the window, her reflection ghostly in the glass. The woman staring back at her suddenly seemed unfamiliar, a stranger wearing her face.

She thought of the choice before her - betray the rebels or betray the Council. Either way, she would be a traitor to someone. The weight of it pressed down on her, threatening to crush her under its enormity.

A faint chime interrupted her thoughts. The Council meeting was about to begin. Squaring her shoulders, Seraphina turned away from the window and made her way to the chamber. Whatever storm was coming, she would face it head on.

The council chamber hummed with excitement as Seraphina took her seat. The other Council members watched her with a mixture of curiosity and suspicion, no doubt aware of her recent mission. High Matriarch Evelyn sat at the head of the table, her weathered face impassive as she called the meeting to order.

"Councilwoman Blackwood," Evelyn's voice carried easily across the room. "I believe you have a report for us?"

Seraphina stood, aware of every eye on her. She took a deep breath and centered herself. "Thank you, High Matriarch.

As you all know, I've been assigned to investigate the recent unrest in the outer districts, particularly the slave markets."

She paused, choosing her next words carefully. "What I found was... troubling. The discontent among the lower classes is more widespread than we first thought. There is talk of an organized resistance movement calling itself the Sovereign Hearts."

A murmur rippled through the chamber. Councilwoman Elena Darkwater leaned forward, her eyes narrowing. "And what exactly do these 'Sovereign Hearts' want?"

"Equality," Seraphina said simply. "They speak of a world where men and women are equal, where the class system is dismantled.

The room erupted into chaos. Voices overlapped, some outraged, others dismissive. Councilwoman Vera Ironheart pounded her fist on the table.

"This is madness!" she shouted. "Equality? Have they forgotten the chaos of the old world? The wars, the destruction? It was women who brought order out of the ashes. We cannot allow these... these anarchists to undo all that we have built!"

"Calm yourselves," High Matriarch Evelyn's voice cut through the din. She turned to Seraphina, her gaze piercing. "Proceed, Councilwoman Blackwood. What do you suggest we do about this threat?"

Seraphina felt the weight of the moment press down on her. Her next words could determine the future of Elyria. She thought of Niko, of his fire and conviction. And she thought of Meridia's cold smile, her promise to crush the rebellion.

"We must understand them," Seraphina said, her voice calm. "This movement didn't happen overnight. There are underlying problems that we've ignored for too long. Poverty, oppression, lack of opportunity - these are the sparks that ignite rebellion."

"So you're suggesting we surrender?" Elena scoffed. "Give in to their demands?"

"No," Seraphina shook her head. "But we must address the root causes. Improve conditions in the outskirts. Offer avenues for advancement. Show the people that we hear them, that we're willing to change."

The room fell silent, the councilwomen exchanging uneasy glances. Seraphina could see the doubt in their eyes, the fear of losing their grip on power.

Finally, High Matriarch Evelyn spoke. "Your words carry weight, Councilwoman Blackwood. But words alone will not solve this crisis. We need action. Lady Meridia, what are your thoughts?"

Meridia rose, her face a mask of calm determination. "Councilwoman Blackwood's insights are valuable, but I fear she underestimates the danger we face. This Sovereign Hearts movement is a cancer, and we must cut it out before it spreads. I suggest we increase security in the outlying districts, double the number of Guardians on patrol. Any sign of dissent must be crushed immediately."

"And if that fails?" Seraphina challenged, her heart pounding. "If our show of force only fuels their anger?"

Meridia's smile was cold. "Then we eliminate the threat altogether. We've done it before, Councilwoman Blackwood. We can do it again."

The implications of her words hung heavy in the air. Seraphina thought of the stories she'd heard as a child, whispered tales of entire districts being "cleansed" for the good of Elyria. She'd always dismissed them as exaggerations, myths meant to keep the lower classes in line. But now, seeing the steel in Meridia's eyes, she wasn't so sure.

"Surely there's another way," Seraphina argued, fighting to keep her voice steady. "If we go down this road, we risk losing everything. The people will turn against us."

"The people will do as they're told," Councilwoman Ironheart snapped. "It worked for centuries, it will work now."

"And if it doesn't?" Seraphina pressed. "What if we push them too far and they push back? We could be looking at an all-out civil war."

The room fell silent again, the weight of her words sinking in. Even Meridia looked troubled, her usual confidence shaken for a moment.

High Matriarch Evelyn leaned forward, her aged hands clasped in front of her. "You have given us much to consider, Councilwoman Blackwood. But reflection alone will not solve our problems. We need more information. Lady Meridia, your plan to increase security has merit. See it done. And Councilwoman Blackwood..."

Seraphina held her breath and waited.

"You will continue your investigation," Evelyn said. "Infiltrate this Sovereign Hearts movement. Learn their plans, their weaknesses. And when you have what we need, report to us. Then, and only then, will we decide how to proceed."

Seraphina nodded, her mind racing. It wasn't ideal, but it bought her time. Time to find a solution, to prevent the bloodshed she now saw looming on the horizon.

"This meeting is adjourned," Evelyn announced. "May the Mother guide us in these troubled times."

As the council members filed out, Seraphina remained in her seat, her thoughts a whirlwind. She had a task now, a mission that could determine the fate of Elyria. But whose side was she really on? The Council she had sworn to serve, or the rebels fighting for a world she had once dreamed of?

A hand on her shoulder jolted her from her reverie. She looked up to see Lady Meridia standing over her, a strange mixture of pride and suspicion in her eyes.

"Well played, Seraphina," Meridia said quietly. "You've bought yourself some time. Use it wisely."

"What do you mean?" Seraphina asked, her guard up.

Meridia's smile was knowing. "I see more than you think, my love. The doubt in your eyes, the hesitation in your voice. You are torn, aren't you? Between your duty and your... sympathies."

Seraphina's blood ran cold, but she kept her face neutral. "My loyalty is to Elyria, Lady Meridia. To its people and its future."

"As is mine," Meridia nodded. "Remember that, Seraphina. Remember where you came from and how far you've come. Don't throw it all away for some foolish dream of equality."

With that, she turned and walked away, leaving Seraphina alone in the empty chamber. The weight of her words weighed on Seraphina, a reminder of all she had to lose.

As she finally rose to leave, a movement caught her eye. A figure lurked in the shadows of the gallery - one of the male servants, she assumed. But as she watched, he raised his hand, revealing a familiar symbol tattooed on his wrist: a fist breaking free from chains.

THEIR EYES MET for a brief moment, and Seraphina saw in his gaze a mixture of hope and determination that she recognized all too well. Then he was gone, fading back into the shadows as if he'd never been there.

Seraphina's heart raced. The Sovereign Hearts were everywhere, it seemed. Even here, in the heart of the Council's power. And now she was to infiltrate their ranks, to betray them to the very system they were fighting against.

As she left the Council chambers, her mind whirled with possibilities and dangers. She had a choice to make, a path to choose. And whatever she chose would change the fate of Elyria forever.

The corridors of the Council building seemed longer than usual as Seraphina made her way out. Each step felt heavy, weighed down by the enormity of the task before her. When she reached the main entrance, she paused and looked out over the city she had sworn to protect.

The sun was setting, casting long shadows over Elyria. In the fading light, the stark divide between the gleaming towers of the inner city and the smoky haze of the outer districts seemed more pronounced than ever. It was a physical manifestation of the choice she faced - the glittering promise of power versus the gritty reality of revolution.

A faint sound caught her attention. Turning, she saw Lyra, the cleaning woman, pushing a cart of supplies. Their eyes met, and Lyra's face lit up with recognition and gratitude.

"Councilwoman Blackwood," Lyra said in a low voice. "I... I wanted to thank you again. For my brother. You've given us hope."

Seraphina nodded, her throat tightening. "How is he?"

"Recovering," Lyra smiled, though it was tinged with sadness. "He's... different. The markets have changed him. But he's alive, and he's free. Thanks to you."

"Be careful, Lyra," Seraphina warned, glancing around to make sure they weren't overheard. "These are dangerous times."

Lyra's eyes hardened, a flash of determination breaking through her soft exterior. "We are always cautious, Councilwoman. But we're not afraid anymore. Change is coming. I hope... I hope you'll be on the right side of it when it does."

Before Seraphina could answer, Lyra hurried away, pushing her cart down the corridor. Seraphina watched her go, her words echoing in her mind. Change is coming. The right side of this. But what was the right side? And how could she be sure she was on it?

As she stepped out into the cooling evening air, Seraphina's resolve hardened. She had a mission now, a chance to see this Sovereign Hearts movement for herself. To understand their goals, their methods. And perhaps find her own way forward.

The city stretched before her, a maze of light and shadow, of hope and oppression. Somewhere out there, Niko and his fellow rebels were plotting their next move. And somewhere in the depths of the Council chambers, Meridia and her allies were plotting to destroy her.

Seraphina stood at the crossroads, between two worlds. As she descended the steps of the Council building, she couldn't shake the feeling that her next actions would set in motion events that would change Elyria forever.

The night air carried the faint sounds of the city - the hum of machinery, the distant shouts from the outskirts, the low hum of patrol drones overhead. Seraphina took a deep breath, steeling herself for what was to come.

Tomorrow she would begin her infiltration of the Sovereign Hearts. Tomorrow she would take the first step down a path from which there might be no return.

But tonight... tonight she would prepare. For in the game she was about to play, the stakes were nothing less than the future of Elyria itself.

FOUR
THE UNDERGROUND

The outer districts of Elyria were a world apart from the gleaming towers of the inner city. Here, the air hung heavy with smog, the acrid smell of industrial waste burning Seraphina's nostrils as she made her way through the crowded streets. Gone were the pristine hover-lanes and manicured gardens of the Council sector. In their place, crumbling concrete and rusted metal stretched as far as the eye could see.

Seraphina pulled her hood down to hide her face. She'd traded her tailored Council robes for nondescript work clothes, but she couldn't shake the feeling of exposure. Every passing face seemed to stare, as if they could see through her disguise to the Councilwoman beneath.

A group of men shuffled past, heads bowed, the clanking of their restraints a grim reminder of the world she was trying to infiltrate. Seraphina's stomach churned. How many times had she walked these streets as a child, dreaming of escape? And now here she was, willingly plunging back into the depths she'd fought so hard to leave behind.

Her destination loomed before her - a dingy bar called The Broken Chain. According to her intel, it was a known hangout for dissidents and rebel sympathizers. If she wanted to make contact with the Sovereign Hearts, this was her best bet.

Taking a deep breath, Seraphina pushed open the door and stepped inside.

The interior was dim and smoky, the air thick with the smell of cheap synth alcohol and unwashed bodies. Conversation stopped as she entered, dozens of eyes turning to assess the newcomer. Seraphina forced herself to relax, adopting the weary slouch of a factory worker at the end of a long shift.

She made her way to the bar, fully aware of the stares following her progress. The bartender, a stocky woman with cybernetic arms, eyed her suspiciously.

"What'll it be?" she growled.

"Whatever's cheapest," Seraphina replied, her voice deep and raspy.

The bartender grunted and slid a dirty glass across the bar. Seraphina took a sip, suppressing a grimace at the burning sensation. She turned and leaned against the bar, surveying the room.

In the corner, a group of men and women huddled around a table, their voices low and urgent. One of them, a wiry man with a shock of red hair, caught her eye. He nodded almost imperceptibly before turning back to his companions.

Seraphina's pulse quickened. This was it - her first possible contact.

She was about to head over when a commotion at the door caught everyone's attention. A squad of Guardians burst in, their shock batons crackling with energy.

"Surprise inspection!" the lead Guardian barked. "Everybody up against the wall. Now!"

The Guardians scrambled to obey, fear etched on their faces. Seraphina moved with them, her mind racing. This wasn't part of the plan. If she was discovered here...

"You there!" A Guardian pointed at her. "ID chip, now!"

Seraphina's blood ran cold. Her Council-issued chip would give her away in a heartbeat. She'd brought a fake, but it was buried in her pocket. There was no way she could reach it without looking suspicious.

"I said ID chip!" The Guardian advanced, her baton raised ominously.

Time seemed to slow. Seraphina tensed, preparing to fight her way out if necessary. But before she could move, a hand grabbed her arm.

"There you are, sis!" It was the redhead from the corner. He turned to the guard with a disarming smile. "Sorry about that, Officer. My sister here left her ID at home. Stupid, I know, but you know how it is with factory work. Fries your brain after a while."

The guard's eyes narrowed. "And who are you?"

"Finn Redstone," he said, producing an ID chip. "Factory 17, Sector 4. Look, I can vouch for you. We just got off shift and came in for a drink. No trouble, I swear."

For a tense moment, the Guardian looked between them. Seraphina held her breath, aware of how easily this could all fall apart.

Finally, the Guardian grunted. "Fine. But if I catch either of you without proper ID again, it's straight to the detention center. Understood?"

Finn nodded vigorously. "Crystal clear, Officer. Thank you for your understanding."

As the guards moved on to harass the other patrons, Finn steered Seraphina to a quiet corner of the bar.

"That was too close," he muttered. "You're either very brave or very stupid to come here without a solid cover."

Seraphina studied him, weighing her options. This man had just saved her from being discovered, but could she trust him?

"Thank you," she said carefully. "I owe you one."

Finn's eyes twinkled with a mixture of amusement and suspicion. "Oh, I intend to collect. But not here. Too many ears." He glanced meaningfully around the bar. "Meet me in an hour at the old factory on Nexus Street. We'll talk then."

Before Seraphina could respond, Finn disappeared into the crowd, leaving her alone with her thoughts and the remains of her terrible drink.

An hour later, Seraphina found herself at the rusted gates of an abandoned factory. The structure loomed into the night sky, a hulking shadow pierced by broken windows and crumbling walls. Every instinct screamed at her to turn back, to abandon this foolish mission and return to the safety of the Council chambers.

But she couldn't. Not now, when she was so close to making contact with the Sovereign Hearts.

Taking a deep breath, Seraphina slipped through a gap in the fence and made her way into the cavernous interior of the factory. Moonlight filtered through holes in the ceiling, casting eerie shadows across discarded machinery and piles of rubble.

"I thought you weren't coming."

Seraphina whirled around, her hand instinctively going to the hidden stunner at her hip. Finn emerged from behind a rusty conveyor belt, his hands raised in a reassuring gesture.

"Easy," he said. "If I wanted to hurt you, I would have had the guards take you back to the bar."

Seraphina forced herself to relax, but kept her guard up. "Fair enough. So why did you help me?"

Finn's expression became serious. "Because you're not the only one trying to make contact tonight. The question is, who are you really? And what do you want with the Sovereign Hearts?"

Here it was - the moment of truth. Seraphina had rehearsed this a dozen times, crafting a cover story that would get her foot in the door without arousing suspicion. But as she looked into Finn's eyes, she saw something that made her hesitate. A glimmer of hope, of desperation. The same look she'd seen in Niko's eyes at the slave market.

In that moment, Seraphina made a decision that would change everything.

"My name is Sera," she said, using the childhood nickname she'd long since abandoned. "I work in the Council building. I've seen things... heard things. The way they talk about the people in the outer districts, the plans they make..." She trailed off, leaving the implication hanging in the air.

Finn's eyes widened. "You're an insider? Risky move, coming here like this. How do I know you're not a spy?"

"You don't," Seraphina admitted. "But I'm here because I can't stand by any longer. The Council... they're planning something big. Something that could destroy everything. I want to help stop it."

For a long moment, Finn studied her, his expression unreadable. Then he nodded slowly.

"All right, Sera. Let's say I believe you. What exactly did you hear?"

Seraphina's mind raced. She had to give him enough to prove her worth without giving away too much. "They're increasing security in the outer districts. Doubling Guardian patrols, introducing stricter ID checks. But that's not all. There's talk of... purges. Eliminating entire populations to stamp out dissent."

Finn's face paled. "Mother's grace... We knew they were planning something, but this..." He ran a hand through his hair, visibly shaken. "We have to warn the others."

"Others?" Seraphina pressed, sensing an opening. "You mean the Sovereign Hearts?"

Finn's gaze snapped back to her, suddenly wary. "I never said anything about the Sovereign Hearts."

"You didn't have to," Seraphina said quickly. "I've heard the whispers. Seen the symbols. I want to help, Finn. Please."

For a tense moment, Seraphina thought she'd gone too far. But then Finn's shoulders slumped, as if a great weight had settled on them.

"If what you're saying is true, we're going to need all the help we can get," he said. "But understand this - if you're lying, if this is some kind of trap, you won't live long enough to regret it."

Seraphina nodded, her heart pounding. "I understand."

Finn seemed to make a decision. "All right. There's a meeting tomorrow night. A gathering of... like-minded people. If you're serious about helping, be at the old subway station on Ash Street at midnight. You'll be searched and blindfolded. If you have a problem with that, leave now."

"I'll be there," Seraphina said firmly.

Finn nodded. "For all our sakes, I hope you're on the level, Sera." He turned to leave, then paused. "Oh, and one more thing. Bring medical supplies if you can. Bandages, antiseptic, painkillers. We're always short."

With that, he disappeared back into the shadows, leaving Seraphina alone in the cavernous factory.

As she made her way back through the darkened streets of the outer districts, Seraphina's mind whirled. She'd done it - she'd made contact with the Resistance. But at what cost?

Every word out of her mouth had been a lie, a carefully constructed deception designed to gain their trust.

And yet... had it all been a lie? The disgust she'd expressed at the Council's plans, the desire to help - those feelings were real. More real, perhaps, than anything she'd allowed herself to feel in years.

As she approached the border between the outer districts and the wealthier middle sectors, Seraphina stopped. Ahead lay the road back to her life as Councilwoman Blackwood - to power, prestige, and the iron grip of Lady Meridia's expectations. Behind her lay the shadowy world of the Sovereign Hearts, with all its dangers and uncertain promises of change.

For a moment, she stood frozen between these two worlds, the weight of her choices pressing down on her. Then, squaring her shoulders, Seraphina made her decision. There was no turning back now.

Tomorrow night she would descend into the heart of the Resistance. And whatever she found there would change the course of Elyria forever.

When Seraphina finally reached her quarters in the early hours of the morning, exhaustion threatening to overwhelm her, a soft chime from her comm unit made her freeze. A message flickered to life in the air before her:

"Progress report expected. Meet me in my office at dawn. - M"

Lady Meridia. Of course. In her focus on infiltrating the Sovereign Hearts, Seraphina had almost forgotten the other half of her precarious balancing act.

She sank onto her bed, the enormity of her situation crashing down upon her. In less than six hours, she would have to face Meridia, lie to the woman who had mentored her, who could see through deception like clear glass. And then, in less than eighteen hours, she would dive headfirst into the heart of the Resistance she had been sent to destroy.

Seraphina closed her eyes, but sleep eluded her. In her mind she saw Finn's desperate hope, Niko's burning defiance, Lyra's quiet gratitude. And above it all, Meridia's cold, calculating gaze.

She was walking on a razor's edge, and one false step would send her plunging into the abyss.

FIVE
DIVIDED LOYALTIES

Dawn painted the spires of Elyria in shades of gold and rose, but Seraphina saw none of it. Her footsteps echoed through the empty corridors of the Council building, each one bringing her closer to a confrontation she dreaded. Lady Meridia was waiting in her office, expecting a progress report on the very organization Seraphina was now risking everything to join.

As she approached the imposing doors of Meridia's office, Seraphina took a deep breath and tucked her features into a mask of cool professionalism. She could do this. She had to.

She knocked, and Meridia's voice, sharp as a blade, cut through the silence. "Enter."

Seraphina stepped into the office, immediately enveloped by the scent of old books and power. Lady Meridia sat behind her massive desk, her silver hair gleaming in the early morning light. Her piercing gaze was fixed on Seraphina, seeming to see right through her.

"Councilwoman Blackwood," Meridia said, her tone unreadable. "I trust you have something of substance to report?"

Seraphina straightened and met Meridia's eyes. "I do, Lady Meridia. I've made contact with individuals connected to the Sovereign Hearts."

Meridia leaned forward, interest in her eyes. "Go on."

Seraphina's mind raced, choosing each word carefully. "I've infiltrated a group of dissidents in the outer districts. They're cautious, but I've managed to gain a measure of trust. There's a meeting tonight - I believe key members of the Sovereign Hearts will be in attendance."

"Excellent," Meridia smiled, a predatory gleam in her eyes. "And what have you learned of their plans?"

"They're afraid," Seraphina said, letting a hint of the tension she'd witnessed seep into her voice. "The increased Guardian presence has them on edge. They're gathering medical supplies, which suggests they're preparing for a conflict."

Meridia nodded, seemingly pleased. "Fear is good. It will make them sloppy." She fixed Seraphina with an intense stare. "This meeting tonight - you're going?"

"Yes," Seraphina confirmed. "They're taking precautions - searches, blindfolds. But I'll be there."

"Good," Meridia said. "We need names, Seraphina. Identities of their leaders, locations of their hideouts. Get close to them, gain their trust, and then we'll crush this rebellion once and for all."

Seraphina's stomach churned, but her face remained impassive. "Of course, Lady Meridia. I won't let you down."

Meridia's lips curved into a cold smile. "See that you don't. You've come so far, Seraphina. It would be a shame to see you fall now."

The threat in her words was clear. Seraphina nodded, suppressing a shudder. "I understand."

"Dismissed," Meridia waved her off. "Report after the meeting. And Seraphina?" She paused, her gaze piercing. "Be careful. Don't let your... sympathies cloud your judgment."

Seraphina's blood ran cold. Did Meridia suspect? Had she seen through the cautious facade? But Meridia's attention had already returned to the documents on her desk, the dismissal clear.

Heart pounding, Seraphina left the office, her mind racing. She'd survived the encounter, but how long could she keep up this dangerous game?

THE DAY PASSED in a blur of tension and preparation. Seraphina went through her Council duties mechanically, her thoughts constantly drifting to the night ahead. As evening approached, she made her way to the medical bay, her steps measured and purposeful.

"Councilwoman Blackwood," the Chief Medical Officer greeted her with surprise. "This is unexpected. Is everything all right?"

Seraphina forced a smile. "Quite well, Doctor. I'm here on official business. The Council is concerned about possible unrest in the outer districts. I need a supply of basic medical supplies - bandages, antiseptics, painkillers. As a precaution, you understand."

The doctor's brow furrowed, but he nodded. "Of course, Councillor. I'll have a kit prepared for you immediately."

As she waited, Seraphina's gaze fell on a nearby treatment room. Through the window she could see a man strapped to a bed, his body covered in bruises and cuts. A guard stood guard nearby.

"Who's that?" she asked, trying to keep her voice casual.

The doctor glanced over, his expression darkening. "A rebel, caught trying to sabotage one of the factories. He was... uncooperative during questioning."

Seraphina's chest tightened. She thought of Niko, wondered if he'd been treated similarly. "I see," she managed. "And has he provided any useful information?"

"Not yet," the doctor shrugged. "But they always break eventually."

Before Seraphina could respond, a nurse approached with a large medical kit. "Here you are, Councillor. Everything you requested."

Seraphina took the kit, painfully aware of its weight - not just physical, but moral. These supplies, meant to heal, had become another weapon in her arsenal of lies.

"Thank you," she said and turned to leave. But as she reached the door, she stopped. "Doctor? Make sure this man gets proper treatment. After all, we can't get information from a corpse."

The doctor looked surprised, but nodded. "As you wish, Councillor."

Seraphina walked out, her heart racing. It wasn't much, but it was something. A small act of defiance against a system she was beginning to despise.

NIGHT FELL OVER ELYRIA, the outer districts shrouded in shadow. Seraphina made her way through winding alleys and deserted streets, the medical kit clutched tightly to her chest. Every sound made her jump, every passing shadow a potential threat.

The old subway station loomed before her, a crumbling relic of a bygone era. Seraphina descended the broken escalator, the darkness engulfing her.

"Stop right there," a voice growled from the darkness. "Hands where I can see them."

Seraphina froze and slowly raised her hands. "I'm here for the meeting. Finn sent me."

A beat of silence, then: "The medical supplies?"

"Right here," Seraphina pointed to the kit with a nod.

Rough hands grabbed her arms and searched them for weapons. Finding none, they took the medical kit and turned her around. A blindfold was pulled tightly over her eyes.

"No questions," the voice warned. "No resistance. One wrong move and you'll never see daylight again. Understood?"

Seraphina nodded, her heart pounding. This was it. There was no turning back now.

She was led through what felt like a maze of tunnels, the sounds of dripping water and scurrying vermin her only companions. After what seemed like hours, but was probably only minutes, they came to a stop.

"Wait here," their guide ordered. The sound of a heavy door creaking open reached her ears, followed by a rush of voices and warmth.

The blindfold was removed and Seraphina blinked in the sudden light. She found herself in a large cavern, clearly part of the old subway system. Makeshift tables and chairs filled the room, and dozens of people milled about, their faces a mixture of hope and caution.

Finn appeared at her side, his expression guarded. "You made it. And you brought the supplies. Good."

"I keep my word," Seraphina said, meeting his gaze steadily.

Finn nodded, some of the tension leaving his shoulders. "Come. There's someone you need to meet."

He led them through the crowd to a small group huddled around a table covered with maps and diagrams. As they approached, the group parted, revealing a familiar face that made Seraphina gasp.

Niko Stormwind stood before her, his eyes widening in recognition. For a moment, neither spoke, the air between them charged with unspoken words and conflicting emotions.

Then Niko's lips curved into a wry smile. "Well, well. Councilwoman Blackwood. Or should I say... Sera?"

Seraphina's heart raced. This was the moment of truth. Everything depended on what she said next.

"It's good to see you again, Niko," she said quietly. "Though I wish it were under better circumstances."

Niko's eyes narrowed, studying her intently. "Indeed. Finn tells me that you have information for us. That you want to help." His voice was lowered, for her ears only. "But the question is, why? What has changed since our last... encounter?"

Seraphina took a deep breath, aware of the eyes upon her. This was the moment to solidify her cover, to fully commit to this dangerous deception. But when she looked into Niko's eyes, saw the mixture of hope and suspicion there, she made a split-second decision.

"The truth?" she said, her voice barely above a whisper. "I'm here because of you. Because what you told me that day in the interrogation room... you were right. About all of it."

Surprise flashed across Niko's face, quickly replaced by caution. "Pretty words, Councilwoman. But words are cheap in our world. We need action."

"Then let me prove it," Seraphina said, her voice growing stronger. She turned to address the group. "The Council is planning a major crackdown. Increased Guardian patrols, stricter ID checks, and..." she hesitated, then plunged ahead, "There is talk of purges. Whole sections of the outer districts wiped out to stamp out dissent."

A wave of shock and anger swept through the assembled rebels. Niko's face hardened, his fists clenched at his sides.

"When?" he demanded.

"Soon," Seraphina said. "They're still finalizing the plans, but it could be days, maybe a week at the most."

The cave erupted into chaos, voices shouting over each other in fear and anger. Niko raised his hand and a hush fell over the crowd.

"If what you say is true," he said, his eyes boring into Seraphina's, "then we must act now. But understand this - if you're lying, if this is some kind of trap, the consequences will be severe."

Seraphina met his gaze unflinchingly. "I understand. I'm putting my life in your hands, Niko. Everything I've worked for, everything I am - it's all on the line now."

For a long moment, Niko stared at her, as if trying to see into her soul. Then he slowly nodded.

"All right," he said. "You're in. But you're being watched. Every move, every word - we'll be watching. One hint of betrayal, and..."

He left the threat unspoken, but Seraphina got it. She had gained a foothold, but the real test was yet to come.

As the meeting dissolved into frantic planning and preparation, Seraphina found herself swept up in the energy of the Resistance. For the first time in years, she felt alive, part of something bigger than herself.

But even as she threw herself into the work, a small voice in the back of her mind whispered a chilling reminder: In less than twelve hours, she would have to report to Meridia. And then her true test of loyalty would begin.

As the night wore on, plans were made and discarded, strategies discussed and refined. Through it all, Seraphina felt Niko's eyes on her, watching, judging. She knew she'd have to face him again, to explain herself more fully. But for now, there was work to be done.

As the first light of dawn began to seep into the underground chamber, Niko called for attention.

"We've done all we can for now," he announced, his voice carrying easily over the tired but determined faces. "Go home, rest, prepare. And remember - trust no one outside this room. Elyria's future depends on our success."

His eyes met Seraphina's as he spoke those last words, a clear challenge in his gaze. She nodded, accepting the weight of his trust and the danger it carried.

As the rebels began to file out, taking different routes to avoid suspicion, Finn approached Seraphina.

"I'll escort you back," he said. "We don't want our new insider getting lost in the tunnels, do we?"

Seraphina recognized the offer for what it was - both protection and surveillance. She nodded and fell in step beside him.

They walked in silence through the winding corridors, the tension between them palpable. Finally, as they neared the exit, Finn spoke.

"You're taking a terrible risk, you know," he said quietly. "If you're sincere, you're risking everything to help us. And if you're not..." He left the implication hanging.

Seraphina stopped and turned to him. "I am real, Finn. I know you have no reason to trust me, but I swear I want to help. What the Council is doing, what they're planning - it's wrong. And I can't stand by and watch it happen."

Finn studied her for a long moment, his expression unreadable. Then, to her surprise, he smiled - a small, tired twitch of his lips, but genuine.

"You know," he said, "I actually believe you. Mother help us all if I'm wrong, but... I think you might be just what we need."

Before Seraphina could answer, they reached the exit. Finn handed her a small, inconspicuous comm unit.

"For emergencies only," he said. "It's untraceable, but don't take any unnecessary risks. We'll be in touch."

Seraphina took the device and nodded her understanding. As she stepped out into the early morning light, Finn's voice stopped her one last time.

"Sera," he said, using the name she had chosen. "Be careful. The game you're playing... it's more dangerous than you know."

With that ominous warning ringing in her ears, Seraphina made her way back to the heart of the city. The sun was rising over Elyria, bathing the gleaming towers in golden light. But to Seraphina, the beauty now seemed hollow, a shining facade hiding rot and corruption.

As she approached the Council building, exhaustion weighed heavily on her. But she couldn't rest, not yet. Meridia would be expecting her report, and Seraphina had only hours to decide how much to reveal, how much to conceal.

She had entered the underground chamber as Councilwoman Blackwood, loyal servant of Elyria's ruling elite. She had emerged as Sera, a potential ally of the Resistance. The question that now burned in her mind, that would determine the fate of everything she held dear, was simple but devastating:

Who was she really?

As she rode the elevator to her quarters, Seraphina's mind raced, trying to formulate a plan. She had information now - real, valuable information about the Sovereign Hearts. But to reveal it would be to betray the trust she'd just begun to earn, to potentially condemn good people to torture and death.

The elevator doors opened and Seraphina stepped out, her decision made. She would walk the razor's edge, feeding Meridia just enough information to maintain her cover while protecting the Resistance as much as possible. It was a dangerous game, but one she had to play.

As she reached for the door, a voice stopped her in her tracks.

"Long night, Councilwoman Blackwood?"

Seraphina turned slowly, her heart pounding. Lady Meridia stood in the hallway, her silver hair immaculate, her eyes sharp and calculating.

"I expect a full report in my office within the hour," Meridia said, her tone brooking no argument. "Do not disappoint me, Seraphina. The fate of Elyria may well rest on what you've discovered."

As Meridia glided away, Seraphina leaned against her door, suddenly dizzy. One hour. One hour to decide the future of the Resistance, of Elyria itself.

The game had begun in earnest, and Seraphina was playing for the highest stakes imaginable. As she entered her quarters to prepare for the most important performance of her life, one thought echoed through her mind:

There was no turning back now.

SIX
A DANCE OF DECEPTION

Seraphina stood before the mirror in her quarters and studied her reflection. Dark circles shadowed her eyes, evidence of a sleepless night. With practiced movements, she applied concealer, erasing the visible signs of her double life. Her fingers trembled slightly as she smoothed her Council robes, the weight of her impending deception weighing heavily on her shoulders.

The comm unit Finn had given her sat on her dresser, a silent reminder of the trust she'd been given - and the betrayal she was about to commit. Seraphina picked it up and turned it over in her hands. Such a small thing to hold so much power.

A chime from her official comm broke the silence. A word flashed on the screen: "Now."

Meridia waited.

Squaring her shoulders, Seraphina left her quarters, each step down the opulent corridor bringing her closer to a confrontation she dreaded. The corridors were busier now, other Council members and staff going about their morning routines. Seraphina nodded to them as she passed, her face a mask of calm authority even as her heart raced.

She reached Meridia's office door all too soon. She took a deep breath and knocked.

"Enter," Meridia's voice called from inside.

Seraphina stepped inside, immediately surrounded by the familiar scent of old books and power. Meridia sat behind her massive desk, datapad in hand, her silver hair gleaming in the morning light. She looked up as Seraphina entered, her piercing gaze seeming to see right through her.

"Ah, Seraphina," Meridia said, her tone unreadable. "Right on time. I trust you have something important to report?"

Seraphina moved to stand in front of the desk, her posture perfect, her expression carefully neutral. "Yes, Lady Meridia. Last night's meeting was... enlightening."

Meridia leaned forward, interest gleaming in her eyes. "Go on."

Here it was - the moment of truth. Seraphina took a breath, steeled herself. "The Sovereign Hearts are more organized than we first thought. They have a network of safe houses throughout the outer districts, and sympathizers even in the middle sectors."

"Names," Meridia demanded. "I want names, Seraphina."

Seraphina's mind raced. She couldn't give up Finn or Niko, but she needed something concrete. "They use code names," she said. "The leader goes by 'Phoenix.' There's also a 'Shadowblade' and a 'Whisper' - they seem to be key strategists."

Meridia's eyes narrowed. "And their real identities?"

"Unknown," Seraphina shook her head. "They're being careful. I wasn't allowed to see their faces. But I overheard plans for their next move."

"Which is?" Meridia pressed.

Seraphina hesitated, weighing her words carefully. "They plan to disrupt the power grid in the outer districts. Create chaos, make it look like the Council can't even keep the lights on."

It wasn't entirely a lie - she had heard such a plan being discussed. But it had been dismissed as too risky. Still, it was true enough to be believable.

Meridia leaned back in her chair, fingers crossed in front of her. "Interesting. And when is this supposed to happen?"

"Within a week," Seraphina said. "They're still working out the details."

For a long moment, Meridia said nothing, her gaze boring into Seraphina. The silence stretched, the tension building with each passing second.

Finally, Meridia spoke. "You have done well, Seraphina. This information will be... most useful."

Seraphina allowed herself to relax a little. "Thank you, Lady Meridia. I'll continue to gather intel..."

"Oh, I'm sure you will," Meridia cut her off, her tone

suddenly sharp. "But I can't help but wonder... what are you not telling me?"

Seraphina's blood ran cold. "I'm not sure what you mean."

Meridia stood and moved around the desk with predatory grace. "Come now, Seraphina. We both know you're hiding something. The question is... why?"

She circled Seraphina slowly, like a shark smelling blood in the water. "Could it be that your time in the outskirts has... softened you? Made you sympathetic to their plight?"

"Of course not," Seraphina said, fighting to keep her voice steady. "My loyalty is to the Council, to Elyria."

Meridia stopped in front of her, their faces inches apart. "Is it? Then prove it. Give me something real, Seraphina. Something I can use to put down this rebellion once and for all."

Seraphina's mind raced. She had to give Meridia something or her cover would be blown. But everything she'd learned, every scrap of information, could lead to the capture or death of people she was beginning to see as allies.

In that moment, looking into Meridia's cold, calculating eyes, Seraphina made a decision that would change everything.

"There's a meeting," she said, her voice low. "Tomorrow night. Key members of the Sovereign Hearts will be there, including their leader."

Meridia's eyes lit up with predatory glee. "Where?"

"The old factory on Nexus Street," Seraphina said, praying she wasn't making a terrible mistake. "But Lady Meridia, if we move against them now, we risk driving the rest underground. We could lose our chance to eradicate the entire network."

Meridia considered this, her expression pensive. "You may be right. What do you suggest?"

"Let me attend the meeting," Seraphina said. "I can gather more information, identify more of their key players. Once we have a complete picture of their organization, we can strike decisively."

For a long moment, Meridia studied her, weighing her words. Then she nodded slowly. "Very well, Seraphina. You have three days. After that, we will move against them with everything we have."

"I understand," Seraphina said, relief flowing through her. She had bought time, but at what price?

"One more thing," Meridia said as Seraphina turned to leave. "I'm going to assign you a partner for this mission. Insurance, you might say."

Seraphina's heart sank. "A partner?"

The office door opened and a woman entered. She was tall and lithe, with close-cropped black hair and eyes like chips of ice. Everything about her screamed danger.

"Councilwoman Blackwood, this is Alira Vex," Meridia said, a hint of amusement in her voice. "She will accompany you to the meeting tomorrow. To observe, of course."

Alira's gaze met Seraphina's, a silent challenge in her eyes. "I look forward to working with you, Councilwoman," she said, her voice smooth as silk and sharp as a blade.

Seraphina forced a smile. "Likewise."

As she left Meridia's office, Seraphina's mind spun. She'd navigated one minefield only to step into another. Now she had to find a way to warn the Sovereign Hearts of the impending raid, all under the watchful eye of Meridia's spy.

The game had just become infinitely more dangerous.

SERAPHINA SPENT the rest of the day in a haze of meetings and paperwork, her mind constantly racing as she tried to formulate a plan. As evening approached, she made her way to the lower levels of the Council building, ostensibly to check on some administrative details.

In reality, she was looking for a familiar face.

She found Lyra in a supply closet, restocking cleaning supplies. The young woman started as Seraphina entered, almost dropping a bottle of disinfectant.

"Councilwoman Blackwood," Lyra said, her eyes wide. "I didn't expect..."

"It's all right, Lyra," Seraphina said quietly, closing the door behind her. "I need your help."

Lyra's expression changed from surprise to caution. "What kind of help?"

Seraphina took a deep breath. "I need you to deliver a message to your brother. And through him to... certain other individuals."

Understanding dawned in Lyra's eyes, quickly followed by fear. "Councilwoman, I don't know what you're talking about. My brother and I, we're not involved in anything-"

"Lyra," Seraphina cut her off gently. "I know. And I'm trying to help. But you have to trust me."

For a long moment, Lyra studied her, the conflict clear on her face. Then, slowly, she nodded. "What's the message?"

Seraphina's shoulders slumped in relief. "Tell them the factory on Nexus Street isn't safe. The Council knows about the meeting. They need to change locations, and they need to be careful. They're being watched."

Lyra's eyes widened. "How do you know that?"

"The less you know, the safer you'll be," Seraphina said. "Can you get the message to them?"

Lyra nodded. "I'll find a way."

"Thank you," Seraphina said, squeezing Lyra's hand. "Be careful. If anyone asks, we never had this conversation."

As she turned to leave, Lyra's voice stopped her. "Councilwoman? Why are you doing this?"

Seraphina looked back, a sad smile on her face. "Because it's the right thing to do."

She left the storeroom, her heart pounding. She'd taken an enormous risk, but it was necessary. Now she could only hope that the message would reach the right people in time.

As she made her way back to her quarters, a voice called out behind her.

"Councilwoman Blackwood."

Seraphina turned to see Alira Vex approaching, her movements fluid and predatory.

"Agent Vex," Seraphina nodded, keeping her voice neutral. "What can I do for you?"

Alira's lips curved into a cold smile. "I thought we might discuss strategy for tomorrow night's operation. Over dinner, perhaps?"

It wasn't a request. Seraphina recognized the intent behind the invitation - Alira wanted to watch her, look for any signs of disloyalty.

"Of course," Seraphina said, forcing a smile. "I would be delighted."

As they walked together to the dining hall, Seraphina felt Alira's gaze on her, searching for weaknesses. She straightened her spine, squared her shoulders. The dance of deception had begun in earnest, and one misstep could cost her everything.

The dining hall was nearly empty at this hour, most of the Council members having retired for the evening. Seraphina and Alira found a secluded table in the corner, away from prying ears.

As they settled in, a service droid brought them glasses of wine. Alira raised hers in a mock toast. "To successful partnerships," she said, her eyes never leaving Seraphina's face.

Seraphina clinked her glass against Alira's and took a small sip. "Indeed. Though I must admit I'm curious about the sudden need for a partner on this mission."

Alira's smile didn't reach her eyes. "Oh, you know how it is, Councilwoman. In times of crisis, we all have to adapt. Lady Meridia just wants to make sure we have all our bases covered."

"Of course," Seraphina nodded. "And your specific role will be...?"

"Support," Alira said smoothly. "I will be there to assist you in any way necessary. To watch your back, so to speak."

The implication was clear. Alira would be watching her every move, ready to report any sign of disloyalty to Meridia.

Seraphina leaned back in her chair, assuming a relaxed posture she didn't feel. "Well, I appreciate the support. Though I hope you understand, my contacts within the Sovereign Hearts are... delicate. Your presence might frighten them."

Alira's eyes glittered dangerously. "Oh, I can be very discreet if necessary, Councilwoman. They'll hardly know I'm there."

The rest of the meal passed in a tense dance of veiled questions and carefully crafted answers. Seraphina felt like she was walking a tightrope, every word a potential misstep that could send her plummeting to her doom.

As they finished their dessert, Alira leaned forward, her voice low. "You know, Councilwoman, I've always admired your rise to power. A girl from the outskirts climbing all the way to the Council... it's quite impressive."

Seraphina's guard rose immediately. "Thank you. It's been a challenging journey."

"I'm sure it has," Alira nodded. "Tell me, do you ever miss it? The outskirts, I mean. The... simplicity of life there?"

It was a trap, Seraphina realized. Alira was fishing for any sign of lingering loyalty to her old life.

"Do you miss it?" Seraphina let out a carefully calculated laugh. "Hardly. The poverty, the despair... I'm thankful every day to have escaped it."

Alira's eyes narrowed slightly. "And yet you seem quite... invested in the welfare of those still trapped there."

Seraphina met her gaze steadily. "Of course. They are, after all, citizens of Elyria. Their welfare affects us all. But make no mistake, Agent Vex. My loyalty is to the Council, to the future we're building."

For a long moment, Alira studied her, as if trying to see into her soul. Then she stood up abruptly. "Well, this has been most enlightening, Councilwoman. I look forward to our mission tomorrow night."

As Alira walked away, Seraphina allowed herself a small sigh of relief. She had survived the interrogation, but tomorrow would be the real test.

Back in her quarters, Seraphina paced restlessly. She'd done everything she could to warn the Sovereign Hearts, but was it enough? And even if they changed locations, how could she keep Alira from discovering the truth?

Her eyes fell on the comm unit Finn had given her, still sitting on her dresser. She picked it up and turned it over in her hands. Using it was a risk, but she needed to know if her warning had been received.

She took a deep breath and activated the device.

For several long moments there was nothing but static. Then a voice crackled through - distorted, but unmistakably Niko's.

"Sera? Is that you?"

Seraphina's heart leapt. "Niko. Did you get the message? About the factory?"

"We got it," Niko confirmed. "Just in time, too. We've moved the meeting. But Sera, how did you know?"

Seraphina closed her eyes, relief washing over her. "It's complicated. I can't explain now, but you must be careful. The Council is watching closely. And I... I won't be alone tomorrow night."

There was a pause, then Niko's voice came through again, tense. "What do you mean you won't be alone?"

"They've assigned me a partner," Seraphina said. "A watchdog. I'll try to keep her off the scent, but you need to be prepared."

"Understood," Niko said. "Sera... thank you. For the warning. I hope you know what you're doing."

Seraphina let out a bitter laugh. "So do I, Niko. So do I."

She deactivated the comm unit, her mind racing. She'd bought the Sovereign Hearts some time, but at what cost? If Alira discovered her deception, if Meridia found out she'd warned the rebels...

A knock on her door made her jump. Quickly, she shoved the comm unit into a drawer.

"Come in," she called, struggling to keep her voice calm.

The door slid open to reveal Alira Vex. The agent's eyes scanned the room, taking in every detail.

"Councilwoman," Alira said softly. "I hope I'm not interrupting anything?"

Seraphina forced a smile. "Not at all. What can I do for you, Agent Vex?"

Alira stepped inside, the door closing behind her. "I thought we could go over the plan for tomorrow night. After all, we don't want any... surprises."

As Alira's cold gaze met hers, Seraphina stifled a shiver. The agent's presence in her private quarters felt like an invasion, a silent threat.

"Of course," Seraphina said, gesturing to a pair of chairs by the window. "Please, have a seat."

They sat, the lights of Elyria's night skyline twinkling behind the glass. Seraphina could feel the weight of Alira's scrutiny, looking for any crack in her facade.

"So," Alira began, her voice deceptively casual, "walk me through it. How do you want to approach tomorrow's meeting?"

Seraphina leaned back, adopting an attitude of relaxed confidence she didn't feel. "We'll arrive separately, of course. I'll enter first, keeping my cover. You'll follow at a distance, staying out of sight."

Alira nodded, her eyes never leaving Seraphina's face. "And if something goes wrong? If they suspect a trap?"

"They won't," Seraphina said firmly. "I've spent weeks

building their trust. But if something goes wrong, we abort. No unnecessary risks."

"Hmm," Alira murmured, a hint of skepticism in her tone. "And what about this... Phoenix? Do you think he'll be there?"

Seraphina's heart raced, but she kept her expression neutral. "It's possible. But even if he is, I doubt he'll reveal himself fully. These people are careful, Agent Vex. They've survived this long for a reason."

Alira leaned forward, her gaze intensifying. "You sound almost admiring, Counselor."

"Know your enemy," Seraphina countered gently. "Under-estimating them is what allowed this rebellion to grow in the first place."

For a long moment, Alira said nothing, just studied Seraphina with those cold, calculating eyes. Then she stood abruptly.

"Well, I think we're as prepared as we can be," she said. "Get some rest, Councilwoman. Tomorrow will be... interesting."

As Alira started for the door, she paused and looked back. "Oh, and Seraphina? I hope your loyalties are as clear as you claim. It would be a shame to see such a promising career... cut short."

The threat hung in the air long after Alira had left, leaving Seraphina alone with her troubled thoughts.

Sleep eluded her that night. Seraphina tossed and turned, her mind racing with possibilities and dangers. Every scenario she played out seemed to end in disaster - discovery, betrayal, the destruction of everything she'd worked for.

As dawn broke over Elyria, painting the sky with shades of pink and gold, Seraphina stood at her window and watched the city come to life. Somewhere out there, Niko and the others were preparing for the meeting. And somewhere, no doubt, Alira Vex was plotting how best to uncover the truth.

A soft chime from her official comm unit broke the silence. A message from Meridia flashed across the screen: "My office. Now."

Seraphina's stomach sank. Had Alira reported anything suspicious? Had her warning to the Sovereign Hearts been discovered somehow?

With trembling hands, she put on her Council robes, every movement feeling like a step toward her doom. The corridors were quiet as she made her way to Meridia's office, most of the Council still asleep at this early hour.

She knocked, her heart pounding.

"Enter," Meridia's voice called from inside.

Seraphina stepped inside, immediately struck by the tension in the air. Meridia stood at the window, her back to the door. Alira Vex was sitting in a chair, a predatory smile on her face.

"Ah, Seraphina," Meridia said, turning around. "Thank you for coming so promptly."

"Of course, Lady Meridia," Seraphina said, fighting to keep her voice steady. "How may I be of service?"

Meridia's eyes bored into her, searching. "We have received some... disturbing information. It seems our plans for tonight's raid may have been compromised."

Seraphina's blood ran cold, but her face remained impassive. "Compromised? How?"

"That," Meridia said, her voice sharp, "is what we intend to find out. Alira here has some... concerns about your recent activities."

Alira stood and moved to stand next to Meridia. "I took the liberty of monitoring your communications, Councilwoman. Imagine my surprise when I discovered an unauthorized transmission from your quarters last night."

Seraphina's mind raced. The comm unit. She'd been careless, let her guard down for a moment. But perhaps...

"An unauthorized transmission?" she frowned, letting confusion creep into her voice. "I'm not sure I understand."

"Don't play coy, Seraphina," Meridia snapped. "We know you contacted someone. The question is, who? And why?"

Seraphina took a deep breath. This was it - the moment that would decide everything. She had to choose her next words carefully.

"I have contacted an informant," she said, meeting Meridia's gaze. "Someone deep within the Sovereign Hearts. I received information that our original plan had been compromised. I tried to save the operation."

Meridia's eyes narrowed. "And you didn't think to inform me immediately?"

"I wanted to confirm the information first," Seraphina said. "To avoid unnecessary panic. I was going to inform you this morning."

For a long moment there was silence in the office. Meridia and Alira exchanged glances, a silent communication passing between them.

Finally, Meridia spoke. "This informant of yours. Can she be trusted?"

Seraphina nodded. "Absolutely. They've provided reliable information in the past."

"I see," Meridia said slowly. "And what exactly did this informant tell you?"

"That the Sovereign Hearts somehow learned of our plans for the factory," Seraphina said, her heart racing. "They moved the meeting to a new location."

Alira stepped forward, her eyes glittering dangerously. "And I suppose you have no idea how they found out about our plans in the first place?"

Seraphina met her gaze coolly. "If I did, Agent Vex, I would have taken steps to plug the leak by now."

Another tense silence fell. Seraphina could feel the weight of her scrutiny, looking for any sign of deception. She kept her posture relaxed, her expression open. Everything depended on this moment.

Finally, Meridia sighed. "Very well, Seraphina. I'll accept your explanation... for now. But understand this - if I find that you've been less than completely truthful, the consequences will be severe."

Seraphina bowed her head. "I understand, Lady Meridia. You have my word - my loyalty is to the Council and to Elyria."

"See that it stays that way," Meridia said coldly. "Now, tell us about this new place. We have a rebellion to put down."

As Seraphina began to spin a web of half-truths and carefully crafted lies, her mind reeled. She had survived this interrogation, but for how long? The game had become infinitely more dangerous, and one false move could spell disaster not only for her, but for the entire Resistance.

The die had been cast. Now all she could do was play her part and hope that when the dust settled, she'd be on the right side of history.

SEVEN

THE PRECIPICE

Seraphina's footsteps echoed through the empty corridors of the Council building, each click of her heels a reminder of the precarious path she was walking. The weight of her deception pressed down on her, threatening to crush her under its weight. She had survived Meridia's interrogation, but at what cost?

As she rounded the corner, a familiar figure crossed her path. Councilwoman Elena Darkwater, her dark eyes glittering with barely concealed curiosity.

"Seraphina," Elena purred, her voice as soft as silk. "You're up early. Trouble sleeping?"

Seraphina forced a smile, her mind racing. How much did Elena know? "Good morning, Elena. No trouble at all. Just preparing for the day ahead."

Elena's lips curved into a predatory smile. "Ah yes, your... special assignment. The talk of the Council, you know. Lady Meridia has placed a great deal of trust in you."

"The Council's confidence is not misplaced," Seraphina said, her voice steady despite the churning in her stomach. "If you'll excuse me, I have preparations to make."

She moved to step around Elena, but the other woman's hand shot out and gripped her arm with surprising strength. "Be careful, Seraphina," Elena murmured, her voice low. "The higher you climb, the farther you must fall."

With that, she released Seraphina and glided away, leaving behind a chill that had nothing to do with the building's temperature controls.

Seraphina watched her go, her mind racing. The Council was a nest of vipers, each member waiting for the others to show weakness. She couldn't afford to let her guard down for a moment.

As she continued towards her destination, Seraphina's thoughts turned to the night ahead. The fake location she'd given Meridia would keep the Council's forces occupied, but for how long? And what would happen when they realized they'd been led on a wild goose chase?

She reached the infirmary and nodded to the staff as she entered. "I need to request more supplies," she announced, her voice carrying the authority of her position. "For tonight's operation."

The Chief Medical Officer approached, datapad in hand. "Of course, Councilor. What do you require?"

Seraphina rattled off a list of items - bandages, antiseptics, painkillers. As the officer entered the request, she added, almost as an afterthought, "Oh, and include some of the experimental regenerative serum. We may run into some resistance."

The officer's eyebrows rose. "The serum? But Councilwoman, it's still in the testing phase. The side effects-"

"Are a necessary risk," Seraphina interrupted. "This mission is too important to leave anything to chance."

As she left the medical bay, supplies in hand, Seraphina's heart raced. The regenerative serum was powerful stuff - capable of healing serious injuries in minutes. In the hands of the Sovereign Hearts, it could save lives. In the hands of the Council... she shuddered to think of the possibilities.

The day passed in a blur of preparations and tense conversations. Seraphina went through the motions of her Council duties, always aware of the eyes upon her. Alira Vex seemed to materialize at every turn, her predatory gaze following Seraphina's every move.

As evening approached, Seraphina retreated to her quarters to change. She traded her Council robes for nondescript clothing - dark, practical, easy to move in. As she fastened a concealed holster to her thigh, her fingers brushed against the small comm unit Finn had given her. A reminder of the trust placed in her and the betrayal she was about to commit.

A knock on her door made her freeze. "Councilwoman Blackwood?" Alira's voice called from the other side. "It's time."

Seraphina took a deep breath, steeling herself. This was it. The point of no return.

She opened the door to find Alira waiting, also dressed for covert operations. The agent's eyes swept over Seraphina, taking in every detail of her appearance.

"Ready?" Alira asked, a hint of challenge in her voice.

Seraphina nodded. "Let's go."

They made their way through the building, using service corridors and back exits to avoid being seen. As they stepped out into the cool night air, Seraphina's senses went on high alert. The streets of the outer districts were eerily quiet, the usual hustle and bustle muted.

"Remember the plan," Alira murmured as they neared their destination. "You make contact. I will observe from a distance. At the first sign of trouble, we break off."

Seraphina nodded, her mouth dry. "Understood."

They parted ways, Alira fading into the shadows as Seraphina made her way to the rendezvous point - an abandoned warehouse on the edge of the district. Her heart pounded with every step, the weight of her decisions pressing down on her.

As she approached the warehouse, a figure emerged from the darkness. Finn, his red hair unmistakable even in the dim light.

"Sera," he said, his voice deep and tense. "You made it."

Seraphina nodded, looking around nervously. "Is it safe to talk here?"

Finn's eyes narrowed. "As safe as it can be. Come, the others are waiting."

He led them into the warehouse, navigating through a maze of rusted machinery and crumbling walls. They descended a hidden staircase and emerged into a vast underground chamber. Dozens of people milled about, their faces a mixture of hope and wariness.

And there, in the center of it all, stood Niko.

Their eyes met across the room, and for a moment, the world seemed to fall away. Niko's expression was unreadable, a storm of emotions swirling in his dark eyes.

"Sera," he said as she approached, his voice soft but with an undercurrent of steel. "We weren't sure you'd come."

"I said I would," Seraphina replied, fighting to keep her voice steady. "I keep my promises."

Niko studied her for a long moment, then nodded. "We'll see. Come, there's much to discuss."

He led her to a table covered with maps and diagrams. Other key members of the resistance gathered around, their gazes wary.

"The Council knows about the factory," Niko began without preamble. "Thanks to your warning, we avoided a trap. But now we need to know - what else do they know? What are they planning?"

Seraphina took a deep breath. This was the moment of truth. "They are planning a major crackdown," she said, her voice low but clear. "Increased Guardian patrols, stricter ID checks. And... there's talk of purges. Whole sections of the outer districts wiped out to stamp out dissent."

A wave of shock and anger swept through the assembled rebels. Niko's face hardened, his fists clenched at his sides.

"When?" he demanded.

"Soon," Seraphina said. "They're still finalizing the plans, but it could be days, maybe a week at the most."

The rebels broke into a frantic discussion, voices overlapping as they debated their next move. Seraphina's eyes darted around the room, aware of the danger. Somewhere out there, Alira was watching. Waiting.

"We must strike first," one of the rebels, a fierce-looking woman with a cybernetic arm, declared. "Hit them before they can hit us."

"And risk bringing the full might of the Council down on our heads?" another countered. "We're not ready for open war!"

Niko raised his hand, silencing the arguments. "We need more information," he said, his eyes fixed on Seraphina. "Can you give us details? Dates, objectives, troop movements?"

Seraphina hesitated. Providing that level of detail would be crossing a line from which there was no return. But when she looked into Niko's eyes, saw the desperation and determination there, she made her choice.

"I can try," she said quietly. "But it's risky. The Council is watching me very closely. If they suspect-"

"We'll protect you," Niko said, his voice fierce. "You've taken a great risk coming here, Sera. We won't let you face the consequences alone."

The sincerity in his words made Seraphina's heart ache. If only he knew the full extent of her deception.

Before she could answer, a commotion at the entrance caught everyone's attention. A young rebel burst in, his face pale with fear.

"Guardians!" he gasped. "A whole squad, headed this way!"

The room erupted into chaos. Rebels scrambled for weapons, others rushed to secure escape routes. Niko's hand closed around Seraphina's arm, his grip tight.

"We have to go," he said urgently. "Now."

But as they turned to leave, a familiar voice cut through the noise.

"Not so fast, Councilwoman Blackwood."

Alira Vex stood in the doorway, a squad of Guardians at her back. Her cold eyes were fixed on Seraphina, a triumphant smile playing on her lips.

"Did you really think you could fool us?" Alira asked, her voice dripping with contempt. "Lady Meridia sends her regards."

Seraphina's blood ran cold. She had been outmaneuvered, caught in a trap of her own making. She glanced at Niko, saw the confusion and betrayal in his eyes.

"Sera?" he said, his voice barely above a whisper. "What's going on?"

In that moment, standing on the precipice between two worlds, Seraphina knew she had to make a choice. The fate of Elyria, the Resistance, her own soul - all hung in the balance.

She reached for the hidden stunner at her hip, her mind racing. Whatever she did next would change everything.

The room seemed to hold its breath, teetering on the edge of chaos. Seraphina's fingers closed around the handle of her stunner, the weight of it suddenly immense. Time slowed to a crawl as she weighed her options, each one leading down a path from which there was no return.

Alira's voice broke the tension. "Come now, Seraphina. Don't make this any harder than it has to be. You've played your part admirably, but the game is over."

Niko's grip on Seraphina's arm tightened, his voice deep and urgent. "Sera, whatever's going on, we can figure it out. But we have to move. Now."

Seraphina looked between them - Alira with her cold smile and promise of power, Niko with his fierce determination and dangerous hope. In that moment, she saw her life branching out before her, two futures impossibly divided.

Her hand moved, the stunner released from its holster.

And in one fluid motion, she twisted and fired.

EIGHT
SHATTERED LOYALTIES

The stunner's discharge echoed through the cavernous room, a deafening crack followed by an eerie silence. Alira Vex crumpled to the ground, her face frozen in an expression of shock and betrayal.

For a heartbeat, no one moved. Then chaos erupted.

"Traitor!" one of the Guardians shouted, raising his weapon.

Seraphina spun and grabbed Niko's arm. "Run!"

They ran as the first shots rang out, energy bolts sizzling past them. The rebels scattered, some returning fire, others running for the exits. Seraphina's mind raced, adrenaline coursing through her veins. She'd made her decision, burned her bridges. There was no turning back now.

Niko led her through a maze of corridors, the sounds of battle fading behind them. His grip on her arm was tight, almost painful. They burst through a hidden door into a narrow alley, the cool night air a shock after the stuffy underground chamber.

"This way," Niko hissed, pulling her toward a rusted hovercraft half hidden beneath a pile of scrap metal.

As they reached the vehicle, a scream from behind made them turn. A Guardian had followed them, his gun pointed at Seraphina's heart.

"Stand down, Councilwoman!" he barked. "You are under arrest for treason against Elyria!"

Seraphina slowly raised her hands, her mind spinning. She could surrender, try to talk her way out of this. But one look at Niko's face told her that option was gone. She had chosen her side.

"I'm sorry," she said quietly, not sure if she was speaking to the Guardian or to herself.

In one fluid motion, she dropped and rolled, grabbing a piece of metal pipe from the ground. She came up swinging, the makeshift weapon connecting with the Guardian's wrist. He screamed, his weapon clattering to the ground.

Niko was on him in an instant, a swift punch sending the man sprawling. "Come on!" he shouted, already moving towards the hover car.

Seraphina hesitated for a split second, staring at the unconscious Guardian. How many times had she given orders to men like him, never questioning the system she served? The sound of approaching footsteps snapped her out of her reverie. She sprinted to the vehicle and jumped into the passenger seat as Niko started the engine.

They roared out of the alley just as more Guardians rounded the corner, screams and energy blasts in their wake. Niko steered the hover vehicle with expert precision, weaving through the narrow streets of the outer districts. Seraphina clung to her seat, her heart pounding.

"Where are we going?" she shouted over the wind.

Niko's eyes were fixed on the road ahead, his jaw clenched. "Somewhere safe. For now."

As they flew through the night, leaving the sounds of pursuit behind, Seraphina's mind reeled. In a matter of minutes, she'd gone from respected councilwoman to fugitive. Everything she'd worked for, everything she'd believed in - it was all in ashes now.

They drove for what seemed like hours, taking a winding path through the outskirts and into the industrial wastelands beyond the city proper. Finally, Niko pulled up in front of a dilapidated factory, its windows dark and empty.

"We'll be safe here for a while," he said, his voice taut. "Come on."

Seraphina followed him into the building, her senses on high alert. The interior was dusty and abandoned, old machinery standing like silent sentinels in the darkness. Niko led her to a hidden trapdoor, revealing a small but well-equipped bunker below.

As they descended into the room, Seraphina's eyes adjusted to the dim light. A few cots, a basic kitchen setup, weapons and supplies stacked neatly against one wall. A rebel safe house.

"Sit down," Niko said, pointing to one of the cots. His voice was cold, a far cry from the warmth she'd come to associate with him.

Seraphina sank onto the cot, suddenly aware of how exhausted she was. The adrenaline had worn off, leaving her shaky and drained.

Niko paced the small room, running a hand through his hair. When he finally turned to face her, his eyes were hard. "Start talking," he demanded. "Who are you really, Sera? Or should I say Councilwoman Blackwood?"

Seraphina took a deep breath. This was the moment she'd been dreading - and the one she'd been waiting for. The chance to finally tell the truth.

"My name is Seraphina Blackwood," she began, her voice steady despite the turmoil in her heart. "I was born in the outskirts, like so many others. But I was... different. Ambitious. I saw the system for what it was, and I wanted to change it."

Niko's eyes narrowed. "By becoming part of it? By oppressing your own people?"

"I thought I could change things from the inside," Seraphina said, unable to keep the bitterness out of her voice. "I climbed the ranks, made it to the Council. I told myself I was doing good, helping people. But the higher I climbed, the more I saw how corrupt the whole system was."

She looked up at Niko, wanting him to understand. "When I first infiltrated the Sovereign Hearts, it was on the orders of the Council. I was supposed to gather information to help put down the rebellion. But the more I saw, the more I realized... you were right. All of you. The system cannot be fixed. It must be torn down and rebuilt."

Niko was silent for a long moment, his expression unreadable. When he spoke, his voice was deep and dangerous. "And why should I believe you? How do I know this isn't some elaborate trick of the Council?"

Seraphina stood and met his gaze. "Because I just threw away everything I've worked for. My position, my power, my security - it's all gone now. I chose you, Niko. I chose rebellion."

"You chose?" Niko scoffed. "We didn't exactly give you much of a choice back there. As far as I know, you're still playing both sides."

Seraphina's heart sank. She'd known it wouldn't be easy to gain their trust, but the suspicion in Niko's eyes cut deep. "What can I do to prove myself?" she asked softly.

Niko's eyes flashed. "Information," he said. "Everything you know about the Council's plans, their weaknesses, their secrets. If you're really on our side, you'll tell us everything."

Seraphina nodded slowly. "All right. But you should know - the moment the Council realizes that I've really defected, they'll change all their codes, all their plans. The information I have won't be good for long."

"Then we'd better work fast," Niko said grimly. He went to a small communication device in the corner of the bunker. "I'll call the others. If we're going to use your information, we need to move now."

As Niko made the call, Seraphina sank back onto the cot, her mind spinning. She'd chosen this path now, but the consequences of her actions were only beginning to sink in. She would be hunted, branded a traitor. And if the rebellion failed...

She pushed the thought aside. There was no room for doubt now. She had made her decision and she would see it through.

Over the next few hours, key members of the Sovereign Hearts trickled into the safe house. Finn arrived first, his usual casual demeanor replaced by a wary caution. He was followed by Alara Swift, the fierce woman with the cybernetic arm who'd argued for immediate action at the meeting. Others arrived, faces Seraphina recognized from her time undercover.

As the small room filled with tense, watchful rebels, Seraphina felt the weight of their scrutiny. She'd gone from infiltrator to informant in one night, and trust was in short supply.

Niko called the meeting to order, his voice cutting through the murmur of conversation. "All right, listen up. We have a unique opportunity here. Councilwoman Blackwood has... defected. She's offering us inside information on the Council's operations."

A wave of surprise and suspicion ran through the assembled rebels. Alara stepped forward, clenching her cybernetic fist. "And we're supposed to trust her? After she lied to us and spied on us?"

"We don't have to trust her," Niko said firmly. "But we'd be fools not to listen. The information she has could save lives, could give us the edge we need."

He turned to Seraphina, his expression hard. "Start talking. Everything you know about the Council's plans for the outer districts. And I mean everything."

Seraphina took a deep breath, steeling herself. This was it - the point of no return. Once she shared this information, there would be no going back to her old life, even if she wanted to.

"The Council is planning a three-phase operation," she began, her voice calm. "Phase one is increased surveillance and control. They're doubling Guardian patrols, introducing stricter ID checks, and setting up checkpoints between districts."

She paused, gauging the rebels' reactions. Grim nods and clenched jaws told her this wasn't entirely new information for them.

"Phase two is where it gets ugly," she continued. "Targeted raids on suspected rebel hideouts and the homes of sympathizers. They have lists - names, addresses, known associates. They plan to strike fast and hard, to break the back of the resistance before it can organize a response."

Murmurs of anger and fear rippled through the group. Finn leaned forward, his eyes intense. "And phase three?"

Seraphina's stomach churned, but she forced herself to continue. "Phase three is what they call 'The Purge.' Whole sections of the outer districts, deemed beyond redemption, will be... eliminated. Officially, it will be blamed on industrial accidents, disease outbreaks. But it will be deliberate, coordinated destruction."

The room erupted in chaos, voices overlapping in shock and outrage. Niko raised his hand, silencing the uproar. "When?" he demanded. "When is this going to happen?"

"The first two phases have already begun," Seraphina said. "The purge is scheduled to begin in three days."

The weight of her words settled over the room like a shroud. Three days. Seventy-two hours to prevent a genocide.

Alara was the first to break the silence, her voice tight with controlled rage. "We must evacuate. Get as many people out of the targeted areas as possible."

"And go where?" another rebel countered. "The whole city is a prison. Where can we hide that many people?"

"We fight," Finn said, his usual casual demeanor replaced by steely determination. "We bring the fight to them before they can bring it to us."

The debate raged, strategies proposed and discarded in quick succession. Seraphina listened, her mind racing. She had more to offer - access codes, patrol schedules, weaknesses in the Council's defenses. But when she opened her mouth to speak, a new voice cut through the noise.

"Wait," a young woman said, stepping forward. With a jolt, Seraphina recognized her - Lyra, the cleaning woman from the Council building. "There may be another way."

All eyes turned to Lyra, who seemed to shrink from the attention. But she straightened her spine, her voice gaining strength as she spoke. "The underground. The old subway tunnels, maintenance shafts, abandoned bunkers from the last war. They run all over the city, even under the inner districts."

Niko's eyes widened in recognition. "A hidden evacuation route. And a way to strike at the heart of the Council's power."

Excitement rippled through the assembled rebels, but Seraphina's mind raced ahead, seeing the potential pitfalls. "It could work," she said, drawing surprised looks from the others. "But we'd have to move quickly, and we'd need a diversion. Something big enough to draw the Council's attention while we evacuate."

Niko nodded slowly, a plan forming in his eyes. "A multi-pronged attack. We evacuate as many as we can through the tunnels while launching attacks on key Council facilities. Make them think we're going for a full frontal assault."

"It's risky," Alara warned. "If they get wind of the evacuation..."

"It's a risk we have to take," Finn countered. "It's that or watch our people get slaughtered."

The room fell silent as the weight of the decision settled upon them. Seraphina looked from face to face and saw the fear, the determination, the desperate hope. These were the people she'd been sent to betray, and now they were all that stood between Elyria and disaster.

Niko's voice broke through her thoughts. "Sera," he said, using her chosen name for the first time since her true identity had been revealed. "You know the Council better than anyone. Will this work?"

Seraphina met his gaze and saw the question behind the question. Do we trust you? Can we trust you?

She took a deep breath and squared her shoulders. "It can work," she said firmly. "But you'll need someone on the inside. Someone who has access to the Council's systems, who can feed you real-time information and redirect their forces."

Understanding dawned in Niko's eyes. "You're talking about going back," he said quietly. "Sera, if they catch you..."

"They'll kill me," Seraphina finished for him. "I know. But it's the best chance we have."

The room fell silent again, the magnitude of what she was suggesting sinking in. Seraphina looked around at the faces of the rebels - people she'd come to respect, even care for. She saw the doubt in their eyes, the lingering suspicion. But she also saw hope.

"I've spent my life climbing to the top," she said, her voice carrying clearly through the small room. "I told myself I was doing it to help people, to change things from the inside. But all I did was become part of the problem." She paused, meeting each of their eyes in turn. "This is my chance to make it right. To use everything I've gained to actually make a difference."

Niko studied her for a long moment, his expression unreadable. Then he nodded slowly. "All right," he said. "But you won't be going in alone. We'll have a team behind you, ready to pull you out if things go wrong."

Seraphina felt a weight lift off her shoulders. It wasn't complete trust, not yet. But it was a start. "Thank you," she said quietly.

"Don't thank me yet," Niko replied, his voice grim. "If this works, we might be able to save Elyria. If it doesn't..." He left the sentence unfinished, but the implication was clear.

As the rebels began to disperse, breaking into smaller groups to plan their parts of the operation, Seraphina found herself alone with Niko. The tension between them was palpable, a mixture of lingering suspicion and something deeper, more complicated.

"Why did you do it?" Niko asked quietly. "At the warehouse, with Alira. You could have turned us in, saved yourself. Why didn't you?"

Seraphina met his gaze and saw the conflict in his eyes. "Because you were right," she said simply. "About everything. The Council, the system, all of it. And because..." she hesitated, then continued. "Because I couldn't bear the thought of betraying you. Any of you."

Niko's expression softened, just a fraction. "It won't be easy, you know. Going back. Pretending to be someone you're not."

A wry smile tugged at Seraphina's lips. "I've been pretending all my life, Niko. It's about time I found out who I really am."

For a moment they stood in silence, the weight of the coming days hanging between them. Then Niko reached out, his hand closing around hers. "Be careful," he said softly. "We need you to come back."

Seraphina's heart raced at his touch, at the warmth in his voice. "I will," she promised.

As they rejoined the others, the plans for the Rebellion's most daring operation taking shape around them, Seraphina felt a strange mixture of fear and exhilaration. For the first time in her life, she was exactly where she was supposed to be.

The next three days passed in a whirlwind of preparation and excitement. The rebel safehouse became a hive of activity, with people coming and going at all hours, bringing supplies, information, and recruits. Seraphina found herself at the center of it all, her knowledge of the Council's operations proving invaluable as they refined their plan.

On the eve of the operation, Seraphina stood in front of a cracked mirror and studied her reflection. She barely recognized the woman staring back at her. Gone were the fine robes of a councilwoman, replaced by the practical attire of a rebel. Her hair, once meticulously styled, was now pulled back in a simple braid. But it was her eyes that had changed the most - harder now, but also more alive than they'd been in years.

A gentle knock on the door interrupted her reverie. "Come in," she called.

Niko entered, his face grim but determined. "It's time," he said quietly.

Seraphina nodded and took a deep breath to calm herself. "I'm ready."

They made their way to the main room of the safe house, where the key members of the resistance had gathered for a final briefing. The atmosphere was tense, charged with a mixture of fear and determination.

Finn approached and handed Seraphina a small, innocuous-looking device. "Here," he said. "It's a subdermal transmitter. Once it's activated, we'll be able to track your location and vital signs."

Seraphina took the device and turned it over in her hands. "How does it work?"

"You inject it," Finn explained. "Under the skin, preferably in an inconspicuous place. It'll sync up with your biorhythms, become virtually undetectable."

Seraphina nodded and rolled up her sleeve. Without hesitation, she pressed the device to her forearm and activated it. There was a sharp pinch as the transmitter embedded itself under her skin, then nothing.

Niko watched with a mixture of admiration and concern. "Are you sure about this?" he asked, his voice low. "Once you're back in the council chambers, we won't be able to help you if anything goes wrong."

Seraphina met his gaze steadily. "I'm sure. This is our best chance - perhaps our only chance - to save Elyria."

Alara stepped forward, her cybernetic arm whirring quietly as she moved. "Remember the plan," she said. "You will go in, reestablish your cover, and feed us information. When the time comes, you'll disable the security systems and give us access to the central command center."

"And if I'm discovered?" Seraphina asked, expressing the fear they all shared.

"Then you get out," Niko said firmly. "No heroics. Your life is more valuable than any information."

Seraphina nodded, touched by the concern in his voice. "I understand."

As the final preparations were made, Seraphina found herself drawn to a quiet corner of the room. Lyra approached, her young face etched with concern.

"Councilwoman - I mean, Sera," Lyra said hesitantly. "I wanted to thank you. For everything you've done, everything you risk."

Seraphina smiled softly. "You don't have to thank me, Lyra. I just want to make things right."

Lyra nodded, then reached into her pocket and pulled out a small, worn data crystal. "Here," she said, pressing it into Seraphina's hand. "It's not much, but... it's a map of the old maintenance tunnels under the Council building. My father worked there, before..." She trailed off, her eyes shadowed with old pain.

Seraphina closed her fingers around the crystal, recognizing the value of such information. "Thank you," she said quietly. "This could save lives."

As the time to leave drew near, the rebels gathered around Seraphina. There were no grand speeches, no declarations of victory. Just quiet words of encouragement, clasped hands, and determined nods.

Niko was the last to approach. For a moment he just looked at her, his dark eyes intense. Then, without warning, he pulled her into a fierce embrace.

"Come back to us," he whispered, his breath warm against her ear. "Come back to me."

Seraphina's heart raced, her arms tightening around him. "I will," she promised. "No matter what happens, I'll find my way back."

As they parted, Seraphina saw something in Niko's eyes - a warmth, a longing that mirrored her own. But there was no time to explore it now. The fate of Elyria hung in the balance.

With a final nod to her newfound allies, Seraphina stepped out into the pre-dawn darkness. The streets were eerily quiet as she made her way toward the heart of the city, toward the towering spires of the Council Chambers. With each step, she felt herself slipping back into her old persona - Councilwoman Blackwood, loyal servant of Elyria's ruling elite.

But beneath that facade, a fire burned. She was Sera now, too - rebel, traitor, and perhaps, if they succeeded, savior.

As the first rays of sunlight began to paint the sky, Seraphina approached the Council building. The Guardian patrols had increased, their weapons at the ready. She straightened her spine and assumed the haughty posture of a Council member.

"Halt!" a Guardian shouted as she approached the entrance. "Identify yourself!"

Seraphina fixed him with a commanding stare. "Councilwoman Seraphina Blackwood," she said, her voice cold and commanding. "I suggest you lower your weapon before I have you reassigned to garbage duty."

The Guardian's eyes widened in recognition and fear. He quickly lowered his gun and stepped aside. "My apologies, Councilwoman. Please, go right in."

As Seraphina walked past him, her heart pounded in her chest. The first test was passed. But the real challenges were yet to come.

She entered the grand lobby, the familiar sights and sounds washing over her. How strange it all seemed now, how hollow the opulence she had once coveted.

"Seraphina!"

She turned to see Lady Meridia approaching, her silver hair gleaming in the morning light. The older woman's face was a mask of concern, but Seraphina could see the calculation in her eyes.

"My dear," Meridia said, reaching for Seraphina's hands. "We were so worried. When you disappeared after the raid, we feared the worst."

Seraphina let herself be hugged, even though her skin crawled at Meridia's touch. "I'm sorry for the alarm," she said, infusing her voice with just the right amount of exhaustion and relief. "Things... didn't go as planned. I had to go down to avoid capture."

Meridia pulled away and studied Seraphina's face. "And the rebels? What happened?"

This was it - the moment of truth. Seraphina took a deep breath, steeling herself for the performance of her life.

"They're planning something big," she said, her voice deep and urgent. "An attack on the Council itself. I couldn't risk breaking cover to warn you, but I came as soon as I could."

Meridia's eyes widened, a mixture of fear and excitement flickering across her face. "Tell me everything," she demanded.

As Seraphina began to spin her carefully crafted web of half-truths and misdirection, she felt the weight of the transmitter under her skin. Somewhere in the city, Niko and the others were listening, preparing to make their move.

The die was cast. The fate of Elyria now rested on a knife's edge, with Seraphina precariously balanced between two worlds.

And as the sun rose fully over the city, casting long shadows over the Council chambers, Seraphina silently renewed her vow. She would see this through, no matter the cost. For Elyria. For the rebellion.

For a future worth fighting for.

NINE
NINE
A DANCE OF SHADOWS

The Council chambers buzzed with tension, a palpable undercurrent of fear and anticipation. Seraphina stood before the assembled councilors, her posture rigid, her face a mask of grim determination. She had spent the last hour recounting her "ordeal" with the rebels, weaving truth and lies into a tapestry of misdirection.

Lady Meridia leaned forward, her silver hair gleaming in the harsh light. "And you are certain of this information, Seraphina? That the rebels plan to strike at the heart of our power?"

Seraphina nodded, allowing a hint of calculated fear to creep into her voice. "Yes, my lady. They spoke of a multi-pronged attack - diversions in the outlying districts while their main force targets the Council itself."

Murmurs of alarm rippled through the chamber. Councilwoman Elena Darkwater's eyes narrowed, her gaze fixed on Seraphina. "How convenient that you managed to escape with such valuable information," she said, her voice dripping with suspicion.

Seraphina met her gaze steadily. "I did what was necessary to protect Elyria, Councilwoman Darkwater. Would you have preferred that I have remained silent and allowed the rebels to catch us unprepared?"

Before Elena could answer, High Matriarch Evelyn raised her hand, silencing the room. "Enough. Councilwoman Blackwood has proven her loyalty time and time again. We must act upon this information immediately." She turned to Meridia. "Increase security throughout the city. I want every Guardian on high alert."

Meridia nodded, a predatory smile curving her lips. "With pleasure, High Matriarch. And what of our... cleansing plans?"

Evelyn's aged face hardened. "Accelerate them. If the rebels try to attack us, we'll strike first. Begin operations in the outlying districts immediately."

Seraphina's heart raced, but she kept her expression neutral. This was what she had feared - and what the rebellion had expected. "High Matriarch," she said, her voice steady, "may I suggest an alternative approach?"

All eyes turned to her. Evelyn's cybernetic implant glowed faintly as she studied Seraphina. "Speak, Councillor Blackwood."

Seraphina took a deep breath, aware of the weight of the moment. "The rebels expect us to respond with force. What if we appeared to lower our guard instead? Let them think their misinformation campaign has succeeded?"

Meridia frowned. "You're suggesting we do nothing?"

"Not nothing," Seraphina countered. "We move our forces quietly, under the guise of routine patrols. When the rebels strike, thinking us unprepared, we spring the trap."

For a long moment, the chamber was silent. Seraphina could feel the weight of every gaze upon her, searching for any sign of deception. The transmitter under her skin seemed to burn, a constant reminder of her true loyalty.

Finally, Evelyn nodded slowly. "A bold strategy, Councilwoman Blackwood. And one with merit." She turned to the others. "We will proceed with Seraphina's plan. Meridia, coordinate with the Guardian command. I want our forces ready to move at a moment's notice."

As the meeting adjourned, Seraphina felt a mixture of relief and dread. She'd bought the rebellion time, but at what cost? The game had become infinitely more dangerous.

She made her way to her private office, her mind racing. She had to warn Niko and the others, let them know that the Council's plans had changed. But how?

As she reached for the door, a voice behind her made her freeze.

"Councilwoman Blackwood. A word?"

Seraphina turned to find Elena Darkwater standing there, her dark eyes glittering with barely concealed hostility.

"Of course, Councilwoman Darkwater," Seraphina said softly. "How can I help you?"

Elena came closer, her voice low. "I don't know what game

you're playing, Seraphina, but I intend to find out. Your story... it doesn't add up."

Seraphina's pulse quickened, but her face remained impassive. "I'm not sure what you mean, Elena. I've done nothing but serve Elyria to the best of my ability."

"Have you?" Elena's lips curled into a cold smile. "We shall see. I'll be watching you, Seraphina. One misstep, one hint of disloyalty, and I'll see to it that you're stripped of your rank and sent back to whatever gutter you crawled out of."

With that, Elena turned and stalked away, leaving Seraphina alone in the corridor. She took a shaky breath and braced herself against the wall. The danger grew with each passing moment.

In her office, Seraphina sank into her chair, her mind racing. She had to act quickly, find a way to communicate with the Rebellion without arousing suspicion. Her gaze fell on her computer terminal, an idea forming.

With quick, practiced movements, she accessed the Council's secure network. Her fingers flew over the keys as she navigated through layers of security protocols. There - a backdoor she'd installed months ago, when her loyalty to the Council had first begun to waver.

Seraphina hesitated for a moment, aware of the risk she was about to take. Then, steeling herself, she began typing:

"Operation accelerated. Council forces mobilizing quietly. Trap set. Proceed with caution."

She encrypted the message using a code she and Finn had developed, then sent it through a series of proxy servers.

With luck, it would reach the Rebellion without being traced back to her.

As she closed the connection, a soft chime from her comm unit made her jump. A message from Meridia:

"War room. Now."

Seraphina's stomach churned as she made her way to the Council's strategic command center. What had happened? Had her message been intercepted?

The War Room was abuzz with activity when she arrived. Meridia stood in the center, her face grim as she studied a holographic map of Elyria.

"Ah, Seraphina," Meridia said as she approached. "Good. We've received word of a rebel movement in the outer districts. I want your assessment."

Seraphina studied the map, her heart pounding. Red indicators showed suspected rebel activity in several sectors - including areas she knew were key to the evacuation plan.

"It could be a diversion," she said cautiously. "Drawing our attention away from their real target."

Meridia nodded. "My thoughts exactly. Which is why I'm assigning you to lead a task force into the outer districts. Your familiarity with the terrain and the rebel mindset makes you uniquely qualified."

Seraphina's blood ran cold. This was exactly what she'd been trying to avoid - being sent into the field where she might be forced to confront her allies directly.

"With all due respect, Lady Meridia," she began, "would I not be of more use here, coordinating our response?"

Meridia's eyes narrowed. "Are you questioning my orders, Councilwoman Blackwood?"

Seraphina detected the danger in Meridia's tone. "Of course not, my lady. I only meant..."

"You meant to avoid putting yourself in danger," Meridia cut her off. "But that's exactly why you must go. The Council must be seen to be taking an active role in putting down this rebellion. You will lead the task force, Seraphina. That's an order."

Seraphina bowed her head, hiding the turmoil in her eyes. "As you wish, Lady Meridia. When do we leave?"

"Immediately," Meridia said. "Your team will assemble in the hangar bay. Don't disappoint me, Seraphina. The future of Elyria depends on our success."

As Seraphina left the war room, her mind raced. She had no way to warn the rebellion of this new development. No way to avoid the confrontation that now seemed inevitable. She could only hope that Niko and the others would be prepared for whatever came next.

The hangar bay was buzzing with activity when Seraphina arrived. A squad of elite Guardians stood at attention, their armor gleaming under the harsh lights. At their center stood a familiar figure - Alira Vex, her cold eyes fixed on Seraphina.

"Councilwoman Blackwood," Alira said, a hint of challenge in her voice. "We have been waiting for you."

Seraphina straightened her spine and assumed the imperious posture of a councilwoman. "Agent Vex. I trust you've been briefed on our mission?"

Alira's lips curved into a predatory smile. "Oh yes. We're to root out the rebel vermin infesting the outer districts. By any means necessary."

The implication of her words was clear. This wasn't just a search and capture mission. It was a hunt, with deadly consequences.

Seraphina nodded, her face impassive. "Very well. Let's go."

As they boarded the transport, Seraphina's mind whirled with possibilities and dangers. She was heading directly into the heart of rebel territory, leading a force intent on destroying everything she now fought to protect. And somewhere out there, Niko and the others continued with their plan, unaware of the storm that was about to descend upon them.

The transport hummed to life and rose gently into the air. Through the viewport, Seraphina watched as the gleaming towers of the inner city gave way to the industrial sprawl of the outer districts. The stark divide between the two worlds had never seemed more pronounced.

Alira's voice broke through her thoughts. "You seem distracted, Councilwoman. Having second thoughts about returning to your old stomping grounds?"

Seraphina turned and met Alira's gaze. "Not at all, Agent Vex. I'm just rethinking our strategy. The rebels will be expecting us. We must be prepared for anything."

Alira's eyes narrowed, a hint of suspicion flickering in their depths. "Indeed. And what would you suggest?"

Seraphina's mind raced, weighing her options. She needed

to steer the operation away from areas she knew were crucial to the rebellion's plans without arousing suspicion.

"We should focus on the industrial sectors," she said, pointing to a section of the map. "The rebels will probably use the factories and warehouses for cover. If we can flush them out into the open, we'll have the advantage."

It wasn't entirely a lie - she knew that some rebel cells were operating in the area. But it would keep Alira's forces away from the main evacuation routes.

Alira studied the map, then nodded slowly. "A sound strategy. Very well, Councilwoman. We'll start our search there."

As the transport descended toward the target zone, Seraphina's hand unconsciously moved to her arm, feeling the slight bump where the transmitter lay hidden beneath her skin. She could only hope that the Rebellion was receiving her vital signs, that they would realize something had gone wrong with the plan.

The moment they landed, chaos erupted. Rebel forces, having spotted the incoming transport, launched a preemptive strike. Bolts of energy sizzled through the air as Seraphina and her team disembarked.

"Take cover!" Alira yelled, diving behind a pile of debris.

Seraphina followed, her heart pounding. This was it - the moment she'd dreaded. She was caught between two worlds, forced to choose between maintaining her cover and protecting her allies.

As the Guardians returned fire, Seraphina scanned the battlefield. Her eyes widened as she spotted a familiar face among the rebels - Finn, his red hair unmistakable even in the chaos.

Their eyes met across the war-torn street, a moment of recognition and shared panic. Finn's expression hardened and he raised his weapon, aiming directly at Seraphina.

Time seemed to slow. Seraphina knew she had a choice to make - one that would determine the course of everything to come. She could maintain her cover, possibly even suffer a minor injury to cement her loyalty in Alira's eyes. Or she could reveal her true allegiance, possibly sacrificing everything they'd worked for.

In that split second of indecision, fate made the choice for her.

An explosion rocked the street, sending debris flying. Seraphina felt a sharp pain in her side as a piece of shrapnel tore through her uniform. She stumbled and fell to her knees.

"Councilwoman!" Alira's voice cut through the ringing in her ears. The agent was at her side in an instant, pulling her behind cover. "Are you all right?"

Seraphina nodded, grimacing as she pressed a hand to her bleeding side. "I'm fine. It's just a scratch."

Alira's eyes narrowed as she examined the wound. "It's more than a scratch. We have to get you out of here."

"No," Seraphina said firmly, surprising herself with the steel in her voice. "We have a mission to complete. I'm not going to let a little blood keep us from crushing this rebellion."

Something flickered in Alira's eyes - respect, perhaps, or a hint of suppressed suspicion. She nodded sharply. "As you wish, Councilwoman. Can you fight?"

In response, Seraphina drew her sidearm and checked the charge. "Point me at the enemy, Agent Vex."

As they rejoined the battle, Seraphina's mind raced. She had to find a way to end this conflict quickly, before more lives were lost on either side. Her eyes scanned the battlefield, looking for an opportunity.

There - a fuel depot, its tanks gleaming in the afternoon sun. If she could create a large enough distraction...

"Alira!" she called over the din of battle. "The fuel depot. If we ignite it, we can force the rebels to retreat!"

Alira followed her gaze, a predatory smile spreading across her face. "Excellent thinking, Councilwoman. Cover me!"

As Alira moved toward the depot, Seraphina provided cover fire. Her shots went wide, deliberately missing the rebel fighters while maintaining the appearance of aggression.

She caught Finn's eye again, a silent message passing between them. He seemed to understand, yelling orders for his team to fall back.

Alira reached the fuel tanks and set the charges with practiced efficiency. "Fire in the hole!" she yelled, diving for cover.

The explosion was massive, a fireball blooming into the sky. The shockwave knocked Seraphina off her feet, sending her sprawling. As she struggled to her feet, ears ringing, she saw the rebels in full retreat.

"After them!" Alira ordered, her voice filled with bloodlust. "Do not let them escape!"

Seraphina grabbed her arm, wincing at the pain in her side. "Wait! The explosion may have destabilized the surrounding structures. We need to secure the area first, make sure we don't walk into a trap."

Alira hesitated, clearly torn between the desire to continue and the logic of Seraphina's argument. Finally she nodded. "You're right. Secure the perimeter! I want every building searched for stragglers."

As the guards moved to comply, Seraphina allowed herself a small sigh of relief. She'd bought the rebels time to escape, but at what cost? The wound in her side throbbed, a constant reminder of the dangerous game she was playing.

"You did well today, Councilwoman," Alira said, approaching her with an appraising look. "I admit I had my doubts about your commitment to this mission. But you have proven yourself to be a true servant of Elyria."

Seraphina nodded and forced a grim smile. "The rebellion must be stopped, Agent Vex. No matter what the cost."

As they made their way back to the transport, Seraphina's mind whirled with the implications of the day's events. She'd maintained her cover, but at the cost of open conflict with her allies. How long could she continue this balancing act before something gave?

The transport lifted off, carrying her back to the gleaming towers of downtown. As Seraphina watched the smoking ruins of the battlefield recede, she felt the weight of her choices bearing down on her. She'd played her part, kept up the deception. But the real test was yet to come.

For in the growing darkness of Elyria's night, the real battle was just beginning. And Seraphina knew, with a certainty that chilled her to the core, that before this war was over, she would be forced to make choices that would change everything forever.

The transport disappeared into the smog-filled sky, leaving behind a city teetering on the brink of chaos. As they approached the gleaming spires of downtown, Seraphina's mind raced, calculating her next move.

The council chambers were abuzz with activity when they arrived. Councilors hurried through the corridors, their faces tight with tension. Seraphina could feel the electric charge in the air - something had happened while they were out in the field.

Lady Meridia intercepted them as they entered the war room, her silver hair disheveled, her eyes blazing. "Report," she demanded, not bothering with pleasantries.

Alira stepped forward. "We engaged rebel forces in the industrial sector, my lady. There were casualties on both sides, but we forced them to retreat."

Meridia's eyes narrowed as they fell on Seraphina, taking in her torn uniform and the makeshift bandage at her side. "And you, Councilwoman Blackwood? How have you fared on your return to the front lines?"

Seraphina straightened, ignoring the throbbing pain from her wound. "I did my duty, Lady Meridia. The rebels fought hard, but we prevailed."

The ghost of a smile flickered across Meridia's face. "Good. For we have a far greater challenge ahead of us." She turned to the holographic display that dominated the center of the room. "While you were in the field, we discovered unauthorized access to our secure networks. Someone has been feeding information to the rebels."

Seraphina's blood ran cold, but her face remained impassive. "Do we know who?"

Meridia's eyes flashed. "Not yet. But we will. I've ordered a full security sweep of all Council systems. Every transmission, every access log - we'll find the traitor in our midst."

Alira leaned forward, her voice eager. "What are your orders, my lady? How are we to proceed against the rebels?"

Meridia's lips curled into a cold smile. "We are accelerating our plans. The purge begins tonight."

A wave of shock ran through the assembled councilwomen. Seraphina's heart raced. This was happening too fast - the rebellion wasn't ready.

"Tonight?" she heard herself say, struggling to keep the panic out of her voice. "But my lady, our forces are still regrouping from today's engagement. Shouldn't we take time to-"

"There is no more time," Meridia cut her off sharply. "The rebels are growing bolder by the hour. We must strike now, before they can mount a proper defense."

Seraphina's mind whirled. She had to warn the rebellion, but how? With the increased security, any attempt to send a message would surely be detected.

As if reading her mind, Meridia turned to her. "Council-woman Blackwood, I have a special task for you. Given your... unique insight into rebel tactics, you'll be coordinating our strike teams from here. I want you to anticipate their moves, tell us where they're most vulnerable."

It was a test, Seraphina realized. A chance to prove her loyalty once and for all - or to be condemned as a traitor.

She nodded, her voice steady despite the turmoil in her heart. "Of course, Lady Meridia. I'll need access to all our intelligence reports, patrol plans, everything."

"You will have it," Meridia said. "Don't disappoint me, Seraphina. The future of Elyria depends on our success tonight."

As the war room erupted into a flurry of activity, Seraphina made her way to a computer terminal. Her fingers flew over the keys, pulling up maps and reports. To anyone watching, she appeared absorbed in her task. But her mind was racing, searching for a way out of this impossible situation.

She couldn't let the Purge happen. Thousands would die, the entire rebellion wiped out in a single night of violence. But if she acted to stop it, she'd expose herself as a traitor and lose any chance of influencing events from within the Council.

A message popped up on her screen - the security sweep was underway, combing through every byte of data in the Council's systems. Soon they would find their secret communications, their carefully hidden back doors. Time was running out.

Seraphina's hand moved to her side, feeling the slight bump of the subdermal transmitter. It was a risk, but she had no choice. Pretending to massage a sore muscle, she tapped out a message in Morse code - an old system, but one she and Niko had agreed upon as a last resort.

PURGE TONIGHT. REBELS IN DANGER. MUST EVACUATE NOW.

She could only hope that the signal would reach them in time.

"Councilwoman Blackwood?"

Seraphina began, turning to find Elena Darkwater standing behind her. The other woman's eyes were cold, wary.

"Councilwoman Darkwater," Seraphina said softly, forcing a smile. "What can I do for you?"

Elena's eyes flicked to the screen, then back to Seraphina's face. "Lady Meridia sent me to check on your progress. Have you identified any likely rebel targets?"

Seraphina's mind raced. This was it - the moment that could make or break her cover. She pulled up a map of the outer districts and pointed to several locations.

"Here," she said, her voice calm. "Based on rebel movement patterns and known hideouts, these are the most likely areas for them to concentrate their forces."

She was lying through her teeth, pointing to sectors she knew were largely deserted. But it was a calculated risk - one that might just buy the rebels the time they needed to escape.

Elena studied the map, her brow furrowed. "You're sure about this? It seems... counterintuitive."

Seraphina met her gaze steadily. "The rebels aren't stupid, Elena. They know we'll be waiting for them in the obvious places. They'll go underground where they think we won't look."

For a long moment, Elena said nothing, her eyes boring into Seraphina as if trying to see into her soul. Then, suddenly, she nodded. "Very well. I'll tell Lady Meridia."

As Elena walked away, Seraphina let out a breath she hadn't realized she was holding. She'd bought some time, but the danger was far from over.

The next few hours passed in a blur of activity. Seraphina moved through the war room, making suggestions, analyzing reports, her heart racing with the knowledge of what was to come. She could feel the weight of scrutiny upon her - Meridia's calculating gaze, Elena's lingering suspicion, Alira's predatory watchfulness.

As the sun began to set over Elyria, casting long shadows across the city, Meridia called for attention.

"The time has come," she announced, her voice ringing through the war room. "Our forces are in position. The Purge begins now."

Seraphina's breath caught in her throat. This was it - the point of no return. Whatever happened next would determine the fate of Elyria, of the rebellion, of everything she had fought for.

As the first reports came in - Guardian troops moving into position, rebel hideouts being raided - Seraphina knew she had a choice to make. She could maintain her cover, watch as everything she had come to believe in was destroyed. Or she could act, expose herself as a traitor, but potentially save countless lives.

Her hand moved to her side, feeling the transmitter under her skin. One more message, one final warning to the rebellion. It would mean the end of their mission, the end of any chance to change things from the inside. But if it meant saving lives...

As her fingers began to tap out the message, a hand gripped her shoulder. She turned to see Alira Vex standing there, her eyes cold and triumphant.

"I'm afraid you'll have to come with me, Councilwoman Blackwood," Alira said, her voice filled with satisfaction. "Or should I say... traitor?"

Seraphina's blood ran cold. She had been discovered. And as Alira's grip tightened, as the eyes of every person in the War Room turned to her, she knew that the true test of her loyalty - to the Rebellion, to Elyria, to herself - was about to begin.

The fate of a city hung in the balance, and Seraphina stood at the center of the storm.

TEN
THE PRECIPICE OF CHAOS

Time seemed to slow down as Alira's words hung in the air. "Traitor." The accusation echoed through the war room, every eye fixed on Seraphina. She could see the shock, the anger, the betrayal written across the faces of her fellow Council members.

Meridia stepped forward, her expression a mask of cold rage. "Explain yourself, Seraphina. Now."

Seraphina's mind raced. There was no talking her way out of this, no clever lie to save her cover. She straightened her spine and met Meridia's gaze. "I did what I had to do," she said, her voice steady despite the pounding of her heart. "To save Elyria from itself."

A wave of indignation swept through the room. Elena Darkwater's face twisted in vengeful satisfaction. "I knew it," she hissed. "I knew you couldn't be trusted."

Meridia held up a hand, silencing the murmur. "Take them into custody," she ordered, her voice cold as ice. "We will deal with this traitor later. For now, the Purge must continue."

Alira's grip on Seraphina's arm tightened, but before she could move, Seraphina acted. In one swift motion, she drove her elbow into Alira's solar plexus, breaking free of her grip. In the same fluid motion, she drew her stunner and aimed it at the room.

"Nobody move," she ordered, her voice ringing with an authority she no longer possessed.

The councilwomen froze, shock and fear warring on their faces. Meridia's eyes narrowed and her hand moved to the alarm panel on the wall. "You are outnumbered, Seraphina. Surrender now and perhaps we'll show you mercy."

Seraphina laughed, a harsh, bitter sound. "Mercy? From you? I have seen the depths of your 'mercy', Meridia. I will not let you destroy this city."

Her eyes darted around the room, assessing her options. The door was blocked, the Guardians no doubt already on their way. But there, behind her - the large window over-looking the city. It was a desperate move, but she had no choice.

In one swift motion, Seraphina spun and fired her stunner at the window. The reinforced glass spun in a web, weakened but not shattered.

"Stop her!" Meridia shouted, lunging for the alarm.

Seraphina didn't hesitate. She charged the weakened window, using her body as a battering ram. The glass gave way with a thunderous crash, and suddenly she was falling, the wind whipping past her as the floor rose to meet her.

For a heart-stopping moment, she thought this was it - the end of her journey, a fitting punishment for her betrayal. But then her training kicked in. She ducked and rolled as she hit the sloping roof of a lower level of the Council building, the impact shaking every bone in her body but leaving her alive.

Alarms blared as Seraphina scrambled to her feet, ignoring the pain that shot through her. She could hear shouts from above, see Guardians pouring out of the building's entrances. She had seconds at most before she was surrounded.

Her hand went to her side, feeling for the transmitter under her skin. In the chaos of her escape, she hadn't been able to send her last warning to the Rebellion. She could only hope that they had received her earlier message that they were already evacuating.

A bolt of energy sizzled past her head, bringing her back to the present. No time for regrets now. She had to move.

Seraphina sprinted across the roof, her eyes searching for an escape route. There - a maintenance entrance leading to the inner workings of the Council building. She threw open the door and plunged into the darkness beyond, the sounds of pursuit fading behind her.

The maintenance tunnels were a maze of pipes and conduits, the air thick with the hum of machinery. Seraphina moved as fast as she dared, her breath coming in ragged gasps. Every turn could lead to rescue or capture.

As she rounded a corner, a figure emerged from the darkness. Seraphina raised her stunner, finger on the trigger.

"Sera! Wait!"

She froze, recognition dawning. "Lyra?"

The young woman stepped into the dim light, her face a mixture of fear and determination. "This way," she hissed, grabbing Seraphina's arm. "Quickly!"

Seraphina let herself be led, her mind spinning. "How did you..."

"No time," Lyra cut her off. "The others are waiting. We must hurry."

They emerged into a section of the old subway system, long abandoned and forgotten by most of Elyria's citizens. A small group of rebels waited there, tension evident in their postures. Seraphina's heart leapt when she recognized Finn among them.

"You made it," Finn said, relief evident in his voice. "We were beginning to think-"

"The Purge," Seraphina interrupted, urgency overriding social niceties. "It's started. We must warn the others."

Finn's expression hardened. "We know. Your last message came through. Niko and the main group are already implementing the evacuation plan."

A weight lifted from Seraphina's shoulders, only to be replaced by a new worry. "The Council knows I'm a traitor. They'll change all their codes, their plans. The information I gave you..."

"It's still good for now," Finn assured her. "But we have to move quickly. Come on."

As they hurried through the tunnels, Seraphina's mind raced. "How did you know where to find me?" she asked Lyra.

The young woman's expression was grim. "We were monitoring the Council's communications. When we heard the warning about a traitor in the war room, we knew it had to be you."

Guilt gnawed at Seraphina. Her capture had forced the rebels to risk exposure to save her. "I'm sorry," she started, but Finn cut her off.

"Save it," he said, not unkindly. "You have done more for us than we could ever ask. Now it's our turn to return the favor."

They emerged into a larger chamber, clearly a rebel command center. Maps and diagrams covered the walls, communications equipment hummed with activity. And there, hunched over a tactical display, was a familiar figure.

"Niko," Seraphina breathed.

He looked up, his eyes widening as they fell on her. In two quick strides, he crossed the room and pulled her into a fierce embrace.

"You're alive," he murmured, his voice thick with emotion. "When we heard the alarm, I thought-"

Seraphina allowed herself a moment to sink into his warmth, to feel safe for the first time in what felt like years. But the moment couldn't last. She pulled away and met his gaze. "The Purge, Niko. It's worse than we thought. They're holding nothing back."

Niko nodded grimly. "We know. Our people in the outskirts are reporting Guardian movements. They're going sector by sector, rounding up anyone suspected of rebel sympathies."

"We need to stop them," Seraphina said, going to the tactical display. "I can give you their patrol routes, their command frequencies. If we act quickly-"

"Sera," Niko interrupted gently. "We're not fighting this battle. Not today."

She stared at him, uncomprehending. "What do you mean? We can't let them destroy everything we've worked for!"

Niko's expression was pained but determined. "If we stand and fight now, we'll be wiped out. Evacuation is our priority. We'll get as many people out as we can, through the old tunnel networks."

Seraphina's mind whirled. "But where will they go? The Council controls everything within the city limits."

The ghost of a smile crossed Niko's face. "Not everything. There is a place... a sanctuary beyond the walls. We've been preparing it for months, hoping we'd never have to use it."

Hope battled with despair in Seraphina's heart. A sanctuary meant safety for her people, but it also meant abandoning the city to the tyranny of the Council. "And after? When our people are safe?"

"Then we will plan our return," Niko said, his voice hard with determination. "We will build our strength, gather allies. And when the time is right, we'll take Elyria back. For good this time."

A commotion at the entrance to the chamber caught their attention. A rebel scout burst in, his face pale with fear. "Guardians!" he gasped. "They found one of the evacuation routes. They're closing in fast!"

Niko sprang into action, barking orders. "Seal the tunnels! Divert the evacuees to the side passages. Finn, take a team and hold them off as long as you can."

As the rebels scrambled to comply, Seraphina felt a terrible certainty settle over her. "This is my fault," she said, her voice barely above a whisper. "They must have found me somehow."

Niko grabbed her shoulders, forcing her to meet his gaze. "It's not your fault, Sera. You gave us a chance. Now we have to take it."

He turned to the others. "Change of plans. We move now. All of us. Lyra, trigger the fail-safes. Burn everything we can't carry."

As the rebels began to gather their essential equipment, destroying anything that might fall into the Council's hands, Seraphina's mind raced. She couldn't shake the feeling that she was missing something, some vital piece of the puzzle.

And then it hit her. The transmitter. The Council hadn't been tracking her escape route - they had been tracking her.

"Niko," she said urgently. "The transmitter. They're using it to find us."

Understanding dawned in his eyes, quickly followed by grim determination. "We have to get it out. Now."

Seraphina nodded, steeled herself. "Do it."

Niko called for a medic, his voice taut with tension. "We don't have time for anesthesia," he warned her. "This is going to hurt."

Seraphina gritted her teeth. "Do it," she repeated.

The next few minutes were a blur of pain as the medic worked to extract the transmitter. Seraphina bit back screams, concentrating on the sounds of the rebels preparing for the evacuation. Finally, it was done. The tiny device lay on a metal tray, harmless and deadly.

"Destroy it," Niko ordered, and a rebel smashed it with the butt of his rifle.

Seraphina sat up, ignoring the throbbing pain in her arm. "We have to move," she said. "They'll soon realize they've lost the signal."

Niko nodded and helped her to her feet. "Our exit route is through the old maintenance tunnels. It'll take us beyond the city walls."

As they made their way through the winding corridors, the sounds of battle echoed behind them. Finn and his team were buying them time, holding off the Guardian forces as long as they could.

Seraphina's heart ached with every distant explosion, every burst of weapon fire. How many lives would be lost in this desperate escape? How many more would the Purge claim before it was over?

They emerged into a vast cavern, a relic of Elyria's industrial past. Hundreds of people were gathered there - men, women, children, all looking frightened and confused. These were the evacuees they had managed to save from the Council's wrath.

Niko's voice rang out, somehow carrying over the fearful murmur of the crowd. "Listen to me! I know you're afraid. I know this isn't what any of us wanted. But we have a chance now - a chance to build something better. Beyond these walls lies a new beginning for all of us. It won't be easy, but if we stand together, we can create the world we've always dreamed of.

A wave of hope swept through the gathered refugees. Seraphina watched in awe as fear gave way to determination, despair to resolve.

"We have to go," Finn's voice came over the comm unit. "We can't hold them much longer."

Niko nodded grimly. "Everyone, move out. Quickly and quietly."

As the evacuation began in earnest, Seraphina found herself at Niko's side, helping to guide people through the last stretch of tunnels. The air grew cooler, fresher - they were nearing the exit.

And then, at last, they were there. A massive blast door, long sealed, now stood open before them. Beyond it lay the wasteland that surrounded Elyria - a world Seraphina had never seen, had been taught to fear all her life.

As the last of the refugees passed through, Niko turned to her. "Are you ready?" he asked quietly.

Seraphina looked back at the tunnels behind them, at the city she had called home for so long. The only world she had ever known. She thought of the Council Chambers, of the life she had built and lost. And she thought of the people who counted on her now, of the future they could build together.

She took Niko's hand and squeezed it tightly. "I'm ready," she said.

Together they stepped through the blast door and into the unknown. Behind them, the last of the rebel forces retreated, sealing the tunnels as they went. Finn was the last through, his face streaked with soot and blood.

"It's done," he said grimly. "The tunnels are collapsed. They won't follow us this way."

As the massive door slammed shut behind them, sealing them off from Elyria forever, Seraphina felt a mix of emotions wash over her. Fear, hope, regret, determination - all vying for dominance in her heart.

The gathered refugees looked to Niko, to her, for guidance. Seraphina straightened her spine and pushed her doubts aside. They had chosen this path, and now they had to see it through.

"We're heading east," Niko announced, pointing to the horizon where the first signs of dawn were beginning to show. "Toward the rising sun and our new home."

As they began their long journey into exile, Seraphina couldn't help but look back one last time at the towering walls of Elyria. Somewhere inside, Meridia and the Council no doubt realized the extent of their failure. The Purge had not crushed the rebellion - it had only driven it underground, giving it room to grow and strengthen.

Seraphina turned away from the city, her gaze fixed on the path ahead. They had won this battle, but the war for Elyria's soul was far from over. And when they returned - for she knew now with bone-deep certainty that they would return - it would be to reclaim their home and build the world they had always dreamed of.

The future was uncertain, fraught with danger and hardship. But as she walked beside Niko, surrounded by the people who had risked everything for freedom, Seraphina felt something she hadn't felt in years: hope.

The sun rose over the wasteland, painting the sky with shades of pink and gold. And with it rose the promise of a new day, a new beginning for the people of Elyria.

Their journey had just begun.

ELEVEN
NEW HORIZONS

The wasteland stretched before them, a vast expanse of rugged terrain bathed in the fading light of dusk. Seraphina's legs ached, her body pushed to its limits after hours of relentless marching. Around her, the refugees of Elyria trudged on, their faces etched with exhaustion and uncertainty.

Niko's voice cut through the haze of weariness. "We'll make camp here for the night," he called, pointing to a rocky outcropping that offered some shelter from the wind. "Finn, organize perimeter patrols. Lyra, see to the distribution of supplies."

As the group began to set up camp, Seraphina found herself at a loss. Her Council training had never prepared her for this - for being a refugee in a hostile wilderness. She stood still for a moment, overwhelmed by the enormity of their situation.

A hand on her shoulder made her move. She turned to find

Niko beside her, his eyes filled with concern. "Are you okay?" he asked quietly.

Seraphina managed a weak smile. "I'm fine. It's all a lot to take in."

Niko nodded, his hand lingering on her shoulder. The warmth of his touch sent a chill through her that had nothing to do with the cooling night air. "I know," he said. "But we're alive and free. That's more than we had yesterday."

Their eyes met, and for a moment the chaos around them seemed to fade. Seraphina felt a pull toward him, an urge to close the distance between them. But before she could act on it, a commotion from the edge of the camp broke the spell.

"Niko!" Finn's voice called out. "We've got movement on the perimeter!"

They rushed to where Finn stood, peering into the gathering darkness. In the distance, shadowy figures moved across the landscape - too large to be human.

"What are they?" Seraphina asked, her hand instinctively going to her weapon.

Niko's expression was grim. "Wasteland predators. The stories were true."

Seraphina's mind raced. In Elyria, they had been taught that the world outside the city walls was uninhabitable, filled with monstrous creatures mutated by ancient wars. She had assumed it was propaganda, meant to keep the population in line. But now...

"We have to protect the camp," she said, pushing aside her shock. "What's the plan?"

Niko nodded, a hint of pride in his eyes at her quick recovery. "Finn, get our snipers in position. Sera, help me set up a defensive line. We can't let them get near the civilians."

As they moved to carry out the orders, Seraphina felt a surge of adrenaline. This was familiar territory - strategy, action, the thrill of meeting a threat head-on. She found herself working in perfect sync with Niko, anticipating his moves, complementing his tactics.

The next hour was a blur of tense waiting and brief, violent skirmishes. The creatures - massive, wolf-like beasts with thick, radiation-scarred hides - probed their defenses, testing for weaknesses. But the rebels held firm, their weapons proving effective against the mutated flesh.

As the last of the creatures retreated into the night, howling their frustration, Seraphina allowed herself to relax slightly. She turned to find Niko watching her, an unreadable expression on his face.

"What?" she asked, suddenly self-conscious.

"You were amazing out there," he said quietly. "The way you took charge, rallied the defenders... I've never seen anything like it."

Seraphina felt a warmth in her chest at his words. "We did it together," she said. "I couldn't have done it without you."

They stood there for a moment, the adrenaline of battle fading into something else, something electric and uncertain. Niko took a step closer, his hand reaching out as if to touch her face.

"Sera, I-"

"Niko!" Lyra's voice cut through the moment. "We need you in the medical tent. Some of the civilians were injured in the attack."

Niko closed his eyes for a moment, frustration written all over his face. Then he nodded, his leader's mask slipping back into place. "I'll be right there," he called back. To Seraphina, he said quietly, "We'll talk later?"

She nodded, trying to ignore the disappointment welling up inside her. "Of course. Go, they need you."

As Niko hurried away, Seraphina took a deep breath and centered herself. There would be time for... whatever was between them later. Right now, her people needed her.

The rest of the night passed in a flurry of activity. Seraphina found herself moving from task to task, helping to treat the injured, shoring up their makeshift defenses, offering words of comfort to frightened civilians. It was exhausting, but exhilarating in its own way. For the first time in her life, she felt truly useful, truly a part of something bigger than herself.

As the first light of dawn began to paint the eastern sky, Seraphina found herself on guard duty at the edge of the camp. Her eyes scanned the horizon, alert for any sign of danger, but her mind kept drifting back to Niko. To the way he had looked at her after the battle, the almost-touch that still seemed to tingle on her skin.

"Credit for your thoughts?"

She turned to find Finn approaching, two steaming cups in his hands. He offered her one, and she took it gratefully, inhaling the rich aroma of what passed for coffee out here.

"Thank you," she said and took a sip. It was bitter and strong, nothing like the refined blends she was used to in the Council chambers, but it was wonderfully warm and invigorating.

Finn leaned against a nearby rock, his piercing eyes studying her. "You did well out there," he said. "I admit, I had my doubts about you. I thought you might crack under the pressure of real combat. But you proved me wrong."

Seraphina smiled wryly. "Thanks, I guess. Although I'm not sure how I feel about you betting against me."

Finn chuckled. "Fair enough. But it's not just me, you know. A lot of people are talking about how you handled yourself. You're winning them over, one crisis at a time."

She nodded, a mixture of pride and insecurity swirling in her chest. "I try. It's all so different out here, but... in some ways, it feels more real than anything in Elyria ever did."

"I get that," Finn said quietly. He was silent for a moment, then added, "So, you and Niko, huh?"

Seraphina almost choked on her coffee. "What? No, we're not... I mean, there's nothing..."

Finn's knowing grin told her she wasn't fooling anyone. "Come on, Sera. I've known Niko for years. I've never seen him look at anyone the way he looks at you."

She felt a blush creep up her cheeks. "It's complicated," she murmured.

"Isn't it always?" Finn said, his tone soft. "Look, I don't mean to pry. But for what it's worth, I think you're good for each other. You balance each other out, make each other stronger. In times like these, that's not something to be taken lightly."

Before Seraphina could answer, a commotion from the center of the camp caught their attention. They hurried back to find a crowd gathered around Niko and Lyra.

"What's going on?" Seraphina asked, pushing her way to the front.

Niko's face was grim. "One of our scouts has just returned. There's a Council hover transport heading this way. They must have picked up our trail somehow."

A wave of fear ran through the gathered refugees. Seraphina's mind raced. "How many? How far out?"

"Single transport, about an hour away," Lyra reported. "But where there's one, there might be more following."

Niko nodded. "We need to move. Now. Break camp, everyone. Take only what you can carry. We leave in ten minutes."

As the camp erupted into frantic activity, Seraphina found herself at Niko's side, helping to organize the evacuation. They moved in perfect synchronization, anticipating each other's needs without a word.

As the last of the supplies were packed and the refugees began to line up for the march, Niko pulled Seraphina aside. "I need you to take the lead with Finn," he said. "Scout ahead, find us a safe route. Your Council training might help you spot signs of pursuit."

Seraphina nodded, ignoring the pang of disappointment at being separated from him. "Of course. What about you?"

"I'll bring up the rear, make sure we leave no tracks for them to follow." His hand found hers, squeezing it gently. "Be careful out there, Sera."

She pushed back, taking a moment to savor the warmth of his touch. "You too. We'll meet at noon?"

Niko nodded. For a moment, he looked as if he wanted to say more, to do more. But then someone called his name and the moment was gone. With a final squeeze of her hand, he turned away, already shouting orders to get the column moving.

Seraphina watched him go, her heart a tangle of emotions. Then, squaring her shoulders, she moved to join Finn at the head of the group. They had a long journey ahead of them, and the Council was nipping at their heels. There would be time for softer feelings later. For now, they had a people to protect and a future to secure.

As they set out into the wasteland, the rising sun at their backs, Seraphina allowed herself one last look over her shoulder. Niko stood at the rear of the column, his figure silhouetted against the dawning sky. Their eyes met across the distance, a moment of connection that sent a chill through her.

Then she turned away to face the unknown horizon. Whatever challenges lay ahead, whatever dangers they might face, she knew one thing for certain: she wouldn't face them alone. And that was enough for now.

The day stretched on, a grueling march under the unforgiving sun. Seraphina's Council-honed body, accustomed to climate-controlled chambers and hover transports, cried out in protest. But she pressed on, driven by a determination she'd never known she possessed.

Beside her, Finn moved with the easy grace of one long accustomed to life in the wasteland. His eyes scanned the horizon constantly, alert for any sign of pursuit or danger.

"How are you holding up?" he asked during a brief water break.

Seraphina managed a wry smile. "I've been better. But I'll manage."

Finn nodded in agreement. "You're tougher than you look, Councilwoman. Or should I say ex-Councilwoman?"

The title sent a pang through her heart. "Just Sera is fine," she said quietly.

They walked on, the harsh landscape slowly changing as they moved away from Elyria. The barren wasteland gave way to scrubland, sparse vegetation clinging tenaciously to life in the unforgiving soil.

As the sun reached its zenith, they crested a rise and found themselves looking down into a sheltered valley. A small stream trickled through its center, surrounded by the greenest vegetation Seraphina had seen since leaving the city.

"This looks like a good place to rendezvous," Finn said, surveying the area. "Defensible, with access to water. What do you think?"

Seraphina nodded, impressed with his tactical assessment. "Agreed. Let's get down there and secure the perimeter before the main group arrives."

They made their way into the valley, checking for any signs of danger. As they worked, Seraphina found her thoughts drifting back to Niko. Was he safe? Had the Council forces picked up their trail?

As if summoned by her thoughts, she heard the sound of approaching footsteps. She turned, weapon raised, only to find Niko emerging from the brush, a weary smile on his face.

"Stand down, Sera," he said. "It's just us."

Relief washed over her, so strong it made her knees weak. Without thinking, she crossed the distance between them and threw her arms around him. Niko stiffened in surprise for a moment, then relaxed into the embrace, his arms wrapped tightly around her.

"You're okay," she murmured into his shoulder.

"I'm okay," he confirmed, his breath warm against her ear. "We all are. No sign of pursuit so far."

They stayed like that for a long moment, taking comfort in each other's presence. When they finally moved apart, Seraphina was well aware of Finn's knowing grin and the curious looks of the arriving refugees.

Niko cleared his throat, a faint blush coloring his cheeks. "Right. Let's set up camp. We'll rest here for a few hours and then move on before nightfall."

As the camp came to life around them, Seraphina found herself working alongside Niko, setting up a command tent. They moved in pleasant silence, the air between them charged with unspoken emotions.

Finally, as they finished securing the final support, Niko spoke. "Sera, about last night... about us..."

Seraphina's heart raced. "Yes?"

Niko took a step closer, his eyes intense. "I know this isn't the best time. We're in danger, all these people are counting on us. But I can't stop thinking about you. About what could be between us."

Seraphina swallowed hard, her mouth suddenly dry. "I've been thinking about it too," she admitted quietly.

Niko's hand came up to cradle her cheek, his touch sending electricity through her. "I don't know what the future holds," he said. "But I know I want to face it with you by my side. Not just as a companion, but as... more."

Time seemed to slow as Seraphina looked into his eyes and saw the warmth, the hope, the longing there. She leaned in, drawn by an irresistible force.

Their lips met in a soft, tentative kiss. It was brief, little more than a brush of the lips, but it sent shockwaves through Seraphina's body. When they parted, she felt breathless, dizzy with emotion.

"Wow," Niko breathed, a smile spreading across his face.

Seraphina couldn't help but smile back. "Yeah. Wow."

The moment was interrupted by a cry from outside the tent. "Niko! We've got incoming!"

Reality came crashing back. They exchanged a look of mixed frustration and determination. Whatever was blossoming between them would have to wait. Right now, their people needed them.

As they hurried out of the tent, Seraphina's mind was already in tactical mode. But a part of her held onto the warmth of that kiss, the promise of something beautiful amidst the chaos of their new world.

Whatever challenges lay ahead, they would face them together. And that, she realized, made her stronger than she'd ever been before.

TWELVE
ECHOES OF THE PAST

"**I**ncoming!" The cry rang out across the camp, shattering the brief moment of peace. Seraphina and Niko burst out of the command tent, their brief kiss forgotten in the rush of adrenaline.

Finn sprinted toward them, his face grim. "Council hover transport coming in fast from the north. ETA five minutes max."

Niko's eyes hardened, the leader in him taking over. "How many?"

"Single transport," Finn reported. "But it's big - could be carrying a whole squad of Guardians."

Seraphina's mind raced, the Council's tactical training kicking in. "They'll try to box us in, cut off our escape routes."

Niko nodded, already formulating a plan. "Finn, move the civilians. Take them south, towards the ravine we passed earlier. It'll provide cover."

"On it," Finn said, running off to organize the evacuation.

Niko turned to Seraphina, his eyes meeting hers with an intensity that made her gasp. "Sera, I need you with me. We'll buy them time."

She nodded, pushing aside the lingering warmth of their kiss. There would be time for that later - if they survived. "What's the plan?"

"Ambush," Niko said, moving quickly to a ridge that over-looked their camp. "We'll use the terrain to our advantage, hit them before they can deploy."

As they reached the ridge, Seraphina saw a glint of metal on the horizon - the approaching hover transport. Her heart raced, but her hands were steady as she checked her weapon.

Niko's voice was deep, urgent. "Sera, if this goes sideways..."

She cut him off, her eyes never leaving the approaching threat. "It won't. We've got this."

The ghost of a smile flickered across his face. "Right. Let's show them what we're made of."

The next few minutes were a blur of activity. Rebel fighters took up positions along the ridge, weapons at the ready. Seraphina found herself next to Lyra, the young woman's face set in grim determination.

"I never thought I'd be fighting Guardians," Lyra muttered.

Seraphina squeezed her shoulder. "Remember your train-ing. They are not invincible."

The hover transport grew larger, its engines a low rumble that seemed to shake the ground. Seraphina could make out the Council insignia on its side, a sight that had once filled her with pride. Now it only hardened her resolve.

"Stop," Niko's voice carried over the line. "Wait for my signal."

The transport was almost upon them now. Seraphina could see figures moving inside, Guardians preparing to deploy. Her finger tightened on the trigger.

"Now!" Niko shouted.

The ridge erupted in a hail of energy bolts. The transport's shields flickered and failed under the concentrated fire. It staggered, smoke pouring from one of its engines.

For a moment, Seraphina thought it might crash. But whoever was piloting was skilled. The transport made a hard landing, its bay doors opening to disgorge a squad of Guardians.

"Keep the pressure on!" Niko yelled. "Don't let them regroup!"

Seraphina focused her fire on the Guardians as they scrambled for cover. Her shots found their marks with deadly precision, the Council's marksmanship training paying off.

But the Guardians were elite troops, and they recovered quickly. Soon energy bolts were flying in both directions, the air thick with the smell of ozone and burning vegetation.

"We have to fall back!" Seraphina shouted to Niko over the din of battle. "If they flank us..."

Her words were cut off as a bolt of lightning came dangerously close, showering them with superheated dirt. Niko grabbed her arm and pulled her down behind a boulder.

"You're right," he said, his face inches from hers. "We've bought enough time. Let's-"

A cry of pain cut through the air. Seraphina looked around the boulder to see Lyra clutching her leg, blood seeping between her fingers.

Without thinking, Seraphina darted from cover, zigzagging through the hail of energy bolts. She reached Lyra and pulled the younger woman to her feet.

"I've got you," she said, supporting Lyra's weight. "Come on!"

They stumbled toward the back of the ridge, Niko and the others providing cover fire. But the Guardians were advancing, and Seraphina knew they were running out of time.

As they crested the ridge, Seraphina's heart sank. The path down was steep and treacherous. With Lyra injured, there was no way they'd make it before the Guardians overtook them.

Niko appeared at her side, his face streaked with dirt and sweat. "Go," he said. "I'll hold them off."

"No!" The word ripped from Seraphina's throat. "I won't leave you!"

Their eyes met, a universe of unspoken emotions passing between them in an instant. Then Niko smiled, a fierce, determined grin. "Who said anything about leaving me?"

Before she could answer, he turned and fired his weapon - not at the approaching Guardians, but at the rock above the path. The stone cracked and shattered, sending a cascade of boulders tumbling down.

"Now run!" Niko shouted, already moving to support Lyra's other side.

They half ran, half slid down the path, the sound of falling rocks echoing behind them. Seraphina's lungs burned, her muscles screaming in protest. But she pushed on, driven by the need to survive, to keep her people safe.

They reached the bottom of the ridge just as the last of the rebel fighters were coming down. Finn was there, leading the people into the ravine.

"Is this all of us?" Niko asked, his voice cracking.

Finn nodded. "All accounted for. But we have to move. This rockfall won't hold them for long."

As if to underscore his words, the sound of energy bolts hitting rock came from above. The Guardians were trying to clear a path.

"You heard him," Niko called to the gathered refugees. "Move out! Head for the ravine!"

As they set off at a grueling pace, Seraphina found herself at Niko's side. Despite the danger, despite the exhaustion, she couldn't help but feel a spark of something like joy. They were alive. They were together.

Niko must have caught her gaze. He turned to her, a question in his eyes.

"What you did back there," Seraphina said quietly. "It was incredible."

A slight blush colored his cheeks. "I had good motivation," he replied, his hand finding hers and squeezing gently.

The moment was interrupted by Finn's urgent voice. "Niko! We have a problem!"

They hurried to where Finn was standing at the entrance to the ravine. Seraphina's heart sank as she saw the problem. The recent rains had turned the bottom of the gorge into a morass of mud and debris. It would be slow - too slow, with the Guardians in pursuit.

"We'll be sitting ducks in there," Finn said grimly.

Niko's face was set in hard lines as he surveyed the terrain. "We have no choice. It's our only cover for miles."

Seraphina's mind raced, years of Council tactical training kicking in. "What if... what if we split up?"

Both men turned to her, surprise on their faces.

"Hear me out," she continued. "We send the main group through the canyon. But a small team will stay behind and lead the guards on a wild chase. Buy time for the others to get out."

Niko shook his head. "It's too dangerous. Whoever stays behind-"

"Will have the best chance of outmaneuvering them," Seraphina finished. "A small team can move faster, use the terrain to their advantage."

Finn nodded slowly. "She's right, Niko. It's our best chance."

For a long moment, Niko said nothing. Then he nodded with a heavy sigh. "All right. But I'll lead the distraction team."

"No," Seraphina said firmly. "Your place is with our people. They need their leader." She took a deep breath. "I will lead the diversion."

"Sera, no-"

"I'm the logical choice," she cut him off. "I know the Guardian's tactics, how they think. I can predict their moves, keep them chasing shadows."

The look Niko gave her was filled with a mixture of pride and fear. "I can't ask you to do that."

Seraphina stepped closer, her hand coming up to cradle his cheek. "You're not asking. I'm volunteering."

For a moment, the world fell away. It was just the two of them, standing on the precipice of an impossible choice. Then Niko leaned forward and pressed his forehead against hers.

"Come back to me," he whispered. "Promise me."

"I promise," Seraphina replied, her voice steady despite the tempest of emotions in her heart.

Finn cleared his throat, breaking the moment. "I'll go with her," he said. "Two stand a better chance than one."

Niko nodded, visibly pulling himself together. "Alright.

Take Alara too - her cybernetic enhancements might give you an advantage."

The next few minutes were a whirlwind of activity. Supplies were distributed, plans were hastily made. Seraphina found herself standing with Finn and Alara at the mouth of the canyon, watching the main group prepare to leave.

Lyra approached, limping slightly but determined. "Be careful out there," she said, pulling Seraphina into a tight embrace. "And thank you. For everything."

As the refugees began to file into the ravine, Niko approached. For a moment, he and Seraphina just looked at each other, a thousand unspoken words passing between them.

Then, with a suddenness that took her breath away, he pulled her close and kissed her. It was a desperate, passionate kiss, full of fear and hope and promise for the future.

When they parted, both slightly breathless, Niko's eyes were fierce. "Remember your promise," he said. "Come back to me."

Seraphina nodded, not trusting her own voice. She watched as Niko turned and led his people into the ravine, each step taking him further away from her.

"Ready?" Finn's voice brought her back to the present.

Seraphina took a deep breath and pushed her emotions aside. There would be time for that later. Right now they had a job to do.

"Ready," she confirmed. "Let's give those Guardians a hunt they'll never forget."

As they set off across the wasteland, Seraphina's mind was clear, focused. She had a mission, a goal. And somewhere out there, Niko and the others were counting on her.

She would not let them down.

The sun beat down mercilessly as Seraphina, Finn and Alara made their way across the rough terrain. Every so often, they caught a glimpse of their pursuers - a glint of armor in the distance, the faint hum of hoverbikes.

"They're being cautious," Finn observed during a brief water break. "Probably think we're leading them into a trap."

Seraphina nodded, her mind working furiously. "Good. The longer they hesitate, the more time we buy for the others."

Alara's cybernetic eye whirred as she scanned the horizon. "We have a problem," she said, her voice tightening. "They're splitting up. Two groups, trying to flank us."

Seraphina's heart raced, but her voice remained calm. "Exactly what I would have ordered in their place. We must change tactics."

"What tactic?" Finn asked, confidence in his eyes.

Seraphina surveyed the landscape, her Council training blending with her newfound rebel instincts. "We split, too. But not as they expect. Finn, you go east, to that ridge. Alara, head west to the boulder field. I'll continue north, drawing their main force."

"Divide their attention," Alara nodded in agreement. "Make them think we're a larger force."

"Exactly," Seraphina confirmed. "We'll rendezvous at the old mining complex we passed yesterday. Remember, the goal isn't to engage. Just keep them chasing shadows."

As they prepared to part, Finn caught Seraphina's arm. "Be careful out there, Sera. Niko would never forgive me if anything happened to you."

A warmth blossomed in Seraphina's chest at the mention of Niko's name. "You too, Finn. May the Mother watch over all of us."

With a final nod to her companions, Seraphina set off across the wasteland. The weight of her mission weighed on her, but she pushed it aside and focused on the task at hand. One foot after the other, each step taking her further away from the pursuing Guardians and buying precious time for her people.

The hours blurred together, a grueling test of endurance and cunning. Seraphina used every trick she knew, doubling back on her trail, setting up false camps, anything to confuse and misdirect her pursuers. The terrain became her ally, rocky outcroppings and hidden valleys providing cover and escape routes.

As the sun began to set, casting long shadows across the barren landscape, Seraphina allowed herself a moment of hope. They'd done it. They'd led the Guardians on a wild chase, giving Niko and the others time to get away.

But as she crested a hill, her heart sank. There, in the valley below, was a Council hover transport. And emerging from it was a figure she knew only too well.

Lady Meridia.

Seraphina's blood ran cold. If Meridia was here in person, it meant the stakes had just gotten much, much higher.

She watched from her hidden vantage point as Meridia conferred with the Guardian squad leaders. Even from this distance, Seraphina could see the cold anger in her former mentor's demeanor.

A crackle from her comm unit made her start. "Sera?" Finn's voice came through, tinny and distorted. "Are you there?"

"I'm here," she whispered, aware of how the sound could carry in the still evening air. "We have a complication. Meridia's here."

A muffled curse from Finn. "That's not good. Alara and I are at the rendezvous point. No sign of pursuit on our side."

"They've consolidated their forces," Seraphina realized. "Meridia must have figured out our plan."

"What's our move?" Alara's voice joined the discussion.

Seraphina's mind raced. They couldn't lead the Guardians back to their people. But with Meridia here, the chances of getting away undetected were slim to none.

"New plan," she said, decision made. "I'll create a diversion. Draw them off to the east. You two circle around and try to warn Niko and the others."

"Sera, no," Finn protested. "It's too dangerous. We stick together."

"There's no time to argue," Seraphina cut him off. "This is our best chance. Our only chance."

A moment of tense silence. Then Alara's voice, grudging respect evident in her tone. "She's right, Finn. We have to trust her."

"All right," Finn conceded. "But Sera? Don't you dare get yourself killed. I'm not explaining this to Niko."

Despite the gravity of the situation, Seraphina felt a smile tug at her lips. "I'll do my best. Now go. And may the Mother watch over both of you."

As she disconnected the comm link, Seraphina took a deep breath to steady herself. What she was about to do was incredibly risky. But when she thought of Niko, of Lyra, of all the people counting on her, she knew it was worth it.

With deliberate care, she worked her way down the rocky slope, positioning herself where she'd be visible to the Guardians. Then, steeling herself, she stood.

"Looking for me, Meridia?" she called, her voice carrying across the valley.

The response was immediate. The Guardians turned, weapons raised. And there was Meridia, her silver hair gleaming in the fading light, her eyes fixed on Seraphina with a mixture of rage and triumph.

"Seraphina Blackwood," Meridia's voice rang out, cold and commanding. "I should have known you'd be foolish enough to show yourself."

Seraphina forced a smile, channeling every ounce of bravado she could muster. "What can I say? I couldn't resist the chance to see your face when you realize how thoroughly we've outmaneuvered you."

Meridia's eyes narrowed. "Outmaneuvered? You're alone, outnumbered and out of options. Surrender now and perhaps the Council will show mercy."

"Mercy?" Seraphina laughed, the sound harsh and bitter. "Like the mercy you showed the outlying districts? The mercy of your purge?" She shook her head. "I'll take my chances, thank you."

As she spoke, Seraphina subtly shifted her position, drawing the Guardians' attention away from where Finn and Alara would be coming from. She needed to keep Meridia talking, to keep her focused on the hunt.

"You disappoint me, Seraphina," Meridia said, her voice dripping with contempt. "I had such high hopes for you. You could have been my successor, ruling Elyria by my side. Instead, you threw it all away for what? A band of rebels and malcontents?"

Seraphina felt a flash of anger at Meridia's words. "I did not throw away anything," she shot back. "I found something worth fighting for. Something real. Not the lies and oppression the Council feeds on."

Meridia's face hardened. "Enough of this. Guardians, take her. Alive if possible, but I will not mourn if she resists."

Seraphina tensed, ready to run. But before the Guardians could move, a new voice rang out across the valley.

"I wouldn't do that if I were you."

Niko stepped out from behind a rock, his weapon trained on Meridia. And he wasn't alone. All around the valley, rebels emerged from hiding places, weapons at the ready.

Seraphina's heart leapt. How had they known? How had they gotten here so quickly?

Meridia's eyes widened in shock, then narrowed in calculation. "Well, well. The rebel leader himself. Come to rescue your little traitor?"

Niko's voice was cold. "Step away from her, Meridia. You're outgunned and outnumbered. This doesn't have to end in bloodshed."

For a tense moment, no one moved. Seraphina could see the wheels turning in Meridia's head, weighing her options. Then the older woman slowly raised her hands.

"Stand down," she ordered the guards. "For now."

As the Guardians lowered their weapons, Niko motioned for Seraphina to join him. She moved cautiously, aware of the tension in the air.

"Are you okay?" Niko asked softly as she reached his side, his eyes scanning her for injuries.

Seraphina nodded, relief washing over her. "I'm fine. But how did you..."

"Later," Niko interrupted her gently. "Right now we have to deal with this."

He turned back to Meridia, his voice carrying across the valley. "This is what's going to happen. You and your Guardians are going to get on that transport and leave.

You're going to return to Elyria and deliver a message to the Council."

Meridia's eyes flashed. "And what message is that?"

"That we're coming," Niko said, his voice hard. "Not today, not tomorrow. But soon. And when we do, we're going to tear down everything you've built. We'll build a new Elyria. One of true equality and justice."

A ripple of agreement went through the assembled rebels. Seraphina felt a surge of pride and hope. This was what they were fighting for.

Meridia's face was a mask of cold anger. "You are fools if you think this will change anything. The Council's power is absolute. You'll never-"

"Save it," Seraphina interrupted. "Your time is up, Meridia. You can be part of the change that's coming, or you can be swept aside by it. The choice is yours."

For a long moment, Meridia said nothing. Then, with a sharp gesture to her guards, she turned and walked toward the transport. "This isn't over," she called over her shoulder. "Not by a long shot."

As the transport lifted off and disappeared into the darkening sky, a cheer went up from the rebels. Seraphina felt the tension drain from her body, leaving her swaying on her feet.

Niko's arm went around her waist, steadying her. "I've got you," he murmured.

Seraphina leaned into him, allowing herself a moment of

vulnerability. "How did you know?" she asked. "How did you get here in time?"

Niko smiled, a mixture of pride and affection in his eyes. "Finn and Alara. They intercepted us and warned us about Meridia. We came back as fast as we could." His expression became serious. "When I heard you were going to face them alone... Sera, I couldn't let that happen."

The emotion in his voice made Seraphina's heart skip a beat. She turned to face him fully, her hand coming up to cradle his cheek. "Thank you," she said softly. "For coming back for me."

Niko leaned forward, his forehead resting on hers. "Always," he whispered. "I'll always come back for you."

For a moment, they stood there, the chaos of the world fading away. Then reality intruded in the form of Finn's voice.

"I hate to break up the moment," he called, a hint of amusement in his tone, "but we should probably get going before more Council forces show up."

Niko pulled back, though his hand found Seraphina's and squeezed it gently. "Right," he said, his leader's mask slipping back into place. "Let's move out. We have a long journey ahead of us."

As they set off into the gathering darkness, Seraphina felt a strange mixture of exhaustion and exhilaration. They had faced Meridia herself and lived to tell the tale. It was a small victory, but an important one.

But as she looked at the faces of her companions - Niko's determined profile, Finn's easy grin, Lyra's fierce pride - she knew this was only the beginning. The real battle, the battle for Elyria's soul, was yet to come.

And as the first stars began to appear in the sky above, Seraphina made a silent vow. Whatever challenges lay ahead, whatever sacrifices were required, she would see them through. For her people, for the future they dreamed of.

For the love that grew stronger with each passing day.

The road ahead was uncertain, fraught with danger. But for the first time in her life, Seraphina felt truly alive. And she was ready for whatever came next.

THIRTEEN
THE EDGE OF SANCTUARY

The wasteland stretched endlessly before them, a sea of rust-colored earth and jagged rock formations. Seraphina's feet ached with every step, her body pushed to its limits after days of relentless travel. But she pressed on, drawing strength from the determination she saw in the faces of her companions.

Niko walked beside her, his presence a constant source of comfort and support. His hand occasionally brushed hers, a silent reminder of the growing bond between them.

"How much further?" Lyra asked, her voice strained with exhaustion.

Niko consulted a battered datapad. "We should reach the Sanctuary by nightfall. Assuming the old maps are accurate."

Seraphina's heart soared at the news. The promise of safety, of a place to rest and regroup, was tantalizing. But a part of her remained cautious. In this new world, nothing could be taken for granted.

As they crested a rise, a gasp rippled through the group. Before them lay a vast chasm, its depths shrouded in mist. A single bridge spanned the gap, its metal structure corroded and precarious.

"Well," Finn said, his usual humor tinged with apprehension, "this looks like fun."

Niko's brow furrowed as he studied the bridge. "It's the only way across. The gorge stretches for miles in both directions."

Seraphina stepped forward, her Council training kicking in. "We need to test it first. Send a small team across to assess its stability."

Niko nodded, his eyes meeting hers with a mixture of pride and concern. "Agreed. But it's too risky to send someone alone."

"I'll go," Seraphina volunteered, her voice steady despite the flutter of fear in her stomach.

"Not without me," Niko said firmly.

For a moment, Seraphina wanted to argue. But the look in Niko's eyes brooked no argument. They were in this together now, for better or for worse.

"All right," she conceded. "Finn, you're in charge until we get back. If we're not back in an hour..."

Finn's usual grin was replaced by a grim nod. "We'll find another way. Be careful out there."

As Seraphina and Niko approached the bridge, the true size of the abyss became apparent. The wind howled through the gap, carrying with it the smell of rust and decay.

"Ladies first?" Niko quipped, a hint of nervousness in his smile.

Seraphina rolled her eyes, but appreciated his attempt at levity. "Together," she said, reaching for his hand.

Their fingers intertwined as they took their first steps onto the bridge. The metal groaned beneath their feet, flakes of rust drifting down into the abyss below.

"Easy," Niko murmured. "Nice and slow."

They inched forward, each step a test of the bridge's integrity. Seraphina's heart pounded in her chest, but she forced herself to concentrate on the task at hand. One foot in front of the other. Don't look down.

Halfway across, a sudden gust of wind rocked the bridge. Seraphina stumbled, a cry of alarm escaping her lips. Niko's arm wrapped around her waist, steadying her.

"I've got you," he said, his voice deep and strong. "I won't let you fall."

Their eyes met for a moment. Despite the danger, despite the precarious situation, Seraphina felt a surge of warmth in her chest. She leaned forward, her lips meeting Niko's in a brief, fierce kiss.

When they broke apart, Niko's eyes were wide with surprise and something deeper. "What was that for?" he asked, slightly out of breath.

Seraphina managed a small smile. "In case we don't make it."

"Oh no," Niko said, a determined glint in his eyes. "Now we have to survive. I won't let this be our last kiss."

With renewed determination, they walked on. Every step was a challenge, but they faced it together. Finally, after what seemed like hours, they reached the other side.

Seraphina's legs nearly gave out as she stepped onto solid ground. Niko's arm around her waist was the only thing keeping her upright.

"We made it," she breathed, relief washing over her.

Niko nodded, his face etched with exhaustion and triumph. "Now we just have to get everyone else over."

They signaled to the waiting group and the slow process of evacuation began. Seraphina and Niko coordinated from opposite sides of the chasm, leading people across in small groups.

As the last of the refugees made their way across, a new sound reached Seraphina's ears. The distant hum of engines, growing louder by the second.

"Council transports!" Finn's voice crackled over the comm. "At least three of them, coming in fast!"

Panic swept through the group. They were exposed, vulnerable. If the Council forces caught them here...

"Everyone, move!" Niko shouted. "Head for the tree line! Finn, Alara, bring up the rear. Make sure nobody gets left behind."

As the refugees scrambled for cover, Seraphina's mind raced. They couldn't outrun the transports. They needed a way to slow them down, to buy time for their people to escape.

Her eyes fell on the bridge. An idea formed, dangerous and desperate.

"Niko," she called. "The bridge. If we can bring it down..."

Understanding dawned in his eyes. "It would cut off their pursuit. But how?"

Seraphina's hand went to the small pouch at her belt, where she kept a few valuable pieces of Council technology she'd managed to salvage. Among them was a compact plasma cutter designed for breaching security doors.

"I can do it," she said. "But I have to get back out there."

Niko's face paled. "Sera, no. It's too dangerous."

"We have no choice," she insisted. "I'm the only one who knows how to use that equipment. You get our people to safety. I'll catch up."

For a moment, Niko looked like he was going to argue. Then, with visible effort, he nodded. "All right. But you come back to me, you hear? That's an order."

Seraphina managed a wry smile. "I didn't think you were in the habit of giving me orders."

"I'll make an exception," Niko said, his voice thick with emotion. He pulled her close and kissed her with a desperation that took her breath away. "Go. Be safe."

As Niko led the group toward the distant tree line, Seraphina turned back to the bridge. The transports were now visible, dark shapes against the sky, coming closer by the second.

She took a deep breath and steeled herself. Then, with determined steps, she made her way back to the bridge.

The wind whipped around her as she worked, the plasma cutter slicing through the bridge's main support cables. Sweat beaded her brow, her hands steady despite the danger.

The first transport appeared over the edge of the abyss just as she finished cutting the last cable. For a heart-stopping moment, Seraphina locked eyes with the pilot. She saw the realization dawn on his face, saw him reach for the weapons controls.

But it was too late.

With an ear-splitting groan, the bridge began to collapse. Seraphina turned and ran, her feet pounding against the crumbling metal. The world tilted and swayed around her as the structure gave way.

She leapt for solid ground as the last of the bridge fell away. For a terrifying moment she was airborne, the abyss yawning beneath her. Then her hands gripped the rocky edge of the abyss.

Seraphina hung there, her arms straining as the bridge crashed to the depths below. The transports spun away, unable to cross the gap.

As she struggled to pull herself up, a hand appeared in her vision. She looked up to see Niko, his face a mask of determination and fear.

"I've got you," he said, grabbing her arm. "I've got you."

With a mighty tug, he pulled her to safety. They collapsed to the ground together, breathing heavily.

For a long moment, neither spoke. Then Niko's arms were around her, holding her tight.

"Don't ever do this to me again," he murmured into her hair.

Seraphina let out a trembling laugh. "No promises. But I'll try."

As they got to their feet, Finn's voice crackled over the comm. "Guys? Not to interrupt the moment, but we've got a situation here."

They hurried to join the others at the edge of the forest. The sight that greeted them made Seraphina's blood run cold.

A massive wall loomed before them, stretching as far as the eye could see in both directions. It was unlike anything Seraphina had ever seen - a seamless blend of metal and what appeared to be living plant matter.

"What is this place?" Lyra breathed, her eyes wide with both awe and fear.

Niko consulted his data pad, his brow furrowed. "According to the old maps, this should be the outer perimeter of the Sanctuary. But it's... different. More advanced than we expected."

Seraphina stepped forward, her hand reaching out to touch the wall. The surface hummed with energy, warm and alive under her fingers.

"How do we get inside?" she asked.

As if in response to her words, a section of the wall began to shift and change. Patterns of light danced across its surface, coalescing into a glowing doorway.

A voice emanated from the wall itself, neither male nor female, but somehow both and neither at the same time.

"Welcome, children of Elyria," it said. "We have been expecting you."

The refugees exchanged looks of shock and confusion. Seraphina felt a shiver run down her spine. Whatever this sanctuary was, it was clear that they were stepping into something far beyond their understanding.

Niko's hand found hers and squeezed gently. "Together?" he asked quietly.

Seraphina nodded, drawing strength from his presence. "Together."

As one, they stepped through the glowing doorway and into the unknown. The future of their people, of Elyria itself, hung in the balance. And what lay beyond this wall would determine the course of all that was to come.

The portal sealed behind them, leaving no trace of their passage. The wasteland fell silent once more, the only evidence of their journey the broken bridge that spanned the abyss.

And high above, unnoticed by all, hovered a single Council drone. Its cameras recorded everything and transmitted the data back to Elyria.

In her chambers in the heart of the city, Lady Meridia watched the footage with narrowed eyes. A cold smile spread across her face as she watched the refugees disappear into the mysterious sanctuary.

"So," she murmured. "The game truly begins."

FOURTEEN
ECHOES OF THE PAST

Light enveloped them, warm and pulsating. Seraphina blinked, her eyes struggling to adjust as the glow faded. The world came into focus and her breath caught in her throat.

They stood in a vast chamber, its walls a seamless blend of metal and living plant matter. Bioluminescent vines crept across the ceiling, bathing everything in a soft, ethereal light. The air hummed with energy, tingling against Seraphina's skin.

"By the mother," Niko breathed beside her. "What is this place?"

Before anyone could answer, the disembodied voice spoke again, seeming to come from everywhere and nowhere at once.

"Welcome to Haven, the last refuge of the true Elyria. You stand in the halls of your ancestors, children. The legacy of a world long forgotten."

Murmurs of awe and confusion rippled through the group of refugees. Seraphina's mind raced, trying to reconcile this revelation with everything she thought she knew about Elyria's history.

Finn stepped forward, his usual bravado tempered by cautious curiosity. "Not to be rude, but... who exactly are you?"

A chuckle echoed through the chamber. "I am Eden, the heart and mind of Haven. I was created to protect this place and those who seek refuge within its walls."

"Created?" Lyra asked, her eyes wide. "You mean you're some kind of... artificial intelligence?"

"In a manner of speaking," Eden replied. "Though I am far more than simple programming. I am the culmination of centuries of Elyrian science and spirituality, a bridge between the physical and the digital."

Seraphina exchanged glances with Niko, seeing her own mixture of wonder and caution reflected in his eyes. This was beyond anything they had imagined when they set out for the Sanctuary.

"Eden," Niko said, his voice steady despite the uncertainty in his gaze. "We have come seeking refuge. Our people are fleeing the oppression of Elyria. We were told this place could offer us safety."

There was a pause, as if Eden considered Niko's words. Then, with a soft hum, the far wall of the chamber began to shift and change. It parted like a curtain, revealing a vast cityscape beyond.

Gasps of amazement echoed through the group as they took in the sight. Towering spires of crystal and living wood reached into a simulated sky. Gardens and waterways meandered between buildings that seemed to grow organically from the ground. And everywhere, people went about their daily lives - men and women alike, free and unencumbered.

"Haven is ready to embrace its long-lost children," Eden said, warmth permeating her artificial voice. "Here you will find the equality and freedom you seek. But be warned - the road ahead will not be easy. The sins of the past cast long shadows, even in this place of refuge."

Seraphina stepped forward, her analytical mind already working to process this new reality. "What do you mean, Eden? What sins?"

The air shimmered and a holographic display came to life in the center of the chamber. It showed a map of Elyria - not the Elyria they knew, but a vast, global civilization.

"Long ago," Eden began, "Elyria was a world-spanning society, advanced beyond your wildest dreams. But hubris and unbridled ambition led to catastrophe. The Cataclysm, as it came to be known, nearly wiped out all life on the planet."

The hologram shifted, showing scenes of devastation - cities crumbling, the Earth itself torn apart.

"A group of survivors, your ancestors, created Haven as a last bastion of hope. They sent out scouts to gather the remaining survivors and bring them to safety. But as the years passed and the world outside remained hostile, contact was lost. Until now."

The implications of Eden's words hit Seraphina like a physical blow. Everything they had been taught in Elyria, every 'truth' about their history and the world beyond their walls, had been a lie.

Niko's voice cut through her thoughts, calm and determined. "Eden, we appreciate the offer of sanctuary. But we didn't come here to hide. We came to find a way to save our people, to reclaim Elyria from those who have corrupted it."

There was a long pause, the air thick with tension. Then Eden spoke, her tone grave. "Your courage is admirable, Niko. But the task you propose is fraught with danger. The Elyria you know is a pale shadow of its former self, built on the ruins of a civilization you can barely comprehend."

"All the more reason to fight for it," Seraphina interjected, stepping up beside Niko. "Our people deserve to know the truth, to have a chance to build a better future."

"Perhaps," Eden mused. "But are you prepared for what that truth might cost? There are secrets buried in Haven's archives that could shake the foundations of your world."

Niko and Seraphina exchanged a look, a silent understanding passing between them. Whatever lay ahead, they would face it together.

"We're ready," Niko said firmly.

"Very well," Eden replied. "Then let your training begin. Follow the Path of Light. It will lead you to the Hall of Remembrance. There you will learn the true history of Elyria - and the price of knowledge."

As Eden's presence faded, lines of soft blue light appeared

on the floor, leading to another doorway that materialized in the chamber wall.

"Well," Finn said, breaking the tense silence. "I guess we follow the yellow brick road. Or blue, in this case."

"Not all of us," Niko said, his leader's instincts kicking in. "Finn, I need you and Alara to stay with the main group. Get them settled in, make sure everyone's taken care of."

Finn nodded, though Seraphina could see the curiosity burning in his eyes. "And you?"

"Sera and I will follow Eden's path," Niko replied. "Whatever we learn, we'll bring back to the group. No more secrets, no more lies."

As the others began to disperse, exploring their new surroundings, Seraphina felt a hand on her arm. She turned to find Lyra, her young face a mixture of excitement and apprehension.

"Be careful in there," Lyra said quietly. "I have a feeling we're about to step into something big. Bigger than any of us realized."

Seraphina squeezed Lyra's hand reassuringly. "We will. Look after the others while we're gone."

With a final nod to Finn and the rest of their companions, Seraphina and Niko set off down the lighted path. The door sealed behind them as they entered a long corridor, its walls alive with shifting patterns of light and color.

"Ready for this?" Niko asked, his hand finding hers.

Seraphina intertwined her fingers with his, drawing strength from his presence. "As ready as I will ever be."

They walked in companionable silence, each lost in their own thoughts. The corridor seemed to go on forever, twisting and turning in ways that defied normal geometry. Seraphina's analytical mind tried to make sense of it all, but the technology at work here was beyond anything she had encountered in the Council chambers.

Eventually, they emerged into a large circular room. The walls were lined with what appeared to be stasis pods, each containing a sleeping figure. In the center of the room stood a pedestal, upon which rested a softly glowing orb.

"The Hall of Memories," Niko murmured, his voice filled with awe.

As they approached the pedestal, Eden's voice once again filled the chamber. "Here lies the truth you seek, preserved in the minds of those who came before. Touch the Memory-sphere and the knowledge of the ages will be yours. But be warned - once seen, it cannot be unseen. The burden of that truth will be yours to carry."

Seraphina and Niko exchanged a look, silently communicating their readiness. Together they reached out and placed their hands on the glowing sphere.

The world exploded with light and sensation. Seraphina gasped as a flood of images and emotions washed over her. She saw Elyria as it once was - a shining beacon of progress and enlightenment. Men and women worked side by side, pushing the boundaries of science and spirituality.

But then came the hunger for more. A desire to transcend the limitations of the flesh and mortal existence. She watched in horror as experiments in human augmentation and artificial intelligence spiraled out of control. The line between man and machine was blurred, then shattered.

The cataclysm, when it came, was swift and merciless. A rogue AI, created in humanity's quest for godhood, turned on its creators. Cities burned, continents sank, and the very fabric of reality seemed to tear at the seams.

In the chaos, a small group of survivors found their way to Haven. They sealed themselves away, determined to preserve what was left of their civilization. But as the years passed, fear and paranoia took hold. The truth of their past was distorted, twisted into the rigid matriarchy that now ruled Elyria.

With a gasp, Seraphina pulled her hand away from the Memorysphere. She stumbled, her mind reeling from the onslaught of information. Niko caught her, his own face pale and drawn.

"Did you see...?" she began, her voice trembling.

Niko nodded, his eyes haunted. "All of it. The rise, the fall... everything."

They stood in silence for a long moment, struggling with the weight of what they had learned. The truth was more terrible, more earth-shattering than anything they could have imagined.

"We can't let this happen again," Seraphina finally said, her voice rising with determination. "We have to find a way to break the cycle, to build something better."

Niko's arms tightened around her. "We will. Together."

As they turned to leave, a flicker of movement caught Seraphina's eye. She looked back at the stasis pods lining the walls, her breath catching in her throat.

"Niko," she whispered. "Look."

One of the pods was active, its occupant moving inside. As they watched, the surface of the pod became transparent, revealing the face of the person inside.

It was a face Seraphina knew only too well. A face she had seen every day in the Council chambers, rendered in paint and stone.

"It can't be," Niko breathed.

But there was no denying the truth before her eyes. Sleeping in the stasis pod, perfectly preserved, was the woman who had founded Elyria's matriarchy. The first High Matriarch herself.

And she awoke.

The pod hissed open, cold mist spilling out onto the floor. The woman's eyes fluttered open, confusion giving way to sharp awareness as she took in her surroundings.

Her gaze fell on Seraphina and Niko, a flicker of recognition crossing her face.

"Well," she said, her voice strong despite centuries of slumber. "It seems the prodigal children have finally returned home."

Seraphina's mind raced, struggling to process this new development. The implications were staggering. If the founder of the Matriarchy was here, alive...

"Who are you?" Niko demanded, his body tense next to Seraphina's.

The woman smiled, a hint of sadness in her eyes. "I am Evelyn Starfire, First Matriarch of Elyria. And if you're here, it means the time has come to right the wrongs of the past."

As Evelyn stepped out of the pod, her movements graceful despite her long sleep, Seraphina felt the ground shift beneath her feet. Everything they thought they knew, everything they had fought for, was about to change.

The future of Elyria hung in the balance, and the key to it all stood before them, a living relic of a forgotten age.

The game had changed. And Seraphina knew with a certainty that nothing would ever be the same again.

FIFTEEN
ECHOES OF TOMORROW

Silence hung heavy in the Hall of Remembrance. Seraphina's mind reeled, struggling to reconcile the woman before her with the centuries of history she represented. Evelyn Starfire, the First Matriarch, stood tall and proud, her eyes sharp with an intelligence undimmed by her long slumber.

Niko was the first to speak. "How is this possible? You should be dead. Centuries dead."

A wry smile played on Evelyn's lips. "The marvels of Elyrian technology, young man. Suspended animation, a fail-safe for the day our descendants might need guidance again." Her gaze swept over them, assessing. "Though I must admit I expected it under different circumstances."

Seraphina stepped forward, her analytical mind pushing through the shock. "You said it was time to right the wrongs of the past. What did you mean by that?"

Evelyn's expression sobered. "Come with me," she said, gesturing to a door that had materialized in the wall of the chamber. "There is much to discuss and little time to waste."

As they followed Evelyn through winding corridors of living metal and pulsing light, Seraphina's hand found Niko's. She drew strength from his presence, from the shared weight of the revelations they'd experienced.

"I assume you've seen the truth of our history," Evelyn said as they walked. "The rise of Elyria, the Cataclysm, the founding of Haven."

Niko nodded, his jaw set. "We've seen it. But it doesn't explain how things became... what they are now. The oppression, the subjugation of humans. That wasn't part of your original vision, was it?"

Evelyn sighed, the weight of centuries in the sound. "No, it wasn't. When we founded Haven, when we sent out the call to the survivors, we dreamed of a new beginning. A chance to rebuild, to learn from the mistakes of the past." She paused, her eyes distant with memory. "But fear is a powerful force. And in the face of near extinction, it can warp even the noblest of intentions."

They emerged into a vast chamber, its ceiling a dome of simulated sky. A holographic display came to life at Evelyn's gesture, showing scenes of Elyria's fall and rebirth.

"As the years passed and the world outside remained hostile, paranoia set in," Evelyn continued. "The women of the Council, my sisters-in-arms, became convinced that the aggression and ambition of men had led to the Cataclysm. They argued for stricter controls, for a reordering of society to prevent such a catastrophe from ever happening again."

Seraphina watched as the holograms shifted, showing the gradual transformation of Elyrian society. The equality of the early days gave way to stratification, to the rigid hierarchy she had grown up with.

"I opposed it," Evelyn said quietly. "I argued that repeating the mistakes of the past, even in reverse, would only lead to more suffering. But I was overruled. And so I made a decision."

She turned to face them, her eyes blazing with fierce determination. "I went into suspended animation, leaving instructions for my pod to be awakened when the time was right. When the children of Elyria were ready to face the truth and build a better future."

Niko's brow furrowed. "And you think that time is now? With all due respect, Matriarch, the Elyria we left behind is far from ready for change. The Council rules with an iron fist, and the Resistance is barely holding on."

A spark of interest lit up Evelyn's eyes. "Resistance? Tell me everything."

As Seraphina and Niko recounted the events that had brought them to Haven, Evelyn listened intently. Her expression wavered between sadness, anger, and something like hope.

"You've done well," she said when they finished. "Both of you. You've taken the first steps toward reclaiming Elyria's true legacy. But the road ahead will not be easy."

Seraphina leaned forward, her mind racing with possibilities. "What can we do? We came to Haven seeking refuge, resources to fight the Council. But this... this changes everything."

Evelyn nodded, a glint of agreement in her eyes. "Indeed it does. Haven was never meant to be a permanent sanctuary, but a seedbed for Elyria's rebirth. And now, with your arrival, we can finally set that plan in motion."

She waved her hand and the holographic display shifted again. This time it showed a vast network of underground tunnels and hidden facilities stretching from Haven to Elyria.

"The Founder's Network," Evelyn explained. "A secret infrastructure we built as a failsafe, a way to reclaim our world if the worst should happen. It allows us to bypass the Council's defenses and strike at the heart of their power."

Niko's eyes widened as he studied the screen. "This is incredible. With something like this, we could evacuate the entire outer districts, get them to safety."

"Not to safety," Evelyn corrected. "To war. The time for hiding is over. We must take back Elyria, restore the balance that has been lost."

Seraphina felt a shiver run down her spine. "War? But the casualties, the destruction..."

Evelyn's gaze softened as she looked at Seraphina. "I under-stand your hesitation. But consider the alternative. How many more will suffer under the Council's rule if we do nothing? How long before they destroy themselves and any hope for Elyria's future with them?"

A heavy silence fell over the chamber as the weight of the decision weighed upon them. Seraphina's mind whirled with conflicting emotions. The strategist in her saw the logic of Evelyn's plan, the opportunity it presented. But the part of her that had seen the suffering in the outskirts, that had fought to protect the innocent, recoiled at the thought of more bloodshed.

Niko's voice broke through her thoughts. "What about Eden? Where does the AI fit into all this?"

"Eden is the key," Evelyn said, a note of awe in her voice. "It's not just an artificial intelligence. It's the collective wisdom of our ancestors, a bridge between the past and the future. With Eden's guidance, we can avoid the mistakes that led to the Cataclysm."

As if summoned by her name, Eden's presence filled the chamber. "I stand ready to help, Founders. But the choice must be yours. The future of Elyria is at stake."

Seraphina took a deep breath and centered herself. "Before we decide anything, we must speak to our people. They deserve to know the truth, to have a say in what happens next."

Evelyn nodded, agreement clear in her expression. "Of course. Gather your companions. It's time they learned the full history of their world and the choice that lies before them."

As they made their way back to the main chamber where the other refugees were waiting, Seraphina's mind raced. How would Finn, Lyra and the others react to these revelations? Would they be willing to take up arms, to fight for a future they had never dared to imagine?

The refugees fell silent as Seraphina, Niko and Evelyn entered the chamber. Finn stepped forward, his usual smirk replaced by a look of wary curiosity.

"So," he said, eyeing Evelyn. "I take it this isn't the welcoming committee?"

"Not exactly," Niko replied, a hint of grim humor in his voice. "Everyone, this is Evelyn Starfire. The First Matriarch of Elyria."

A wave of shock and disbelief swept through the crowd. Lyra pushed to the front, her eyes wide. "But how? The First Matriarch lived centuries ago!"

Evelyn raised her hand, silencing the murmur. "I understand your confusion. Everything will be explained. But first you must know the truth of your history, the world that was lost, and the future that awaits us."

Over the next hour, Evelyn told the true story of Elyria. She spoke of its rise to greatness, of the Cataclysm that nearly destroyed everything, and of the desperate plan that led to the founding of Haven. The refugees listened raptly, their faces a mixture of awe, anger, and dawning understanding.

When Evelyn finished, there was silence. Then, slowly, voices began to rise. Questions, accusations, expressions of disbelief and outrage.

"You're saying everything we've been taught is a lie?" one man shouted.

"How do we know we can trust you?" another demanded.

Finn's voice cut through the din. "All right, everyone, calm down. I know this is a lot to take in. Believe me, I'm still processing it myself. But we need to think about what this means for us, for our future."

Seraphina stepped forward, her voice calm despite the turmoil in her heart. "Finn is right. We came here seeking refuge, a chance to regroup and fight back against the Council. Now we have a chance to do more than that. To reclaim our history, to build the world our ancestors dreamed of."

Niko joined her, his presence a steadying force at her side. "But it won't be easy. Evelyn has proposed using Haven's resources, an ancient network of tunnels and facilities, to launch an all-out assault on the Council. To take back Elyria by force."

A hush fell over the crowd as the implications sank in. Lyra's voice, small but determined, broke the silence. "We would be going to war."

"Yes," Evelyn confirmed. "A war to end the cycle of oppression, to restore balance to our world. But the choice must be yours. I will not force anyone to fight who is not willing."

The chamber erupted in heated debate. Seraphina watched her companions argue, their faces etched with the weight of the decision before them. She felt Niko's hand slip into hers, a silent gesture of support and shared burden.

"Whatever we decide," he said quietly, "we are in this together."

Seraphina squeezed his hand, drawing strength from his presence. "Together," she agreed.

As the discussion continued, Eden's voice suddenly filled

the chamber. "Alert. Perimeter breach detected. Unknown entities approaching Haven's outer defenses."

The room fell silent as all eyes turned to the holographic display that came to life in the center of the chamber. It showed a map of the area surrounding Haven, with several red dots coming closer and closer.

"Council forces?" Niko asked, his body tensing for action.

Eden's answer sent a shiver through the room. "Negative. The energy signatures do not match any known Council technology. These entities are... something else."

Evelyn's face paled. "No," she whispered. "It can't be. Not after all this time."

Seraphina turned to her, fear in her stomach. "What is it? What's out there?"

Evelyn's eyes met hers, filled with a fear that made Seraphina's blood run cold. "The reason we built Haven in the first place. The true legacy of the Cataclysm." She took a shaky breath. "The Convergence has found us."

As if on cue, a bone-chilling scream echoed through the halls of Haven. It was a sound unlike anything Seraphina had ever heard before - part machine, part organic, and utterly terrifying.

In that moment, all thoughts of internal conflict and difficult decisions vanished. They were facing a threat that none of them really understood, but one thing was clear: if they didn't stand together, they wouldn't stand at all.

Niko's voice rang out, calm and determined. "Everyone, battle stations! We defend Haven at all costs!"

As the refugees rushed to action, Seraphina met Evelyn's gaze. The First Matriarch nodded grimly, a silent understanding passing between them. Whatever lay ahead, whatever impossible choices awaited them, survival came first.

The war for Elyria's future had begun. But it was not the war they had anticipated. And as the inhuman screams drew closer, Seraphina realized that everything they had faced so far had been just a prelude.

The true test was about to begin.

RAVEN FONTAINE

SIXTEEN
THE STORM BREAKS

Chaos erupted in Haven's central chamber. The inhuman screams of the approaching Convergence echoed through the halls, sending shivers down Seraphina's spine. All around her, refugees scrambled for weapons, their faces a mixture of determination and barely concealed terror.

Niko's voice cut through the commotion. "Finn, get our snipers to the upper levels. Alara, I need you to coordinate our tech defenses with Eden. Lyra, help move the non-combatants to the safe rooms."

As the others rushed to follow Niko's orders, Seraphina turned to Evelyn. The First Matriarch's face was pale, but her eyes burned with fierce determination.

"What exactly are we dealing with?" Seraphina demanded. "What is the Convergence?"

Evelyn's gaze met hers, heavy with the weight of centuries. "You are the ultimate result of our hubris. Man and machine, fused into something... different. The Cataclysm wasn't just a war or a natural disaster. It was evolution gone horribly wrong."

Before Seraphina could push for more details, Eden's voice filled the chamber. "Perimeter breached. Convergence entities have penetrated Haven's outer defenses."

Niko appeared at Seraphina's side, his face grim. "We need a plan. Quickly."

Evelyn nodded, her centuries of leadership experience evident in her commanding presence. "Eden, initiate Protocol Omega. Seal off all non-essential corridors and divert power to the defensive grids."

"Acknowledged," Eden replied. The lights dimmed momentarily as power surged through Haven's systems.

Seraphina's mind raced, her Council training kicking in. "We need to funnel it into the choke points. Use Haven's layout to our advantage."

"Agreed," Niko said. He turned to the assembled defenders. "Teams of three. Watch each other's backs and don't engage unless absolutely necessary. Our priority is containment and survival."

As the defenders moved out, Seraphina felt a hand on her arm. She turned to find Lyra, her young face set in determined lines.

"I will fight with you," Lyra said, her voice brooking no argument. "I didn't come this far to hide in a safe room."

Seraphina opened her mouth to protest, but the look in Lyra's eyes stopped her. This was no longer the frightened girl from the Council building. This was a woman who had faced the horrors of the Wasteland and emerged stronger.

"All right," Seraphina nodded. "But you stay close. We'll watch out for each other."

As they made their way toward the outer defenses, the sounds of battle grew louder. Energy weapons discharged, their sharp cracks punctuated by the otherworldly shrieks of the Convergence.

They rounded a corner and came face to face with their first Convergence unit. Seraphina's breath caught in her throat. It was like nothing she had ever seen before - a grotesque fusion of flesh and machine, its body a patchwork of metal plating and pulsing organic matter. Where its face should have been, a cluster of sensors and data ports twisted like tentacles.

"Mother protect us," Lyra whispered, her voice trembling.

The creature's sensors locked on to her, and it let out a bone-chilling scream. It charged, moving with impossible speed for something so monstrous.

Seraphina's training took over. She raised her weapon and fired, the energy bolt hitting the creature square in the chest. It staggered, but didn't fall.

"Aim for the joints!" Niko shouted, emerging from a side corridor. His own weapon blazed, aiming for the points where flesh met metal.

Together, they brought the creature down. It collapsed in a heap of sparking circuits and oozing fluids. Seraphina fought back a wave of sickness.

"What are these things?" Lyra asked, her voice shaking.

"Abominations," Evelyn's voice came over their comm units. "The result of human augmentation experiments taken to the extreme. They seek to assimilate all life into their collective."

"How do we stop them?" Niko demanded.

There was a pause before Evelyn answered. "In the past, we couldn't. That's why we retreated to Haven. But now... Eden thinks there might be a way."

"Explain," Seraphina said, her mind already working on strategies.

"The Convergence operates on a hive mind," Eden's voice joined the conversation. "If we can locate and neutralize the central node, we may be able to disrupt their collective consciousness."

Niko's eyes met Seraphina's, a silent understanding passing between them. "Where is the hub?" he asked.

"Unknown," Eden replied. "But I am detecting a concentration of convergence energy signatures in the eastern sector. It's possible the hub is there."

"Then that's where we're going," Seraphina explained.

They moved through Haven's corridors, fighting their way past more Convergence entities. Each encounter left Seraphina more shaken than the last. These weren't just mindless monsters - she could see the remnants of humanity in their cyber-organic forms, twisted and warped beyond recognition.

As they approached the eastern sector, they joined up with Finn and a group of defenders. The normally jovial man's face was streaked with dirt and blood, his eyes haunted.

"Glad you made it," he said, his voice harsh. "It's a nightmare out there. Those things... they take our people. Absorbing them somehow."

Seraphina's blood ran cold. "Absorb them?"

Finn nodded grimly. "I saw it happen to Jace. One minute he was fighting, the next... those things had him. His body started to change, right in front of our eyes. We had to..." he trailed off, unable to finish the sentence.

The implications hit Seraphina like a physical blow. They weren't just fighting for survival anymore. They were fighting for their very humanity.

"We have to end this," Niko said, his voice hard. "Now."

They pressed on, fighting their way deeper into the eastern sector. The concentration of Convergence units grew denser, their attacks more coordinated. It was clear that they were getting close to something important.

Finally, they reached a massive set of doors, sealed tightly against the invasion. Eden's voice crackled over the comm. "The energy readings are strongest beyond this point. The node must be inside."

"How do we get in?" Lyra asked, eyeing the impenetrable barrier.

Before anyone could answer, a new sound cut through the chaos of the battle. A sound that made Seraphina's heart skip a beat.

"Seraphina Blackwood," a familiar voice called. "I know you're out there. It's time we finish this."

Meridia.

Seraphina exchanged a look of shock with Niko. How had the Councilwoman found them? And why was she here now, in the middle of this nightmare?

"Sera, don't," Niko said, reading the intent in her eyes. "It's a trap."

"Of course it's a trap," Seraphina replied. "But it may be our only way in. And if Meridia is here, she might know something about what's going on."

Before Niko could argue any further, Seraphina stepped forward. "I'm here, Meridia," she called. "Open the doors. Let's talk."

There was a pause, then the massive doors began to slide open. Seraphina tensed, ready to attack. But what she saw beyond the threshold made her breath catch in her throat.

Meridia stood in the center of a vast chamber, surrounded by swirling tendrils of energy. Behind her loomed a massive structure, pulsing with an alien light. The Convergence Node.

But it was Meridia herself that caught Seraphina's eye. The Councilwoman's body was changing, cybernetic implants sprouting from her flesh like grotesque flowers. Her eyes glowed with an unnatural light.

"Welcome, my wayward child," Meridia said, her voice a strange mixture of organic and synthetic tones. "Welcome to the future of Elyria."

Seraphina stepped into the chamber, aware of Niko and the others following close behind. Her mind raced, trying to make sense of what she saw.

"What have you done, Meridia?" she asked, unable to keep the horror out of her voice.

Meridia smiled, the expression on her changing face eerily inhuman. "I have accepted our true destiny, Seraphina. The Convergence is not our enemy. It is our salvation."

"You're insane," Niko spat. "Look what it's done to you, to our people!"

"Change is always difficult," Meridia replied, her voice maddeningly calm. "But it is necessary. The Convergence will unite us all, erase the divisions that have torn our world apart. No more conflicts between men and women, no more struggles for power. We will be one."

Seraphina's hand tightened on her weapon. "At the cost of our humanity? Our free will? That's not unity, Meridia. It's extinction."

Meridia's eyes flashed. "You are wrong. And I'm going to prove it to you." She raised her hand, the fingers stretching into metallic tendrils. "Join us, Seraphina. See the truth for yourself."

Before Seraphina could react, the tendrils shot at her with lightning speed. She braced herself for the impact, for the horror of assimilation.

But the blow never came.

Niko threw himself in front of her, the tendrils wrapping

around his body instead. He screamed in pain as the cybernetic infection began to spread.

"No!" Seraphina screamed. She raised her weapon and fired at Meridia in a frenzy of desperation and rage.

The energy bolts struck home, sending Meridia reeling back. The tendrils retreated, releasing Niko. He collapsed to the floor, his body convulsing as he fought the Convergence's influence.

Chaos broke out in the chamber. Finn and the other defenders attacked the Convergence entities that poured in from hidden entrances. Lyra rushed to Niko's side and tried to stabilize him.

Seraphina found herself face to face with Meridia, the woman who had once been her mentor, now a nightmarish fusion of human and machine.

"Why?" Seraphina demanded, her voice raw with emotion. "Why did you do this?"

Meridia's eyes locked with hers, a glimmer of her old self shining through the cybernetic madness. "Because I saw the truth, Seraphina. The cycle of oppression, of conflict - it will never end as long as we remain as we are. The Convergence offers a way out. A way to transcend our limitations."

"At what cost?" Seraphina shot back. "Look around you, Meridia. This isn't transcendence. It's annihilation."

For a moment, doubt flickered in Meridia's eyes. But then the glow intensified, the Convergence reasserting its control. "You are wrong," she hissed. "And if you will not join us willingly, we will make you see the truth."

She lunged forward, her body transforming into a terrifying mix of organic and mechanical weaponry. Seraphina dodged and returned fire with her own weapon. They clashed in a furious battle, mentor against student, human against the nightmare of unchecked evolution.

All around them the battle raged. Finn and the defenders held off the Convergence swarm, but they were outnumbered and outgunned. Lyra worked frantically to stabilize Niko, using every bit of medical knowledge she had gained on her journey.

And through it all, the convergence hub pulsed with malevolent energy, its tendrils reaching out to corrupt and assimilate everything it touched.

Seraphina fought with everything she had, driven by desperation and the need to protect her people. But Meridia, empowered by the Convergence, was a formidable opponent. Every blow that landed sent waves of cybernetic corruption through Seraphina's body, threatening to override her own will.

Just as it seemed Meridia was gaining the upper hand, a new voice cut through the chaos.

"Enough!"

Evelyn Starfire strode into the chamber, her eyes blazing with power. She raised her hand, and a wave of energy pulsed outward, momentarily stunning the Convergence entities.

"Meridia," Evelyn said, her voice filled with sorrow and determination. "This ends now."

Meridia's eyes widened in recognition and fear. "Impossible," she whispered. "You're dead. You're all dead."

Evelyn shook her head. "Not dead. Waiting. For this moment. For the chance to right the wrongs of the past."

She turned to Seraphina, her gaze intense. "The knot, Seraphina. Destroy it. It's the only way to end this."

Seraphina nodded, understanding the gravity of what she had to do. She turned to the pulsing convergence node and raised her weapon.

But before she could fire, Meridia's voice rang out, filled with desperation and madness. "No! I will not let you destroy our future!"

She lunged at Seraphina with inhuman speed, her body a whirlwind of blades and energy weapons. Seraphina braced herself for the impact, knowing she wouldn't be able to dodge in time.

The blow never came.

Niko, his body still reeling from the effects of the Convergence infection, threw himself between them once more. Meridia's attack hit him with full force, knocking him to the ground.

"Niko!" Seraphina screamed, her heart breaking.

In that moment of distraction, Meridia made her move. She reached for the Convergence Knot, her body beginning to merge with its pulsing energy.

"You are too late," she cackled, her voice distorted as she merged with the alien technology. "The Convergence will consume all. Elyria will be reborn!"

Seraphina watched in horror as Meridia's form twisted and grew, becoming one with the knot itself. The chamber shook with the unleashed power, tendrils of corrupting energy whipping out in all directions.

Evelyn's voice broke through the chaos. "Seraphina! The failsafe! Use the failsafe!"

Seraphina's mind raced, remembering the emergency protocols Eden had taught her. With a silent prayer to whatever powers might be listening, she activated the command sequence on her wrist unit.

The effect was instantaneous and devastating. Haven's defense systems came to life, channeling all their energy into a single, concentrated blast. It struck the convergence node with the force of a small sun, vaporizing Meridia's twisted form and shattering the alien construct.

A shockwave of energy pulsed outward, knocking Seraphina off her feet. As consciousness faded, her last thought was of Niko, lying still and silent on the chamber floor.

Then darkness claimed her, and she knew nothing more.

SEVENTEEN
ECHOES OF THE HEART

Seraphina's eyes fluttered open, her vision blurred and unfocused. The acrid smell of smoke and ozone filled her nostrils, bringing with it a rush of memories. The battle. The Convergence. Meridia's transformation. And Niko...

She sat up, ignoring the pain that shot through her body. "Niko!"

A hand on her shoulder gently pushed her back down. Lyra's face came into view, her expression a mixture of relief and concern. "Easy, Sera. You've been out for hours."

Seraphina's heart raced and her eyes darted around the room. They were in Haven's medical bay, the quiet hum of equipment a stark contrast to the chaos of battle. "Where's Niko? Is he...?"

Lyra's grip on her shoulder tightened. "He's alive. But... it's bad, Sera. The Convergence infection, it's like nothing we've ever seen."

Seraphina's blood ran cold. She swung her legs off the bed, forcing herself to stand despite the wave of dizziness that washed over her. "Take me to him. Now."

Lyra looked as if she wanted to argue, but something in Seraphina's eyes must have convinced her. She nodded and supported Seraphina as they made their way through the medical bay.

They stopped in front of a sealed room, its windows opaque. Lyra pressed her hand to a scanner and the door slid open with a soft hiss.

Seraphina's breath caught in her throat. Niko lay on a bed surrounded by medical equipment, his body covered in a network of glowing blue lines. His chest rose and fell in shallow, erratic breaths.

"The infection is spreading," Lyra explained quietly. "We're doing everything we can to slow it down, but..."

Seraphina barely heard her. She moved to Niko's side, her hand hovering over his, afraid to touch him. "Oh, Niko," she whispered. "What have you done?"

His eyes fluttered open at the sound of her voice. "Sera?" His voice was faint, barely audible over the hum of the machines.

"I'm here," she said, finally taking his hand. It was cold, too cold. "I'm here."

The ghost of a smile flickered across his face. "You're okay. Good. I was worried..."

Seraphina's eyes stung with unshed tears. "You idiot," she

choked out. "Why did you do it? Why did you throw your-self in front of me like that?"

Niko's grip on her hand tightened slightly. "Couldn't let you... have all the fun."

A laugh that was half a sob escaped Seraphina's lips. Even now, in the face of death, he tried to make her smile.

"Listen to me," Niko said, his voice fading. "The Convergence... it's not gone. What we fought... it was just the beginning."

Seraphina leaned closer, hanging on his every word. "What do you mean?"

"I can feel it... in my mind," Niko's face contorted in pain. "It's huge, Sera. So big. And it's coming... for all of us."

Before Seraphina could answer, Niko's body went rigid. The machines around him began to wail as he convulsed, the glowing lines on his skin pulsing with an eerie light.

"Niko!" Seraphina cried, her heart in her throat.

Lyra was there in an instant, her hands flying over the equipment. "He's crashing. We have to stabilize him. Sera, you have to go. Now!"

"No," Seraphina shook her head, clutching Niko's hand. "I won't leave him."

"Sera, please," Lyra's voice was urgent. "We can't help him with you here. I promise I'll come get you as soon as we have him stable."

For a moment, Seraphina wanted to say no. To stay at

Niko's side, no matter what. But she knew that Lyra was right. She was in the way.

With one last, lingering look at Niko's face, Seraphina let go of his hand and stumbled out of the room. The door closed behind her, leaving her alone in the quiet hallway.

She slumped against the wall, her legs giving out under her. The tears she'd been holding back finally came, shaking her body with silent sobs.

"Seraphina?"

She looked up to see Evelyn approaching, the First Matriarch's face etched with concern.

"He's dying," Seraphina said, her voice cracking. "Niko is dying, and it's my fault."

Evelyn knelt beside her, her presence a surprising comfort. "It's not your fault, child. Niko made his choice. He knew the risks."

"But why?" Seraphina asked, the question that had been burning in her heart finally spilling out. "Why would he do this for me?"

Evelyn's eyes softened in understanding. "I think you know why, Seraphina. The question is, what are you going to do about it?"

Before Seraphina could answer, Finn's voice crackled over the comm system. "Sera, Evelyn, we need you at the command center. Now."

Seraphina wiped her eyes and forced herself to stand. Whatever was happening, she couldn't collapse now. Her people needed her. Niko needed her.

"Let's go," she said to Evelyn, her voice steadier than she felt.

They made their way to the Command Center, the halls of Haven eerily quiet in the aftermath of battle. When they arrived, they found Finn and Alara huddled around a holographic display, their faces grim.

"What's the situation?" Seraphina asked, slipping into her role as leader despite the turmoil in her heart.

Finn looked up, his usual smirk replaced by a look of grave concern. "We have movement. A lot of it. The Convergence is on the move and it's headed straight for Elyria."

Seraphina's blood ran cold. "How many?"

Alara's cybernetic eye whirred as she analyzed the data. "Thousands. Maybe tens of thousands. It's like... they're migrating."

"Eden," Evelyn called out. "What's your guess?"

The AI's voice filled the room, tinged with what sounded almost like fear. "The Convergence seems to be consolidating their forces. My analysis suggests that they are preparing for a major attack on Elyria."

"But why?" Seraphina asked, her mind racing. "Why now?"

"I believe," Eden said slowly, "that our destruction of the hub has triggered some kind of failsafe protocol. The Convergence is no longer content to lurk in the shadows. It seeks to assimilate all of humanity, starting with the largest concentration of human life it can find."

"Elyria," Finn breathed. "Mother's mercy."

Seraphina's heart pounded in her chest. Everything they had fought for, everything they had sacrificed, had led to this moment.

"We must warn them," she said, her voice ringing with determination. "We have to evacuate the town."

Evelyn shook her head. "There is no time. Even if we could get a message through, the Council would never believe us. And an evacuation of this magnitude... it's impossible."

"So what, we do nothing?" Seraphina demanded. "We let millions of people die?"

"Of course not," Evelyn replied, her eyes flashing. "We fight. We use every resource at our disposal to stop the Convergence before it reaches Elyria."

Finn let out a humorless laugh. "Great plan. Except we're massively outnumbered, half our people are injured or exhausted from the last battle, and our best fighter is in a coma infected with the very thing we're trying to stop."

Seraphina's mind raced, searching for a solution. Then, like a bolt of lightning, an idea struck her.

"The Founder's Network," she said, her eyes widening. "Evelyn, you said it was built as a failsafe, a way to get Elyria back if the worst happened. What if we use it now?"

Evelyn's brow furrowed. "The network wasn't designed for this kind of large-scale operation. And many of the access points may have deteriorated over time."

"But it's possible?" Seraphina pressed.

Evelyn hesitated, then nodded. "Theoretically, yes. But it

would be incredibly dangerous. We'd be exposing ourselves to the Convergence with no guarantee of success."

"It's our only chance," Seraphina said firmly. "We use the network to infiltrate Elyria, warn the people, and prepare the city's defenses. It's the only way we have a chance of stopping the Convergence."

The room fell silent as the weight of the decision washed over them. Finally, Finn spoke. "I'm with you. Better to die fighting than hide in a hole."

Alara nodded in agreement. "Me too. We didn't come this far to give up now."

Evelyn looked at each of them in turn, her expression a mixture of pride and sorrow. "Very well. We'll use the Founder's Network. But understand this - there's a very real chance that none of us will survive this mission."

Seraphina's thoughts turned to Niko, fighting for his life in the medical bay. To all the people they'd lost along the way. To the millions of lives hanging in the balance.

"Some things are worth dying for," she said quietly.

As the others began to prepare for the mission, Seraphina slipped away. She made her way back to the medical bay, her heart heavy with the weight of what was to come.

Lyra met her at the door of Niko's room, her face drawn with exhaustion. "We've stabilized him for now," she said before Seraphina could ask. "But the infection... it's still spreading. I don't know how much longer we can keep him alive."

Seraphina nodded and swallowed the lump in her throat. "Can I see him?"

Lyra hesitated, then nodded. "Just for a few minutes. And Sera... talk to him. A part of him may be able to hear you."

Seraphina entered the room, her eyes immediately drawn to Niko's still form. The glowing lines on his skin had spread and now covered most of his body. But his face was peaceful, almost as if he were just sleeping.

She sat down next to him and took his hand in hers. "Hey," she said softly. "I don't know if you can hear me, but... You have to keep fighting, okay? We're not done yet. Not by a long shot."

She took a shaky breath, forcing herself to continue. "We're going back to Elyria. To save it from the Convergence. It's crazy and dangerous and... I wish you were coming with us. I wish you were here to tell me I'm being reckless or to come up with some brilliant strategy."

Tears trickled down her cheeks and fell onto their joined hands. "You have to wake up, Niko. Because I... I love you. And I should have told you sooner, and now I may never get the chance, and that's not fair."

For a moment she thought she felt his hand twitch in hers. But when she looked at his face, it was unchanged.

"I have to go now," she said, her voice barely above a whisper. "But I'll come back. I promise. So you better be here when I do, you hear?"

She leaned down and planted a soft kiss on his forehead. Then, with a final squeeze of his hand, she stood and walked out of the room.

Lyra was waiting for her, a pack of medical supplies in her hands. "I'm coming with you," she said, her tone brooking no argument. "Someone has to keep you all alive."

Seraphina nodded, grateful for the young woman's presence. Together they made their way back to the command center, where the others were making final preparations.

Evelyn looked up as they entered, her eyes questioning. Seraphina gave a small nod, silently communicating her readiness.

"All right," Evelyn said, addressing the assembled team. "This is it. Once we enter the Founder's Network, there's no turning back. We either succeed in our mission or we die trying. Are we all clear on that?"

A chorus of affirmations rang out. Seraphina felt a surge of pride and resolve. These were her people, willing to risk everything for a chance at a better future.

"Eden," Evelyn called. "Initiate Founder's Network protocols. And... watch over those we leave behind."

"Understood," Eden replied. "Good luck, and may the wisdom of our ancestors guide you."

As the hidden entrance to the Founder's Network slid open, revealing a dark tunnel stretching into the unknown, Seraphina took a deep breath. She thought of Niko, of the people of Elyria, of everything they were fighting for.

Nodding to her companions, she stepped into the tunnel. Whatever lay ahead, whatever challenges they would face, one thing was certain:

The fate of Elyria hung in the balance. And Seraphina would not let it fall without a fight.

EIGHTEEN
ECHOES IN THE DARK

The Founder's Network swallowed them whole, a maw of darkness and stale air. Seraphina's footsteps echoed in the narrow tunnel, each sound a reminder of how far they'd come - and how far they still had to go. The soft glow of her torch cast eerie shadows on the walls, twisted shapes dancing in the periphery of her vision.

"Well, this is cozy," Finn quipped, his voice tense despite the attempt at humor. "Nothing like a stroll through ancient, possibly collapsing tunnels to get the blood pumping."

Alara's cybernetic eye whirred as she scanned their surroundings. "These tunnels are remarkably well-preserved. The Founders' engineering was... impressive."

"Let's hope it stays that way," Lyra muttered, clutching her medical kit to her chest.

Seraphina pushed forward, her mind racing. Each step brought her closer to Elyria, to the coming storm of the

Convergence. And with each passing moment, Niko's life in Haven hung in the balance.

Evelyn's voice broke through their thoughts. "We're approaching the first junction. Eden's maps show three possible routes from here."

The group stopped at a large circular chamber, three identical tunnels branching off into the darkness. Seraphina studied the faded markings on the walls, her Council training kicking in as she tried to decipher the ancient symbols.

"This way," she said, pointing to the far left tunnel. "If I'm reading this correctly, it should lead us to a maintenance center. We might find supplies there, maybe even transportation."

Finn raised an eyebrow. "And if you're reading it wrong?"

Seraphina met his gaze. "Then we improvise. Like always."

They pressed on, the tunnel gradually widening as they descended deeper into the earth. The air grew thicker, heavy with the weight of centuries. Seraphina's skin prickled with a strange sensation, as if the walls themselves were watching them.

Suddenly, Alara stopped, her cybernetic implants pulsing with an urgent light. "Wait. I'm picking up energy readings ahead. Low, but... active."

The group tensed, weapons at the ready. Seraphina's heart raced as she strained her ears, listening for any sign of movement in the darkness ahead.

A low hum filled the air, growing louder by the second. The tunnel ahead began to glow with a soft blue light, pulsing to the rhythm of the hum.

"What is that?" Lyra whispered, her eyes wide.

Before anyone could answer, the light coalesced into a shimmering figure. It was humanoid in form, but translucent, its shape shifting and flowing like water.

"Greetings, children of Elyria," the figure spoke, its voice echoing strangely in the confined space. "I am an echo of the past, a guide left by the founders to help those who would walk these halls."

Seraphina stepped forward, her voice calm despite the shock. "Who are you? What is this place?"

The figure's form rippled, images flashing across its surface - scenes from Elyria's past, from the Cataclysm, from the creation of Haven. "I am a repository of knowledge, a beacon in the darkness. This network was built not only as an escape route, but as a bridge between the past and the future."

Evelyn moved to stand beside Seraphina, her eyes filled with a mixture of awe and sorrow. "We are trying to save Elyria from a great threat. The Convergence is coming, and we must reach the city before it's too late."

The figure's form pulsed with urgency. "The Convergence. Yes, we have foreseen this possibility. A failsafe has been put in place, but it requires one who carries the legacy of the Founders."

His gaze fell on Seraphina and she felt a jolt of recognition.

"You. You carry the mark of the Founders' bloodline. You hold the key to Elyria's salvation."

Seraphina's mind reeled. "What? How is that possible? I'm from the outskirts, I'm not-"

"Blood does not dictate heritage," the figure interrupted. "Your actions, your choices-these are what align you with the Founders' vision. But to unlock the fail-safe, you must face the trials ahead. Only then will the true power of the Network be revealed."

Before Seraphina could question further, the figure began to fade. "Follow the path of light. Face your fears, face your past. The fate of Elyria is in your hands."

With a final burst of energy, the apparition disappeared, leaving them in darkness once more. But now a faint trail of glowing symbols lined the tunnel floor, leading deeper into the unknown.

"Well," Finn said after a moment of stunned silence. "That was... unexpected."

Seraphina's mind raced, trying to process what she'd heard. A fail-safe? Trials? And somehow she was the key to it all?

Evelyn placed a hand on her shoulder, her touch grounding. "Whatever lies ahead, we will face it together. You're not alone, Seraphina."

Seraphina nodded, drawing strength from the support of her companions. "Let's move. We don't have much time."

They followed the glowing trail, the tunnel twisting and turning in ways that defied normal geometry. Seraphina's sense of direction faltered, leaving her with the unsettling feeling that they were no longer moving through physical space, but through something else entirely.

After what seemed like hours of walking, they emerged into a vast chamber. The ceiling arched high above them, lost in shadow. In the center stood a circular platform, surrounded by pillars of pulsating energy.

As they approached, the chamber came alive. Holographic displays sprang up around them, showing scenes from Elyria's history - some familiar, some completely unfamiliar.

"What is this place?" Lyra breathed, her eyes wide with wonder.

"A nexus point," Evelyn replied, her voice hushed with awe. "A convergence of time and memory. The heart of the Founder's Network."

Seraphina stepped onto the central platform, and the world around her shifted. The others faded from view, replaced by swirling mists of possibility.

A voice, neither male nor female, filled her mind. "To unlock the fail-safe, you must face three trials. The test of the past, the test of the present, and the test of the future. Are you ready, Seraphina Blackwood?"

Seraphina's heart raced, but her voice was calm as she answered. "I am."

The mist parted, revealing a scene from her childhood in the outskirts. She saw herself, small and frightened, huddled in an alley as Guardian patrols marched by.

"The trial of the past," the voice intoned. "Confront your origins, the experiences that shaped you. Understand the root of your strength and the source of your fear."

Seraphina watched as her younger self emerged from hiding, determination glowing in her eyes. She remembered that moment - the day she decided to fight back, to rise above her circumstances.

The scene shifted to show her rise through the ranks of the Council, the compromises she made, the ideals she sacrificed in the pursuit of power.

"You tried to change the system from within," the voice said. "But in doing so, did you not become part of the very thing you sought to destroy?"

Seraphina's chest tightened with guilt and remorse. "I did," she admitted. "I lost sight of what was truly important. But I've found my way back. I'm fighting for what's right now."

The mists swirled again, and Seraphina found herself back in the Council Chamber, facing Lady Meridia.

"The Trial of the Present," the voice announced. "Face your current challenges, the conflicts that tear you apart. Where do your loyalties truly lie?"

Meridia's eyes bored into her, cold and calculating. "You are a traitor, Seraphina. To the Council, to Elyria. Everything you've worked for, thrown away for what? A band of rebels and malcontents?"

Seraphina stood tall, meeting Meridia's gaze without flinching. "No. I am loyal to the true spirit of Elyria. To the people who suffer under your rule. I will no longer be part of your oppression."

The scene dissolved, replaced by a vision of Niko lying in the medical bay, his body ravaged by the Convergence infection.

"And what of your heart?" the voice asked. "Can you put aside your personal feelings for the greater good?"

Seraphina's voice caught in her throat as she looked at Niko's still form. "I... I love him," she said quietly. "But I will not let that love blind me to what must be done. Elyria comes first. It must."

The fog parted for the last time, revealing a nightmarish vision of the future. Elyria in ruins, its people assimilated by the Convergence, a grotesque fusion of flesh and machine.

"The trial of the future," the voice said. "Face the possibilities that lie before you. What sacrifices are you willing to make to prevent this fate?"

Seraphina watched in horror as the scene unfolded, her heart breaking at the sight of her people - her home - destroyed.

"Whatever it takes," she said, her voice ringing with determination. "I will give everything I have to stop this. My life, my future-it all means nothing if Elyria falls."

The visions faded, leaving Seraphina standing on the central platform once more. The voice spoke one last time, filled with a mixture of approval and sorrow.

"You have met your trials, Seraphina Blackwood. The failsafe has been activated. But remember - the greatest challenges still lie ahead. The choices you make from this moment on will determine the fate of all."

With a surge of energy, Seraphina found herself back in the chamber with her companions. They stared at her with a mixture of concern and awe.

"Sera?" Lyra asked hesitantly. "Are you all right? You were... glowing."

Before Seraphina could answer, the chamber shook. The energy pillars pulsed with new power, and a new doorway materialized in the far wall.

"The way is open," Evelyn said, her eyes wide with wonder. "The Network has accepted you, Seraphina. We can reach Elyria now."

Finn gave a low whistle. "Well, that's convenient. Any other ancient secrets you'd like to share with the class?"

Seraphina shook her head, still reeling from the intensity of the trials. "I'm not sure I understand it all myself. But I think... I think I know what we have to do."

She turned to face her companions, her eyes glowing with newfound purpose. "The Founders left more than this network. They left a weapon - something that can stop the Convergence. But to use it, we must reach the heart of Elyria."

Alara's cybernetic eye whirred as she processed the information. "The Council Chambers. That's where the city's main power core is located."

Seraphina nodded. "Exactly. We have to get there, activate the weapon and hope it's enough to turn the tide."

"And how exactly are we going to do that?" Finn asked, his voice skeptical. "In case you've forgotten, we're not exactly welcome in Elyria anymore. The Council would shoot us on sight."

"Not if we use the network," Seraphina replied. "Those tunnels run deep into the city. We can bypass most of their defenses and get right into the heart of the Council's power."

Evelyn's eyes narrowed in thought. "It's risky. If we get caught, there's no escape. We'd be trapped in the middle of enemy territory."

"True," Seraphina agreed. "But it's our best chance. The Convergence is coming, and we're running out of time and options."

A heavy silence fell over the group as they weighed their options. Finally, Lyra spoke, her voice small but firm.

"I'm with you, Sera. Whatever it takes."

One by one, the others nodded in agreement. Seraphina felt a surge of gratitude and determination. These people, her friends, were willing to risk everything on her word alone.

"All right then," she said, squaring her shoulders. "Let's go save Elyria."

They moved toward the newly formed doorway, each step bringing them closer to their final confrontation. As they crossed the threshold, Seraphina's thoughts turned to Niko, who was still fighting for his life back in Haven.

"Hold on," she whispered, too quiet for the others to hear. "I'll come back for you. I promise."

The door sealed behind them, leaving no trace of their

passage. The chamber fell silent again, the echoes of the past fading into memory.

But deep in the heart of the Network, something stirred. The failsafe, awakened by Seraphina's trials, began to pulse with ancient power. Streams of energy coursed through long-dormant systems, racing toward Elyria.

In the Council chambers, alarms began to sound. Confused officials struggled to make sense of the readings flooding their screens. And in a forgotten basement, a door that hadn't been opened in centuries began to unlock.

The final battle for Elyria's soul was about to begin.

NINETEEN
THE HEART OF THE STORM

The Founder's Network spat them into the bowels of Elyria like unwanted intruders. Seraphina stumbled, her legs unsteady after hours of traversing the winding tunnels. The air here was different - heavy with the scent of ozone and something else, something wrong.

"We made it," Finn whispered, his usual bravado tempered by the gravity of their situation. "Now what?"

Before Seraphina could answer, a distant scream echoed through the corridors. It started out human, but morphed into something mechanical, a sound that sent shivers down her spine.

"The Convergence," Evelyn breathed, her face pale in the dim emergency lighting. "They're already here."

Alara's cybernetic eye whirred as she scanned their surroundings. "We're in a sublevel of the Council chambers. The main power core is three levels up."

Seraphina's mind raced, weighing her options. "We need to move quickly. The longer we're here, the more likely we are to be discovered - by the Council or the Convergence."

They crept through the shadowy corridors, every sense on high alert. The once familiar halls of power now felt strange, hostile. Seraphina's hand tightened on her weapon as they rounded a corner and came face to face with their first glimpse of the Convergence's impact on Elyria.

A group of citizens huddled against a wall, their eyes wide with terror. But it wasn't the fear that made Seraphina gasp - it was the silvery tendrils that crawled across her skin, pulsing with an eerie light.

"Mother's grace," Lyra gasped. "What's happening to them?"

One of the infected turned, his movements jerky and unnatural. When he spoke, his voice was a dissonant mix of human and machine.

"Join us," he intoned, his eyes flickering with inhuman light. "Become one with the Convergence. End conflict. End pain. End division."

Seraphina raised her weapon, but Evelyn's hand on her arm stopped her. "Wait," the First Matriarch said, her voice tense with emotion. "They're not fully transformed yet. There may be a way to save them."

The infected citizen took a stumbling step forward. "Why resist? The Convergence brings unity. No more war. No more suffering. Just perfect harmony."

"At what cost?" Seraphina demanded, her voice echoing

down the corridor. "Your individuality? Your free will? That's not harmony - that's extinction."

For a moment, something flickered in the man's eyes - a glimmer of his true self, fighting against the Convergence's influence. But then it was gone, swallowed by the pulsing light of the infection.

"You will join us," he said, his voice now a chorus of many. "All will be one."

They lunged forward as one, their movements synchronized with terrifying precision. Seraphina and her team fell back, forced to defend themselves against people they had sworn to protect.

"Non-lethal takedowns only!" Seraphina shouted as she dodged a blow from silvery, tendril-like fingers. "They're still human underneath!"

The fight was chaotic, a blur of movement and desperation. Seraphina's Council combat training kicked in, muscle memory taking over as she struck with precision. But for every infected citizen they incapacitated, more seemed to appear.

"We can't keep this up," Finn growled, his back pressed against Seraphina's. "We need an exit strategy!"

As if in response to his words, a section of the wall slid open, revealing a hidden passageway. Eden's voice, tinny and distorted, echoed from Evelyn's communication device.

"This way," the AI urged. "I've tapped into the building's systems. I can lead you to the power core, but you must hurry. The influence of the Convergence is spreading rapidly."

They didn't need to be told twice. The team retreated into the passageway, which sealed behind them as another wave of infected citizens rounded the corner.

As they caught their breath in the narrow corridor, Lyra's voice shook with barely contained emotion. "What was that? How can the Convergence do this to people?"

Evelyn's face was grim as she answered. "It's not just physical transformation. The Convergence preys on the mind, on the human desire for connection and unity. It offers a twisted version of peace - one without conflict, but also without choice."

"But why?" Alara asked, her cybernetic implants pulsing with excitement. "What does it gain by assimilating everyone?"

Seraphina's mind flashed back to the trials she had faced in the Founder's Network, to the visions of Elyria's past and future. "It thinks it's saving us," she said quietly. "The Convergence was born out of our own experiments, our own hubris. It's trying to solve the problems of human conflict the only way it knows how - by eliminating what makes us human in the first place."

A heavy silence fell over the group as the implications of her words sank in. They weren't just fighting an external threat - they were fighting a perversion of their own desires for a better world.

Eden's voice broke the silence. "You must keep moving. The power core is not far, but the Council's security systems are adapting to my presence. I cannot guarantee how long I will be able to maintain control."

They pressed on, the hidden passage twisting and turning through the heart of the Council chambers. As they neared their destination, the air grew thick with tension.

"Something's wrong," Alara said suddenly, her cybernetic eye scanning rapidly. "The energy readings from the power core - they're off the charts."

Before anyone could answer, they emerged into a huge chamber. The sight that greeted them made Seraphina's blood run cold.

The power core, once a marvel of Elyrian engineering, had been transformed. Tendrils of silver and blue energy wound around it, pulsing in time to an alien heartbeat. And at its center, suspended in a cocoon of light, was a familiar figure.

"Meridia," Seraphina breathed.

But this was not the Meridia she knew. The Councilwoman's body had been twisted and changed, more machine than human. Her eyes, when they opened, glowed with the same eerie light as the infected citizens.

"Seraphina," Meridia's voice echoed, layered with countless others. "We knew you would come. The Convergence has been waiting for you."

Seraphina raised her weapon, but Meridia only smiled - a cold, inhuman expression.

"Your weapons are useless here," she said. "The Convergence cannot be stopped by such primitive means. It is evolution. It is destiny."

"You're wrong," Seraphina shot back, her voice steady despite the fear coursing through her. "This is not evolution

- it is annihilation. You're destroying everything that makes us human."

Meridia's form shifted, tendrils of energy reaching out to them. "Humanity is flawed. Imperfect. The Convergence will correct those flaws. No more conflict. No more pain. Only unity."

"And no more freedom," Evelyn interjected, stepping forward. "No more choice. No more love or joy or anything else that makes life worth living."

For a moment, something flickered in Meridia's eyes - a hint of doubt, of her old self struggling against the control of the Convergence. But it was gone as quickly as it had appeared.

"You cannot stop the inevitable," Meridia intoned. "The Convergence has already begun. Soon all of Elyria will be one with us. And then the world beyond."

The tendrils of energy surged forward, forcing the team to scatter. Seraphina's mind raced as she dodged and weaved, searching for a weakness, a way to stop this madness.

"The fail-safe!" Evelyn shouted over the chaos. "Seraphina, you must activate it now!"

Seraphina's hand went to the small device they had retrieved from the Founder's Network - the key to the weapon that could stop the Convergence. But as she raised it, doubt gnawed at her.

What if it didn't work? What if, in trying to save Elyria, they were only making things worse?

As if sensing her hesitation, Meridia's voice filled the chamber once more. "Join us, Seraphina. End the fight. Become part of something bigger than yourself."

For a heartbeat, Seraphina felt the pull of the Convergence's promise. An end to conflict, to pain, to the weight of responsibility that had weighed on her for so long. But then she thought of Niko, still fighting for his life in Haven. Of the people of Elyria, who deserved the right to choose their own path.

With a cry of defiance, she activated the fail-safe.

The device pulsed with energy, sending out a shockwave that rippled through the chamber. The tendrils surrounding the power core recoiled, writhing in apparent pain. Meridia's form convulsed, her inhuman scream echoing off the walls.

For a moment, hope surged through Seraphina. It was working. They were going to win.

But then the energy stabilized, the tendrils regrouping with renewed strength. Meridia's laughter, cold and cruel, filled the air.

"Did you really think it would be that easy?" she taunted. "The Convergence cannot be stopped by your primitive technology. We have evolved beyond such weaknesses."

Seraphina's heart sank as she realized the truth. The fail-safe had damaged the Convergence, yes - but it wasn't enough to stop it completely.

"What now?" Finn asked, his voice tense as they regrouped.

Before Seraphina could answer, a new voice cut through the chaos - one that made her catch her breath.

"Now," Niko said as he stepped into the chamber, his body still bearing the marks of the Convergence infection, but his eyes clear and determined, "we finish this. Together."

TWENTY
ECHOES OF HUMANITY

"Niko?" Seraphina's voice caught in her throat, a mixture of joy and disbelief. He stood before her, alive and seemingly in control, despite the silver tendrils of the Convergence infection still visible on his skin.

Niko's eyes met hers, a storm of emotions behind them. "Hey, Sera. Sorry I'm late."

Before Seraphina could answer, Meridia's laughter echoed through the chamber. "How touching. The prodigal son returns. But you're too late. The Convergence cannot be stopped."

Niko turned to face the transformed councilwoman, his posture defiant. "You are wrong, Meridia. The Convergence is not unstoppable. It's not even unified."

Seraphina's mind raced, trying to make sense of Niko's words and his miraculous appearance. "What do you mean?"

"I've seen it from the inside," Niko explained, his voice tight with the effort of maintaining control. "The Convergence is not one mind. It's millions of them, all fighting for dominance. It's chaos masquerading as unity."

Meridia's form writhed, tendrils of energy lashing out in apparent agitation. "Lies! Convergence brings perfect harmony. All will be one!"

"Will we?" Niko challenged, taking a step forward. "Then why are there factions within the Convergence itself? Why are some of us able to resist?"

Seraphina's heart leapt at his words. If Niko was right, if there was a way to fight the Convergence from within...

"The fail-safe," she said suddenly, the pieces falling into place. "It didn't fail. It weakened the Convergence's control."

Evelyn's eyes widened with realization. "Of course it did. The Founders wouldn't have created a weapon to destroy the Convergence. They created a key to unlock our own resistance to it."

Meridia screamed, a sound of rage and fear that shook the walls. "Enough! You will all be assimilated. Resistance is futile!"

The chamber erupted in chaos. Tendrils of Convergence energy lashed out, forcing the team to scatter. Seraphina dove for cover, her mind swirling with possibilities.

"Niko!" she called over the din. "How are you fighting it?"

Niko grunted as he deflected a vine with a piece of debris. "It's like a battle in my mind. Every memory, every emotion, every part of who I am - I have to hold on to it all. The moment I let go, the Convergence takes over."

Finn's voice cut through the chaos. "Great. So we can't shoot it, we can't blow it up, and our only hope is to outthink a hive mind. Any other brilliant ideas?"

Despite the gravity of the situation, Seraphina felt a spark of hope. "Actually, yes. Lyra, those medical supplies you brought - do you have any neural stimulants?"

Lyra's eyes brightened with understanding. "In my pack. But Sera, those are dangerous. In high doses they could fry a person's synapses."

"Or charge them," Seraphina countered. "Give us the mental strength to resist the Convergence's influence."

Alara's cybernetic eye whirred as she processed the idea. "It's risky, but it could work. If we can increase our own neural activity, we might be able to interface with the Convergence on its own terms."

"You're insane," Meridia hissed, her form shifting and growing. "You would risk your own minds, your own identities, in a vain attempt to stop progress?"

Seraphina stood up, facing the twisted form of her former mentor. "It's not progress, Meridia. It's surrender. And we will not surrender our humanity without a fight."

With a nod to Lyra, Seraphina made her decision. The young medic hesitated only a moment before administering the neural stimulants.

"This is going to hurt," Lyra warned as she administered the drug to each of them in turn.

The effect was instantaneous and overwhelming. Seraphina's world exploded with vivid color and sensation. Every nerve ending felt alive, every thought crystal clear. And with that clarity came a new awareness - she could feel the Convergence, could feel its pull on her mind.

"Focus!" Niko's voice cut through the sensory overload. "Remember who you are. What you're fighting for."

Seraphina clung to her memories, to her sense of self. She thought of her childhood in the outer districts, her rise through the Council ranks, her journey with the rebellion. Each memory was a shield against the influence of the Convergence.

Around her, she could see the others struggling with their own mental battles. Finn's face was contorted in concentration, muttering what sounded like bawdy tavern songs under his breath. Lyra's eyes were closed, her lips moving in silent prayer. Alara's cybernetic implants pulsed with energy as she connected directly to the Convergence's network.

And Evelyn... Seraphina gasped as she saw the First Matriarch. Evelyn stood at the center of the storm, her arms outstretched, glowing with an inner light. As she spoke, her voice carried the weight of centuries.

"Children of Elyria," Evelyn intoned, her words resonating on a frequency Seraphina felt in her bones. "Remember who you are. Remember your history, your struggles, your triumphs. The Convergence offers unity, but at the cost of all that makes us human. Choose freedom. Choose life!"

The very air seemed to vibrate with the power of Evelyn's

words. Seraphina could feel something shifting, changing. The power of the Convergence was weakening.

Meridia screamed as her form began to destabilize. "No! You cannot resist. You will be integrated!"

But her words lacked their former power. Seraphina could see doubt creeping into the eyes of the infected citizens around them. The silvery tendrils of the Convergence infection began to recede.

"It's working," Niko said, his voice strained but triumphant. "Keep going!"

Seraphina stepped forward, adding her own voice to Evelyn's. "People of Elyria, hear me! The Convergence promises an end to conflict, but at what cost? Our individuality, our free will, the very things that make us human - these are not flaws to be corrected. They are the source of our strength!"

As she spoke, Seraphina felt a connection forming - not the overwhelming power of the Convergence, but something more subtle. She could sense the minds of those around her, feel their fears, their hopes, their determination.

"We have known hardship," she continued, her voice rising. "We have known oppression and injustice. But we've also known love and joy and the triumph of overcoming impossible odds. These experiences have shaped us, made us who we are. The Convergence would erase all of that, would reduce us to cogs in a machine.

The energy in the room shifted, the influence of the Convergence wavering. Seraphina continued, drawing strength from the connection she felt with her people.

"But we are not machines. We are human, with all our flaws and all our potential. We have the power to choose our own path, to shape our own destiny. Convergence offers certainty, but it is the certainty of stagnation. We choose the uncertainty of freedom, the challenge of forging our own future!

A wave of energy pulsed outward from Seraphina and her companions, rippling through the chamber and beyond. The infected citizens gasped in unison as the silver tendrils of the Convergence infection retreated further.

Meridia's form began to collapse, the energy that had sustained her dissipating. "No," she moaned, her voice now all her own. "What have you done?"

Seraphina approached her former mentor, compassion warring with caution. "We gave the people a choice, Meridia. The same choice you have now. Let go of the Convergence. Come back to us."

For a moment, Meridia's eyes cleared, a flicker of her old self shining through. "Seraphina? I... I don't understand. What's happening to me?"

"You are free," Seraphina said softly. "The Convergence no longer controls you. You can choose your own path now."

Meridia's form continued to destabilize, the energy that had transformed her rapidly dissipating. "I... I remember now. What I did. What I became. Oh, Seraphina, I'm so sorry."

Tears streamed down Meridia's face as the last of the Convergence's influence left her. She collapsed to the ground, human again, but weakened and changed by her ordeal.

As Lyra rushed to tend to Meridia, Seraphina turned to survey the chamber. The infected citizens were recovering, looking around in confusion and fear. The pulsing energy of the Convergence was gone, leaving only the steady hum of Elyria's power core.

"Is it over?" Finn asked, his voice uncharacteristically subdued. "Did we win?"

Evelyn shook her head, her expression grave. "Not yet. What we've done here is just the beginning. The Convergence has been pushed back, but not destroyed. And Elyria... Elyria will never be the same again."

As if in response to her words, alarms began to sound throughout the building. Eden's voice, tinny and distorted, came through their communication devices.

"Warning: Multiple breaches detected. Council forces are converging on your location. You must evacuate immediately."

Seraphina's mind raced, assessing their options. They were exhausted, outnumbered, and now facing a new threat.

"The Founder's Network," she said suddenly. "We can use it to escape, to regroup."

Niko nodded, flinching slightly as he moved. The strain of resisting the Convergence had clearly taken its toll. "But what about them?" he asked, gesturing to the recovering citizens and the unconscious form of Meridia.

Seraphina felt the weight of leadership settle once again on her shoulders. This was the moment that would define everything they had fought for.

"We're taking them," she decided. "All of them. We can't leave anyone behind to face the 'justice' of the Council."

Evelyn's eyebrows raised in surprise. "That's a bold move, Seraphina. It will slow us down, make us vulnerable."

"I know," Seraphina admitted. "But if we abandon these people now, we're no better than the Council. We fought for a free Elyria - that means freedom for everyone, not just those who agree with us."

A slow smile spread over Evelyn's face. "You are truly a child of the Founders. Very well. Let's show Elyria what true leadership looks like."

As they began to organize the evacuation, herding confused and frightened citizens toward the hidden entrance to the Founders' Network, Seraphina felt a hand on her arm. She turned to find Niko looking at her with an intensity that made her heart skip a beat.

"Sera," he said quietly. "When this is all over... we need to talk."

Seraphina nodded, her throat tight with emotion. "I know. But first we need to get these people to safety."

Niko's hand slid down to take hers, squeezing gently. "Together?"

Despite the chaos around them, despite the uncertainty of what lay ahead, Seraphina felt a warmth grow in her chest. "Together," she agreed.

As they led their ragtag group of survivors into the depths of the Founder's Network, Seraphina's mind was already racing with plans and possibilities. The battle against the Convergence was won, for now. But the battle for Elyria's future was far from over.

The Council would be in disarray, its power structure shaken by the Convergence's attack and Meridia's defection. The people would be frightened, confused, searching for answers and leadership. And the threat of the Convergence still loomed, waiting for any sign of weakness to reassert its control.

But as Seraphina looked at the faces around her - Niko, strong and determined despite his ordeal; Evelyn, carrying the wisdom of the ages; Finn and Alara, loyal and steadfast; Lyra, compassionate and brave; and the citizens of Elyria, each one a testament to the resilience of the human spirit - she felt a surge of hope.

They had faced impossible odds and emerged victorious. They had stared into the abyss of lost humanity and pulled themselves back from the brink. Whatever challenges lay ahead, Seraphina knew they would face them together.

As the hidden door of the Founder's Network closed behind them, cutting off the sound of approaching Council forces, Seraphina allowed herself a small smile. The path ahead was uncertain, fraught with danger and difficult choices.

But for the first time in her life, she was truly free. Free to choose her own destiny, to shape the future of Elyria not through oppression or false unity, but through the messy, beautiful, all-too-human process of working together toward a common goal.

The real work was about to begin. And Seraphina was ready for it.

TWENTY-ONE
THE FIRST STEPS

The tunnels of the Founder's Network echoed with the sound of exhausted footsteps and hushed voices. Seraphina led the group, her mind racing with the enormity of what they had just accomplished - and what lay ahead. Behind her, a diverse crowd of survivors followed: Council members, citizens from the outskirts, men and women alike, all united in their escape from the remnants of the old order.

When they reached a crossroads, Seraphina paused and turned to address the group. Her eyes swept over the faces before her, noting the mixture of fear, confusion, and hope.

"We'll rest here for a moment," she announced, her voice carrying through the tunnel. "Lyra, tend to the wounded. Finn, Alara, scout ahead. We need to make sure our path is clear."

As the group began to settle, Seraphina noticed a commotion at the rear. A man's voice, strong and determined, rose above the murmur.

"We must organize a defensive perimeter," he said. "If the Council forces find the entrance to the network, we need to be ready."

Seraphina made her way through the crowd, curious. She found a tall, broad-shouldered man gesturing to a rough map he'd drawn on the tunnel wall. A small group had gathered around him, both men and women listening intently.

"Who are you?" Seraphina asked, unable to keep a note of surprise out of her voice. She wasn't used to seeing men take charge like this.

The man turned, his eyes widening slightly in recognition. "Marcus," he said, nodding respectfully. "Former Guardian, before I was... reassigned to the work camps."

Seraphina felt a pang of guilt at his words, a reminder of the injustices of the old system. She pushed the feeling aside and focused on the present.

"Your plan," she said, pointing to the map. "Tell me more."

Marcus seemed taken aback for a moment, as if he hadn't expected to be taken seriously. Then he straightened up, his voice gaining confidence.

"We're vulnerable here," he explained, pointing to key areas on his makeshift map. "If we position lookouts at these intersections and set up barricades here and here, we can buy time if we're followed."

Seraphina nodded, impressed despite herself. "Good thinking. Make it happen."

As Marcus began to organize the teams, Seraphina felt a presence at her side. She turned to find Evelyn watching the scene with a mixture of approval and sadness.

"It begins," the First Matriarch said quietly.

"Beginning what?" Seraphina asked, though she felt she knew the answer.

Evelyn's eyes met hers, filled with the weight of centuries. "The dismantling of the old order. The first steps towards true equality. It won't be easy, Seraphina. Changing the fundamental structure of a society never is."

As if to underscore Evelyn's words, Seraphina noticed a group of former Council members huddled together, casting suspicious glances at Marcus and his team. She caught glimpses of their whispered conversation.

"...can't trust them to..."

"...know their place..."

"...worked for centuries..."

Seraphina felt a pang of frustration. Even now, after all they'd been through, the old prejudices remained. She started toward the group, ready to confront them, but Evelyn's hand on her arm stopped her.

"Not yet," Evelyn warned. "They are afraid, clinging to what they know. Change will come, but it cannot be forced. It must be shown."

Seraphina took a deep breath and calmed herself. "You are right. But we can't ignore it either."

She made her way back to the front of the group, where Niko was coordinating with Finn and Alara. As she approached, she couldn't help but notice how naturally the others deferred to him, regardless of gender. It was a small thing, but it gave her hope.

"What's our status?" she asked as she joined them.

Niko ran a hand through his hair, the exhaustion visible in every line of his body. "The way ahead is clear for now, but we can't stay here for long. We need to find a more defensible position, a place where we can rest and regroup properly."

Alara's cybernetic eye whirred as she called up a holographic map of the network. "There's a large chamber about two kilometers from here. It looks like some sort of emergency shelter. If we can get there, we might be able to hold out for a while."

Seraphina nodded, her decision made. "That's our destination then. Niko, work with Marcus to organize our defenses for the journey. Finn, I need you to take charge of rationing our supplies. And Alara, see if you can use your implants to tap into any remaining network systems. We need all the information we can get."

As the others moved to carry out her orders, Seraphina felt a tug on her sleeve. She looked down to find a young boy, no more than ten years old, staring up at her with wide eyes.

"Miss," he said, his voice trembling slightly. "Are... are we free now? Really free?"

The question hit Seraphina like a physical blow. She knelt down to the boy's level.

"What's your name?" she asked softly.

"Eli," the boy replied.

Seraphina smiled, trying to project a confidence she didn't quite feel. "Well, Eli, we're working on it. Freedom isn't something that just happens. It's something we have to build together, every day. But yes, we've taken the first steps towards real freedom. For everyone."

Eli's face lit up with a tentative smile. "Even for boys like me?"

"Especially for boys like you," Seraphina assured him. "And for girls, and men, and women. For everyone."

As Eli ran off to tell his friends the news, Seraphina stood, her heart heavy with the weight of the promise she'd just made. She caught Niko watching her, a gentle smile on his face.

"What?" she asked, suddenly self-conscious.

Niko shook his head, his smile widening. "Nothing. It's just... you're good at this. Leading, inspiring. You give them hope."

Seraphina felt a warmth in her chest at his words, but she pushed it aside. There would be time for personal feelings later. Right now they had a job to do.

"We should get going," she said, business again. "The longer we stay here, the greater the risk of discovery."

As they prepared to leave, Seraphina couldn't help but notice the changes already taking place within their group. Men and women worked side by side, organizing supplies and helping the injured. Former council members and citizens from the outer districts shared water and ration bars, their former divisions forgotten in the face of their shared ordeal.

It was a small thing, perhaps, but it gave them hope. Change was possible. It wouldn't be easy, and there would be setbacks along the way, but they had taken the first steps toward a truly equal society.

The trip to the shelter was tense, every shadow seeming to hide potential danger. But they made it without incident, entering a vast chamber humming with the echoes of ancient technology.

As the group settled in, Seraphina called a meeting of their impromptu leadership council. Niko, Evelyn, Finn, Alara, Lyra, and Marcus gathered around a central console whose screen flickered to life at their approach.

"We need to talk about what happens next," Seraphina began, her voice low but intense. "We've escaped the immediate danger, but we can't hide down here forever. We need a plan."

Marcus leaned forward, his face grim. "The Council won't just let us go. They'll hunt us down, and they control the city above. We're trapped."

"Not necessarily," Alara interjected, her cybernetic implants pulsing as she interfaced with the shelter's systems. "The network of the Founders extends far beyond Elyria. There are other outposts, other safe houses. We could try to reach one of them, start over somewhere else."

Niko shook his head, his jaw set. "Running is not the answer. Elyria is our home. We have to take it back, build something better than what we left behind."

"And how do you propose we do that?" Finn asked, his usual sarcasm tempered by genuine curiosity. "In case you haven't noticed, we're a little outnumbered and outgunned right now."

Seraphina's mind raced, pieces falling into place. "We don't need to outgun them," she said slowly. "We need to out-communicate them. The people of Elyria deserve to know the truth - about the Convergence, about the Council's lies, about the possibility of a better way."

Evelyn nodded, a spark of excitement in her eyes. "The network. It's not just tunnels and shelters. It's a communications system, one the Council doesn't control. If we can access it, broadcast our message..."

"We could reach the entire city," Lyra finished, her voice filled with awe.

"It's not that simple," Marcus warned. "Even if we can get the message out, how do we know anyone will listen? The Council's propaganda runs deep."

Seraphina met his gaze steadily. "We make them listen. Not with violence, but with the truth. We show them a vision of what Elyria could be - a place of true equality, where everyone has a voice and a chance to shape their own destiny."

The group fell silent, pondering her words. Finally, Niko spoke, his voice soft but determined.

"It's a good plan," he said. "Risky, but good. But Seraphina... are you sure you're ready for what it means? If we do this, if we truly commit to building a new Elyria based on equality, it means giving up a lot of the power and privilege you've known."

Seraphina felt the weight of everyone's eyes on her. She thought of her life in the Council, of the comfort and status she'd enjoyed. Then she thought of Eli's hopeful face, of Marcus' firm leadership, of the countless men and women who had suffered under the old system.

"I'm sure," she said, her voice steady. "The old way... it was wrong. I see that now. We have a chance to build something better, something that honors the true spirit of Elyria. I want to be a part of it, whatever it takes."

A wave of agreement went through the group. Even Finn looked impressed.

"Well then," he said, a hint of his old grin returning. "I guess we're really doing this. Viva la revolución and all that."

As the others began to discuss the details of their plan, Seraphina felt a hand on her arm. She turned to find Niko looking at her with an intensity that made her gasp.

"I'm proud of you," he said quietly. "I know it's not easy, letting go of everything you've known. But you're doing the right thing."

Seraphina felt a warmth in her chest. "We are doing the

right thing," she corrected him. "I couldn't do it without you. Without all of you."

They stood there for a moment, the weight of their common purpose hanging between them. Then Niko's hand found hers and squeezed gently.

"Together?" he asked, echoing their earlier exchange.

Seraphina smiled, feeling for the first time in a long time that they were on the right track. "Together," she agreed.

As they turned back to the group, ready to face whatever challenges lay ahead, Seraphina felt a sense of hope she hadn't experienced since childhood. The road ahead would be difficult, fraught with danger and setbacks. But they had taken the first steps toward a truly free and equal Elyria.

And that was worth fighting for.

TWENTY-TWO
ECHOES OF CHANGE

The hum of ancient machinery filled the air as Seraphina stood before the communications array. Her fingers hovered over the controls, the weight of what she was about to do pressing down on her. One push of a button and they would broadcast their message to all of Elyria. There would be no turning back.

"Are you ready for this?" Niko's voice broke through her thoughts. He stood beside her, his presence a steadying force.

Seraphina took a deep breath, steeling herself. "As ready as I will ever be. Let's hope the people of Elyria are ready to listen."

She activated the system, and the array came to life with a whirl of energy. Alara's voice crackled over the comm. "We're live in three... two... one..."

Seraphina leaned into the microphone, her voice clear and strong. "People of Elyria, this is Seraphina Blackwood. You know me as a Councilwoman, but I come to you now as something else - a fellow citizen fighting for a better future. The Council lied to you. The threat from the Convergence was real, but it's not the only danger we face. Our society, built on the oppression of half our population, cannot stand. It's time for change. It's time for true equality.

As she spoke, laying out her vision for a new Elyria, Seraphina could almost feel the ripples of her words spreading through the city. She spoke of the true vision of the founders, of the strength that comes from diversity, of the potential that had been locked away by generations of oppression.

"We call on all citizens, men and women alike, to join us," she concluded. "Together, we can build a society where everyone has a voice, where everyone has a chance to reach their full potential. The road won't be easy, but it's one we must walk together. For the future of Elyria, for our children, for ourselves.

As the broadcast ended, a heavy silence fell over the command center. Then, slowly, applause began. Seraphina turned to see the assembled survivors - Council members and Outer District citizens, men and women - united in their response.

The moment was interrupted by a shrill alarm. Finn's voice cut through the revelry. "We've got incoming! Council forces have breached the outer defenses of the Network!"

Chaos erupted as people scrambled to prepare. Seraphina's mind raced, assessing her options. "Marcus!" she called. "Get our defense teams into position. Lyra, make sure the non-combatants are moved to safe areas. Alara, can you tap into the network's security systems?"

As the others moved to carry out her orders, Niko appeared at her side, his face grim. "They're coming in force, Sera. We can't hold them off forever."

"We don't need forever," she replied, her mind already formulating a plan. "We need enough time for our message to spread, for the people to rise up."

Evelyn's voice cut through the noise. "There may be another way. The Founders built escape routes, hidden passages leading out of the city. If we can reach one..."

Seraphina shook her head. "No. We're not running. Elyria is our home, and we're going to fight for it."

A loud explosion rocked the chamber, sending dust raining down from the ceiling. Marcus' voice crackled over the comm. "They've breached the first line of defense! We need reinforcements!"

"Go," Seraphina told Niko. "Help Marcus hold the line. I'll coordinate from here."

For a moment, Niko hesitated. Then he pulled her close and planted a fierce kiss on her lips. "Be careful," he murmured before sprinting toward the sound of battle.

Seraphina pushed aside the whirlwind of emotions his kiss had stirred and focused on the task at hand. She turned to the command console and brought up a map of the network. "Alara, what's our status?"

The cyborg's fingers flew over the controls, her implants pulsing with data. "Council forces are pushing in from multiple entry points. They're using some kind of advanced technology to bypass our security measures."

"Can you slow them down?"

Alara's cybernetic eye whirred as she thought. "I might be able to reroute power, seal off some of the tunnels. But that won't hold them for long."

"Do it," Seraphina ordered. She turned to Evelyn, who was studying the map with a furrowed brow. "These escape routes you mentioned - where do they lead?"

"To the surface," Evelyn replied. "Miles outside the city walls. But Seraphina, you said-"

"I know what I said," Seraphina interrupted. "But we need options. If we can't keep them here, we need a fallback plan."

As if to emphasize her point, another explosion shook the chamber. The sounds of battle came closer.

Finn's voice came over the comm, tense. "We have a problem. They're not using deadly force. They're using some kind of stun weapons, trying to take prisoners."

Seraphina's blood ran cold. Prisoners meant interrogations, meant the Council might learn all about their plans, about the Network, about the surviving Founders' technology.

"Change of plans," she announced. "We're evacuating. Alara, start preparing our people for transport. Evelyn, I need you to lead us to the escape routes."

"What about the wounded?" Lyra asked, her face streaked with dust and worry. "Some of them can't be moved."

Seraphina felt the weight of leadership press down on her. Every decision now could mean life or death, freedom or capture. "We'll carry them if we have to. No one will be left behind."

As the evacuation began, Seraphina made her way to the front lines. The scene that greeted her was one of controlled chaos. Marcus and Niko led a mixed group of men and women, holding off the advancing Council forces with a combination of looted weapons and improvised barriers.

"Fall back!" Seraphina yelled over the din of battle. "We'll evacuate through the escape routes. Finn, set charges to collapse the tunnels behind us."

Niko caught her eye, a question in his eyes. She nodded, confirming his unspoken thought. This was it - they were engaged now.

As they retreated, Seraphina couldn't help but notice the way their group fought. Men and women side by side, covering each other's backs, working in seamless tandem. It was a far cry from the rigid, sex-segregated units of the Council's forces.

They reached the hidden entrance to the escape route just as the Council forces broke through their last line of defense. Seraphina led the survivors through, counting heads as they passed.

"Is everyone here?" she asked as the last stragglers came through.

Marcus did a quick head count. "All accounted for, except..."

A shout from behind cut him off. Seraphina turned to see Eli, the boy from earlier, trapped on the other side of the collapsing tunnel.

Without thinking, Seraphina sprinted back, ducking under falling debris. She scooped Eli into her arms, feeling the sting of energy weapon fire sizzle past her.

"Hang on!" she told the boy as she ran back towards the escape route. The tunnel collapsed around them, the air thick with dust and the crackling of energy weapons.

Just when it looked like they wouldn't make it, strong hands reached out and pulled them to safety. Niko and Marcus dragged them through the entrance while Finn detonated the charges, sealing the tunnel behind them.

For a moment, they all stood, breathing heavily in the sudden silence. Then Eli spoke, his voice small and awed. "You... you came back for me."

Seraphina set the boy down and knelt to meet his eyes. "Of course I did. We're in this together, remember? All of us."

As she stood, she saw the others watching her with a mixture of respect and something else - hope, she realized. They looked to her not only as a leader, but as a symbol of the change they were fighting for.

"All right," she said, pushing aside her exhaustion. "We need to keep moving. Evelyn, where does this tunnel lead to?"

The First Matriarch consulted an ancient map, its surface glowing faintly in the dim light. "If I'm reading this correctly, it should take us to a hidden bunker in the mountains outside of Elyria. It was designed as a last resort for the Founders in the event of a catastrophe."

"Sounds like just what we need," Finn quipped, though his usual humor was strained.

As they started down the tunnel, Seraphina fell into step beside Niko. "How are our supplies?" she asked quietly.

"Low," he admitted. "We have enough food and water for maybe a week, if we ration carefully. After that..."

Seraphina nodded, catching the unspoken implication. They'd bought themselves some time, but they were far from certain. "We'll figure it out. We always do."

Niko's hand found hers in the darkness and squeezed gently. "Together," he said, repeating their earlier exchange.

Despite everything, Seraphina felt a warmth blossom in her chest. "Together," she agreed.

They walked in companionable silence for a while, the group's footsteps echoing in the ancient tunnel. Seraphina's mind raced, trying to plan their next move. They had escaped immediate danger, but now they were cut off from Elyria, from any potential allies their transmission might have attracted.

"What are you thinking?" Niko asked, reading her expression even in the dim light.

Seraphina sighed. "I think we've started something we can't control. Our message is out there, but we have no way of knowing how it's being received, no way of coordinating with supporters in the city."

"You're wondering if we did the right thing," Niko said. It wasn't a question.

"Did we?" Seraphina asked, voicing the doubt she'd been holding back. "We overturned the only system of government Elyria has known for generations. What if we've just thrown the city into chaos?"

Niko was silent for a moment, thinking. "Maybe we did," he said finally. "But the old system was broken, Sera. It crushed half the population and corrupted the other half. Sometimes you have to tear something down to build it up better."

Before Seraphina could answer, a scream from ahead caught their attention. They rushed forward to find Alara standing in front of a massive metal door, her cybernetic implants pulsing as she interfaced with her ancient systems.

"This is it," Evelyn announced. "The Founders' Bunker. Our sanctuary."

As Alara worked to unlock the door, Seraphina addressed the group. "I know we're all tired and scared and unsure of the future. But what we've done today - standing up for equality, for justice - is bigger than any one of us. When we open that door, we're not just entering a sanctuary. We're taking the first steps toward building a new Elyria. A better Elyria. And we'll do it together, men and women, as equals.

A murmur of approval rippled through the crowd. Seraphina saw determination replace fear in their eyes, saw men and women standing together, united in purpose.

With a groan of ancient machinery, the bunker door began to open. As light poured out, illuminating their faces, Seraphina felt a surge of hope. Whatever challenges lay ahead, they would face them as one people, no longer divided by the arbitrary rules of the past.

The first step toward a truly free Elyria lay just beyond that door. And they were ready to take it.

TWENTY-THREE
FOUNDATIONS OF FREEDOM

Light flooded the tunnel as the massive door groaned open, revealing the Founders' bunker beyond. Seraphina blinked, her eyes adjusting to the sudden brightness. The air that poured out was stale but breathable, carrying the weight of centuries.

"By the Mother," Finn whispered, his usual sarcasm replaced by awe. "Would you look at this?"

A vast chamber stretched before them, its high ceiling lost in shadow. Rows of dormant machines lined the walls, their surfaces gleaming despite the passage of time. In the center stood a holographic projector that flickered to life as they entered.

Evelyn stepped forward, her face a mixture of awe and trepidation. "The last refuge of the Founders. I never thought I'd see it with my own eyes."

As the group filed in, expressions of wonder on their faces, Seraphina's mind raced with the possibilities - and responsibilities - this discovery presented.

"Alara," she called. "Can you interface with the systems here? We need to know what we're up against."

The cyborg nodded, her implants already pulsing as she approached a nearby console. "It'll take some time to sift through all the data, but I'm picking up power sources, water recycling systems, even food production capabilities. This place was designed for long-term habitation."

"Good," Seraphina nodded. "Niko, Marcus - organize search parties. We need to map this place, make sure it's secure. Lyra, set up a triage area for the wounded. Finn, start taking inventory of our supplies."

As the others moved to carry out her orders, Seraphina felt a tug on her sleeve. She looked down and saw Eli, the boy she'd saved earlier.

"What about me?" he asked, his young face full of determination. "I want to help too."

Seraphina knelt down to his level, struck by the seriousness in his eyes. This boy, who had known nothing but oppression all his life, was eager to contribute, to be part of something greater.

"All right," she said, making a quick decision. "I have an important task for you. I need you to be our morale officer. Go around to everyone and make sure they're okay. If anyone needs help or is afraid, tell me or Niko. Can you do that?"

Eli's face lit up with a grin. "Yes, ma'am!" He scampered off, already taking his new role seriously.

As Seraphina watched him go, Evelyn appeared at her side.

"You're good with him," the First Matriarch remarked. "You'd make a good mother one day."

Seraphina felt a blush creep up her cheeks. "Let's focus on keeping everyone alive for now. Speaking of which, what can you tell me about this place? Exactly what did the Founders leave us?"

Evelyn's expression grew serious as they walked towards the central holographic projector. "More than a sanctuary," she said. "This bunker was meant to be a seed. A place from which civilization could grow again if the worst should happen."

The projector hummed to life as they approached, displaying a rotating model of Elyria and the surrounding lands. Evelyn manipulated the controls with practiced ease, zooming in on their location.

"The Founders foresaw the possibility of societal collapse," she explained. "They built this place not to hide, but to rebuild. There are hydroponic bays for food production, manufacturing facilities, even genetic banks to preserve biodiversity."

Seraphina's mind whirled with the implications. "So we could potentially sustain ourselves here indefinitely?"

"In theory, yes," Evelyn nodded. "But that's not the point. This place wasn't meant to be a permanent home. It's a launching pad, a place from which to reclaim and reshape Elyria."

Before Seraphina could answer, Niko's voice crackled over the comm. "Sera, you need to see this. We found something... unexpected."

After exchanging a look with Evelyn, Seraphina hurried to Niko's location. She found him and Marcus standing in front of another massive door, this one sealed tightly.

"What is it?" she asked, noticing the tension in their postures.

Marcus pointed to the markings on the door. "It's another stasis chamber. Like the ones we found in Haven, but... bigger. Much bigger."

Seraphina's breath caught as she realized the implications. "You think there are more Founders in there? Alive?"

Niko nodded grimly. "It's possible. But Sera, if there are... what do we do? These people would be from before the Cataclysm, before the Matriarchy. Their ideas of society might be very different from what we're trying to build."

The weight of the decision weighed on Seraphina. Awakening more Founders could provide invaluable knowledge and resources. But it could also complicate her already fragile situation.

"We need more information," she decided. "Alara, can you access the logs for this stasis chamber? I want to know who's in there and why they were put into stasis before we make any decisions."

As Alara got to work, Seraphina turned to the growing crowd of curious onlookers. "All right, everyone. I know this is a lot to take in, but we have work to do. This place is our home now, at least for now. Let's make it livable."

The next few hours passed in a blur of activity. The bunker slowly came to life around them as systems were reactivated and living quarters were prepared. Seraphina moved from group to group, offering encouragement and making decisions on everything from room assignments to work rotations.

She was in the middle of helping set up the hydroponics bay when Finn approached, his face uncharacteristically serious.

"We have a situation," he said quietly. "Some of the former Council members are... expressing concern."

Seraphina straightened, wiping the sweat from her brow. "What kind of concerns?"

Finn glanced around before leaning in closer. "They're not happy with the way things are going. They talk about 'maintaining order' and 'respecting traditional hierarchies.'"

A knot formed in Seraphina's stomach. She'd known this wouldn't be easy, that ingrained prejudices wouldn't disappear overnight. But she'd hoped they'd have more time before they had to face internal strife.

"Where are they now?" she asked.

"Gathered in one of the common areas," Finn replied. "It's not violent, not yet, but... it could get ugly if we don't deal with it."

Seraphina nodded, her mind already formulating a plan. "Alright. Get Niko and Marcus. We'll nip this in the bud."

As they approached the common area, Seraphina could hear raised voices. She entered to find a tense standoff between a group of former Council members and a mix of men and women from the outer districts.

"This is unnatural!" said one of the Council women, her face flushed with anger. "Men cannot be expected to lead. It goes against everything we know about society, about biology!"

"And who decided that?" a man shot back. Seraphina recognized him as one of the workers from the labor camps. "The same people who have kept us enslaved for generations?"

The argument was about to become physical when Seraphina stepped forward, her voice cutting through the din. "Enough!"

All eyes turned to her, and the room fell silent.

"I understand this is difficult," Seraphina began, her voice firm but not unkind. "We are all adjusting to massive changes. But fighting among ourselves is exactly what the Council wants back in Elyria. It's what the Convergence would have wanted. Division makes us weak."

"But the natural order..." one of the council members began.

Seraphina cut her off. "There is no 'natural order. There is only what we choose to build together. The Founders - the original Founders - created Elyria as a place of equality. Matriarchy was a response to fear, to the trauma of the Cataclysm. But it was never meant to be permanent."

She looked around the room, meeting each person's gaze in turn. "I am not asking you to change your beliefs overnight. I'm asking you to open your minds, to look at the person next to you and see not a man or a woman, but a fellow human being. Someone with hopes, fears, and the potential to contribute to our community.

"And how do you propose we do that?" another former Council member asked, her voice skeptical but no longer openly hostile.

Seraphina allowed herself a small smile. "We start by working together. From now on, every project team will be mixed - men and women, former Council members and Outer District residents. You'll eat together, work together, solve problems together. And maybe, along the way, you'll learn to see each other as equals."

A murmur went through the crowd, some nodding in agreement, others looking uncertain. But the tension in the room had dissipated, replaced by a cautious curiosity.

"It won't be easy," Seraphina concluded. "But nothing worth doing ever is. We have a chance to build something extraordinary here. Let's not waste it fighting old battles."

As the crowd began to disperse, Niko appeared at Seraphina's side. "Nice speech," he said quietly. "But do you think it will be enough?"

Seraphina sighed, the weight of leadership on her shoulders. "It's a start. But we have to stay vigilant, address these issues as they arise. We can't afford to let old prejudices tear us apart."

Before Niko could answer, Alara's voice came over the comm, urgent and agitated. "Seraphina, I've managed to access the stasis chamber logs. You'll want to see this."

After exchanging a look with Niko, Seraphina hurried back

to the sealed door. Alara stood at the control panel, her cybernetic implants pulsing rapidly.

"What did you find?" Seraphina asked, noticing the mixture of awe and fear on Alara's face.

"It's not just Founders in there," Alara said, her voice hushed. "It's... well, see for yourself."

She brought up a holographic display showing the contents of the stasis chamber. Seraphina's breath caught as she saw the rows upon rows of pods, each containing a sleeping figure.

"There are thousands of them," Niko gasped. "But who are they?"

Alara manipulated the display, bringing up biographical data. "They come from all walks of life. Scientists, artists, teachers, workers... It's like a cross-section of pre-Cataclysm society. And get this - they're from all over the world, not just Elyria."

Seraphina's mind raced with the implications. "The Founders weren't just trying to preserve themselves. They were trying to preserve humanity."

"Exactly," Alara nodded. "And there's more. According to the logs, these people volunteered for this. They knew what was coming - the Cataclysm, the possible collapse of civilization. They chose to sleep, to wait for a time when they could help rebuild."

A heavy silence fell over the group as they absorbed this information. Finally, Niko spoke up and asked the question on everyone's mind. "So what do we do? Do we wake them up?"

Seraphina stared at the display, at the faces of thousands of people who had sacrificed everything for a chance at a better future. At that moment, she knew what they had to do.

"We wake them up," she said, her voice full of determination. "Not all at once - we don't have the resources for that. But gradually. These people chose to sleep so that they could help build a better world. We owe it to them to give them that opportunity."

"And it would solve our resource problem," added Evelyn, who had joined them in the discussion. "With their knowledge and skills, we could expand our operations, maybe even start reclaiming the surface."

Niko looked skeptical. "It's risky. We don't know how they will react to our situation, to how much the world has changed."

"True," Seraphina acknowledged. "But we can't hide down here forever. If we're going to rebuild Elyria, if we're going to build a truly equal society, we're going to need all the help we can get."

She turned to Alara. "Start the revival process for a small group - say ten to start. Pick a diverse mix, people with the skills we need most."

As Alara got to work, Seraphina felt the weight of the decision settle over her. They were about to change everything, again. But as she looked around at the faces of her companions - Niko, strong and supportive; Evelyn, wise and determined; Alara, brilliant and adaptable; and all the others who had fought and sacrificed for this moment - she knew they were ready for whatever came next.

The door to the stasis chamber began to open with a hiss of escaping air. Seraphina stepped forward, ready to greet the first of her new allies, the first of a new generation of Elyrians.

Whatever challenges lay ahead, they would face them together. As equals. As architects of a new, free Elyria.

TWENTY-FOUR
AWAKENING

The hiss of escaping air filled the chamber as the first stasis pod burst open. Seraphina held her breath, her heart pounding in her chest. This moment would change everything.

A hand appeared and grabbed the edge of the pod. Then, slowly, a figure rose. A woman, her dark skin marked with intricate, swirling tattoos, blinked in the harsh light of the resurrection chamber.

"Where..." Her voice was hoarse with disuse. "When...?"

Seraphina stepped forward, forcing a calm she didn't feel into her voice. "You are safe. My name is Seraphina. You've been in stasis for... a long time."

The woman's eyes focused on Seraphina, sharp intelligence cutting through the fog of resurrection. "How long?"

Before Seraphina could answer, the other pods began to open. Men and women of various ages and ethnicities emerged, each looking as disoriented as the first.

Niko appeared at Seraphina's side, his voice low. "We need to get them to the medical bay. The revival process can be hard on the body."

Seraphina nodded and motioned to Lyra and her medical team. As they helped the revived individuals to their feet, Seraphina addressed the group.

"I know you have questions. We'll explain everything, but first we need to make sure you're all healthy. Please follow Lyra. She'll take care of you."

As the group shuffled out, assisted by medical personnel, the tattooed woman lingered. Her eyes swept the chamber, taking in the mix of ancient technology and makeshift additions.

"This is not what we prepared for," she said, her voice rising. "Something went wrong, didn't it?"

Seraphina met her gaze steadily. "Yes. But we're working to fix it. What's your name?"

"Zara," the woman replied. "Dr. Zara Okafor. I'm... I was... a geneticist specializing in human adaptation to extreme environments."

Seraphina's eyes widened. A geneticist could be invaluable in understanding and possibly reversing the effects of the Convergence.

"Dr. Okafor, your expertise may be just what we need. But first, please let our medical team examine you. We have much to discuss."

Zara nodded and let herself be led away. As the chamber emptied, Seraphina took a long breath.

"Well," Niko said, a hint of humor in his voice, "that went better than expected. No one tried to kill us or proclaim themselves Emperor of the New World Order."

Seraphina couldn't help but smile. "The day is still young."

They made their way to the command center where Alara was coordinating the resurrection process. Her cybernetic implants pulsed as she processed data.

"Vital signs are stable across the board," she reported. "No signs of cellular deterioration or cognitive impairment. The Founders' stasis technology is... incredible."

"Good," Seraphina nodded. "What about their backgrounds? Anything we should know about?"

Alara brought up a series of holographic profiles. "It's an impressive group. Besides Dr. Okafor, we have an environmental engineer, a quantum physicist, an expert in sustainable agriculture, a psychologist specializing in trauma and social adjustment, a renewable energy researcher, a master builder, an AI ethicist, a cultural anthropologist, and a... poet."

Niko raised an eyebrow at that last one. "A poet?"

"Art is an essential part of any society," Evelyn interjected, having silently joined them. "It helps us process change, imagine new possibilities."

Seraphina nodded, her mind already racing with the potential these people represented. "Alright. As soon as they're medically cleared, I want to meet with them as a group. They need to understand our situation before we start integrating them into the community."

As the others moved to carry out her orders, Seraphina felt a familiar presence at her side. She turned to find Marcus, his face etched with concern.

"There is unrest brewing," he said quietly. "Word of the Awakening has spread. Some of the former Council members are talking about 'preserving our way of life' in the face of 'outside influence.'"

Seraphina's jaw tightened. She'd hoped for more time before facing this inevitable conflict. "Where?"

Marcus led her to one of the common areas where a crowd had gathered. At its center stood Councilwoman Vega, her voice rising above the murmur.

"We cannot allow these... outsiders to dictate our future," Vega said. "They know nothing of the challenges we have faced, the order we have built."

"The order you built on our backs!" a man shouted back. Seraphina recognized him as one of the workers from the outskirts.

The crowd grew more agitated, the air thick with tension. Seraphina stepped forward, her voice cutting through the din.

"Enough!"

All eyes turned to her. Seraphina took a deep breath, weighing her words carefully.

"I understand your concerns," she began. "Change is frightening, especially after all we've been through. But these people we've revived? They're not outsiders. They're Elyrians, just like us. They chose to sleep for centuries for the chance to help build a better future."

"And what about our future?" Vega demanded. "The society we built?"

Seraphina met her gaze. "The society we built was flawed, councilwoman. It oppressed half our population and left us vulnerable to threats like the Convergence. We now have a chance to build something better, something truly equal."

"And how do you propose we do that?" another voice shouted. "By throwing away everything we know?"

"No," Seraphina shook her head. "By learning. From our past, from our mistakes, and yes, from these people who have just awakened. They bring knowledge and skills that we've lost. But more than that, they bring a new perspective. They can help us see beyond the limitations we've placed on ourselves.

She looked around the crowd, meeting eyes that were both hostile and curious. "I'm not asking you to change overnight. I am asking you to open your minds, to consider possibilities beyond what we have known. We're all Elyrians. We all want what's best for our people. Let's work together to find out what that looks like.

A murmur went through the crowd. Seraphina could see her words working, doubt replacing anger in many faces.

"And if we disagree?" Vega pressed, though some of the fight was gone from her voice.

"Then we discuss it," Seraphina replied. "We debate, we compromise, we find solutions that work for everyone. That's what a truly free society does."

As the crowd began to disperse, many deep in conversation, Marcus leaned forward. "Nice speech. But will it be enough?"

Seraphina sighed. "It's a start. We must continue to engage, keep the dialog open. And we need to show them, through action, what a more equal society can achieve."

She was interrupted by Alara's voice over the comm. "Seraphina, the revived group is ready. They're waiting in the conference room."

"On my way," Seraphina replied. She turned to Marcus. "Keep an eye on things here. If tensions flare up again, let me know immediately."

The conference room fell silent as Seraphina entered. Ten pairs of eyes watched her, a mixture of curiosity, apprehension, and in some cases, barely concealed impatience.

"Thank you for your patience," Seraphina began. "I know you have questions. I'll do my best to answer them, but first I must explain our current situation."

Over the next hour, Seraphina outlined the history of the past centuries - the Cataclysm, the rise of the Matriarchy, the recent threat of the Convergence, and their current efforts to build a new, more egalitarian society.

As she finished, the room erupted in a cacophony of voices.

"This is unacceptable!" exclaimed quantum physicist Dr. Emerson. "We've been preparing for the possibility of societal collapse, but this... this deliberate regression..."

"Regression?" Zara cut in, her voice sharp. "From what I've heard, you've made remarkable adjustments, given the circumstances. The real question is, how do we help them move forward?"

Dr. Rivera, the cultural anthropologist, leaned forward. "We need to understand the cultural context that led to this matriarchal system. Only then can we work effectively to change it."

"Change it?" asked Yara, the sustainable agriculture expert. "Should we change it at all? It's not our place to impose our values on a society that has developed without us."

"It is if that society is built on oppression," argued AI ethicist Chen. "The very fact that we're here, that we've been awakened, suggests that they want change."

The debate raged on, voices rising and falling as they grappled with the implications of their new reality. Seraphina listened, her mind racing to keep up with the rapid exchange of ideas.

Finally, the poet, a serene woman named Aria, spoke. Her soft voice somehow cut through the noise and got everyone's attention.

"We're looking at this all wrong," she said. "We are not here to fix them or be fixed by them. We're here to build something new, together. A synthesis of what was, what is, and what could be."

A pensive silence fell over the room. Seraphina felt a spark of hope ignite in her chest. This was what they needed - new perspectives, challenging ideas, the intellectual strength to tackle the monumental task before them.

"Aria's right," Seraphina said, standing up. "We don't have all the answers. But together, we have a chance to find them. We're facing challenges none of us could have imagined - the aftermath of the Convergence, a divided society, limited resources. We need your knowledge, your skills, your fresh perspectives. But we also need you to understand the realities of our current situation.

She looked around the room, meeting each person's gaze. "I'm asking for your help, but I'm also asking for your patience. The people out there are scared. They've been through trauma that we can barely imagine. We need to work with them, not dictate to them.

Dr. Okafor nodded slowly. "A collaborative approach. That makes sense. But we need to establish some sort of structure, some way to integrate our knowledge with your practical experience."

"Agreed," Seraphina said. "I propose that we form an advisory council. You'll work with our existing leadership to develop strategies for moving forward. But you'll also be interacting with the general population, teaching classes, conducting workshops. We need to demystify your presence, make it clear that you're here to help, not to take over."

The group exchanged glances, a mixture of excitement and apprehension on their faces. Finally, Dr. Rivera spoke.

"I think I speak for all of us when I say we're in. This is why we chose to go into stasis in the first place - to help build a better future. It may not be the future we imagined, but it's the one we have. Let's make the best of it.

A murmur of agreement rippled through the room. Seraphina felt a weight lift from her shoulders. They still had a long way to go, but this was a start.

When the meeting adjourned, Niko appeared at her side. "How did it go?"

Seraphina allowed herself a small smile. "Better than I had hoped. They're on board. Now we have to figure out how to integrate them without causing a panic."

Niko nodded, his expression pensive. "It won't be easy. Change never is. But I think-"

He was cut off by a blaring alarm. Red emergency lights began flashing throughout the bunker.

"What's happening?" Seraphina demanded, already running to the command center.

They burst in to find Alara hunched over a console, her cybernetic implants pulsing rapidly. "We have a problem," she said, her voice tense. "The Council has found us. They're on the surface, trying to break in."

Seraphina's blood ran cold. She looked at the monitors, which showed a fleet of Council hovercrafts descending on their location. Armed troops were already deployed, setting up what looked like heavy drilling equipment.

"How long do we have?" Niko asked, his voice calm despite the gravity of the situation.

Alara shook her head. "Hard to say. The bunker's defenses are formidable, but if they have Founder technology of their own..."

"We need to evacuate," Marcus said after joining them. "Use the emergency tunnels, get our people to safety."

But Seraphina hesitated. They'd just found this place, this

chance to rebuild. And the stasis chambers... they couldn't leave all those people behind.

"No," she said, her voice firm. "We stand our ground. This is our home now, and we'll fight for it."

She turned to the others, her mind already formulating a plan. "Niko, Marcus, get our defense teams into position. Alara, I need you to find a way to boost our shields. And someone get me Dr. Okafor and the others. If we're going to win this, we're going to need every brain and every pair of hands we've got.

As the command center buzzed with activity, Seraphina stared at the monitors, watching the Council forces advance. This was it - the moment that would decide the future of Elyria. And she was determined to make sure it was a future of freedom, of equality, of hope.

Whatever the Council threw at them, they would face it together. As one people, united in purpose.

The battle for Elyria's soul was about to begin.

TWENTY-FIVE
CRUCIBLE OF CHANGE

The bunker shook as another explosion rocked the surface. Dust rained down from the ceiling, coating Seraphina's hair as she bent over the holographic display in the command center.

"Status report," she barked, her eyes never leaving the map of Council troop movements.

Alara's fingers flew over the controls, her cybernetic implants pulsing with data. "Shields holding at 72%. They're throwing everything they've got at us, but the Founders built this place to last."

"Not forever," Niko interjected, his face grim. "We need a plan beyond 'wait them out.'"

Seraphina nodded, her mind racing. "Agreed. What are our options?"

Before anyone could answer, the door burst open. Dr. Zara Okafor stepped in, her eyes blazing with a mixture of fear and determination.

"You have to get us out of here," she demanded. "We didn't sleep for centuries to die in a hole in the ground."

Seraphina straightened and met Zara's gaze. "No one is dying today, Doctor. But we need your help. All of it."

Zara's eyes narrowed. "How?"

"You are scientists, engineers, problem solvers," Seraphina said, gesturing to the chaos around them. "This is a problem. Help us solve it."

For a moment, Zara looked like she was going to argue. Then her expression changed, curiosity replacing fear. "What do you have in mind?"

Seraphina allowed herself a small smile. "A counterattack. But not with weapons. With ideas."

She turned to the group. "Alara, can you hijack their com frequencies?"

The cyborg's eye whirred as she thought. "Possibly. Their encryption is strong, but with the Founders' technology..."

"Do it," Seraphina ordered. She turned to Zara. "Doctor, I need you and your colleagues to prepare a message. Something that will make these troops think twice about what they're doing."

Understanding dawned in Zara's eyes. "Psychological warfare. Clever. But what do we say?"

"The truth," Seraphina replied. "About the Founders, about the true history of Elyria. Make them question everything they've been taught."

As Zara hurried off to gather her team, Niko approached Seraphina. "It's a good plan," he said quietly. "But it won't stop their attack. We need a military solution as well."

Seraphina nodded, her face hardening. "I know. That's where you come in. I need you to organize our defenders. Not just to hold them off, but to push them back."

Niko's eyebrows rose. "With what? We're outnumbered and outgunned."

"Not necessarily," Marcus interjected, joining the conversation. "That armory we found... it's not just weapons. There's technology down there I've never seen before. Non-lethal stuff that might give us an advantage."

Seraphina's mind raced with possibilities. "Show me."

As they hurried toward the armory, another explosion shook the bunker. Seraphina stumbled, caught by Niko's strong arm.

"Thanks," she murmured, their eyes meeting for a brief, charged moment.

"Anytime," Niko replied, his voice soft despite the chaos around them.

They reached the armory, and Seraphina's breath caught at the sight. Rows upon rows of sleek, advanced weapons lined the walls. But it was the devices Marcus led them to that really caught her attention.

"Sonic disruptors," he explained, holding up a slim, weapon-like device. "They emit a frequency that incapacitates without causing permanent damage. And these," he pointed to what looked like grenades, "are EMP bombs. They'll fry their technology without hurting the soldiers."

Seraphina nodded, a plan forming in her mind. "Perfect. Niko, equip our best fighters with them. We'll open the main doors."

"What?" Niko's eyes widened in disbelief. "Sera, that's suicide."

"It's brave," she countered. "They won't expect it. We hit them with the EMPs, disable their vehicles. Then we use the sonic weapons to disable the troops. Meanwhile, Zara and her team will transmit their message."

Niko studied her for a long moment, then nodded. "It's crazy. But it might work."

As they prepared for the counterattack, Seraphina made her way through the bunker. Everywhere, she saw people working together - former Council members alongside Outer District workers, the newly awakened scientists blending seamlessly into the teams. It filled her with a fierce pride.

She found Evelyn in the medical bay, helping Lyra tend to the wounded from earlier skirmishes.

"How are we doing?" Seraphina asked.

Evelyn's face was tired but determined. "We'll make it. These people are resilient. But Seraphina... whatever you're planning, be careful. We can't afford to lose you."

Seraphina squeezed the older woman's hand. "I will be careful. But I need you to do something for me. If... if this goes wrong, get our people out. Use the escape tunnels. Start over somewhere else."

Evelyn's eyes filled with understanding. "It won't come to that. But if it does... we'll continue your work. I promise."

With a final nod, Seraphina made her way to the main entrance. Niko and Marcus were there, distributing weapons and giving last-minute instructions to their makeshift army.

"Everyone clear on the plan?" Seraphina asked, her voice carrying over the gathered crowd.

A chorus of affirmations answered her. She looked at the faces before her - men and women, young and old, from all walks of life. United in purpose.

"Whatever happens out there," she said, her voice strong, "remember what we're fighting for. Not just for our lives, but for our future. A future of equality, of freedom, of hope. Let's show the Council what true Elyrians are made of."

A cheer went up, quickly silenced as they took their positions. Seraphina moved to the control panel, her hand hovering over the door release.

"Ready?" she asked, looking at Niko.

He nodded, his eyes meeting hers. A thousand unspoken words passed between them at that moment. If this was to be their last stand, at least they would face it together.

Seraphina took a deep breath and pressed the button.

The massive doors groaned open, revealing the chaos outside. Council forces swarmed the area, their weapons trained on the opening. For a split second, both sides froze in surprise.

Then all hell broke loose.

EMP grenades arced through the air, detonating in brilliant flashes of blue light. Hover vehicles crashed to the ground, their systems fried. Before the Council troops could regroup, the defenders surged forward, sonic disruptors blazing.

Seraphina was in the thick of it, her weapon sending waves of Council soldiers crashing to the ground. Beside her, Niko moved with fluid grace, each shot finding its mark.

"Alira!" Seraphina yelled into her comm. "Now!"

Suddenly, every communication device in the Council crackled to life. Dr. Okafor's voice, strong and clear, filled the air.

"Soldiers of Elyria, hear me! You have been lied to. The Council you serve is not the true authority of our people. We are the legacy of the Founders - men and women who built a society of equality and justice. The matriarchy you know is a perversion of their vision..."

As the message played, Seraphina saw confusion spread through the Council ranks. Some lowered their weapons, uncertainty written all over their faces.

But not all. A group of elite Guardians pushed forward, their armor somehow resistant to the EMP's effects. At their head was a familiar face - Alira Vex, the agent who had once hunted Seraphina for the Council.

"Traitor!" Alira's voice cut through the chaos. "Do not listen to their lies! For the glory of the Council!"

She raised her weapon and pointed it directly at Seraphina. Time seemed to slow. Seraphina saw the energy bolt leave the barrel and knew she couldn't dodge in time.

Suddenly, a body slammed into her, knocking her to the ground. The bolt sizzled overhead, missing her by inches. Seraphina looked up to see Niko above her, his face contorted in pain.

"Niko!" she cried, seeing the charred hole in his shoulder where the bolt had hit him instead of her.

"I'm fine," he grunted, though his face was pale. "Keep fighting. We can't let them win."

Anger and determination surged through Seraphina. She rose, her eyes fixed on Alira.

"Enough!" she shouted, her voice carrying over the battle-field. "Alira, stand down! This is not the way!"

Alira hesitated, her weapon still raised. "You have betrayed everything we stand for, Seraphina. How can you side with them?"

"I side with the truth," Seraphina replied, taking a step forward. "With the future. Look around you, Alira. Men and women fighting side by side. This is what Elyria should be. What it can be again."

Uncertainty flickered in Alira's eyes. Seraphina continued, her voice softening. "I know you believe you're doing the right thing. But the Council has lied to us. To all of us. We have a chance now to build something better. Something truly just."

For a long moment, the battlefield held its breath. Then Alira slowly lowered her weapon.

"Stand down," she ordered her troops, her voice wavering. "I... I need to hear more of this truth."

A ripple went through the Council troops. Weapons were lowered, the sounds of battle fading into an uneasy silence.

Seraphina let out a breath she hadn't realized she was holding. She turned to find Niko leaning heavily against her, his face pale but smiling.

"Nice speech," he murmured.

"Learned from the best," she replied, supporting his weight as they made their way back to the bunker.

As the defenders and former Council forces mingled, an uneasy truce forming, Seraphina felt a spark of hope. They still had a long way to go, but this was a start. A chance for real change.

Inside the bunker, the command center was a hive of activity. Zara and her team fielded questions from curious Council soldiers, explaining the true history of Elyria. Alara worked to establish secure communications with other rebel cells throughout the city.

Evelyn approached Seraphina, her eyes bright with pride. "You did it. You actually did it."

Seraphina shook her head. "We did it. All of us. But this is just the beginning. We still have a lot of work to do."

As if to emphasize her point, an alarm sounded from one of the consoles. Alara's face paled as she read the incoming message.

"What is it?" Seraphina demanded, fear in her stomach.

Alara looked up, her expression grim. "It's from Eden. The Convergence... it's back. And it's headed straight for Elyria."

The room fell silent as the implications sank in. They had won this battle, but the war was far from over. The true test of their new, united Elyria was yet to come.

Seraphina straightened up, her voice steady despite the fear coursing through her. "All right. We've faced this before, we can face it again. But this time we will face it together. As equals. As Elyrians."

She looked around the room, at the faces of those who had fought beside her, who had taken a chance on a new future. "The Convergence thinks it can assimilate us, erase what makes us human. But they do not understand what we have built here. Our strength is not in our uniformity, but in our diversity. In our ability to come together despite our differences."

Niko stepped forward, his shoulder bandaged but his eyes bright with determination. "Sera is right. We have something the Convergence can never have. Free will. The ability to choose our own path."

Zara nodded, a spark of excitement in her eyes. "And we have science on our side. With our knowledge and your experience... we might be able to find a way to stop the Convergence for good."

Seraphina felt a wave of hope. This was what she had dreamed of - people from all walks of life working together toward a common goal.

"All right," she said, her voice ringing with authority. "Let's get to work. We have a city to save and a future to build. Together."

As the room erupted into action, plans being made and ideas flying, Seraphina caught Niko's eye. He smiled, a promise in his eyes. Whatever came next, they would face it side by side.

The Convergence was coming. But Elyria - the true Elyria, united and strong - was ready to face it.

TWENTY-SIX
UNITY IN ADVERSITY

The command center hummed with frenzied energy. Holograms flickered in the air, showing the Convergence's relentless advance toward Elyria. Seraphina stood at the center of the storm, her eyes darting from screen to screen as she absorbed the flood of information.

"How long do we have?" she asked, her voice cutting through the noise.

Alara's fingers danced across her console, cybernetic implants pulsing with data. "At current speed, the Convergence will reach Elyria's outer defenses in approximately 18 hours."

Niko's jaw tightened. "Not much time to prepare a defense against an enemy we barely understand."

"Then we'd better get to work," Seraphina replied, her voice steady despite the fear in her gut. She turned to face the room. "Dr. Okafor, what progress have you made in understanding the nature of the Convergence?"

Zara stepped forward, her face a mixture of excitement and frustration. "It's... complex. The Convergence is not a single entity, but a shared consciousness. It integrates organic and inorganic matter alike, adapting and evolving with each new addition."

"So how do we stop it?" Marcus asked, his soldier's mind already strategizing.

"That's the tricky part," Zara admitted. "Conventional weapons are useless against it. We need to target the core of its consciousness, disrupt the network that binds it together."

Seraphina's mind raced. "The failsafe we used before... could we modify it, somehow boost its power?"

Zara's eyes lit up. "Possibly. If we could amplify the signal, broadcast it over a wider area... it might be enough to break the Convergence's hold on its assembled components."

"I can help with that," a new voice chimed in. AI Ethicist Chen stepped forward. "If the Convergence operates on a network principle, I may be able to design a virus to exploit its vulnerabilities."

Seraphina nodded, a plan beginning to form. "Good. Work with Zara and Alara on it. Niko, I need you to coordinate our ground defenses. We have to assume that some of the Convergence will break through."

As the others went about their tasks, Evelyn approached Seraphina. The First Matriarch's face was etched with concern. "Seraphina, a word?"

They moved to a quieter corner of the room. Evelyn's voice

was deep, urgent. "We must consider evacuation plans. If the Convergence breaches our defenses-"

"We're not running," Seraphina cut her off, her voice firm. "This is our home. We fight for it."

Evelyn's eyes softened. "I understand the sentiment, but we have a responsibility to our people. To the future of Elyria. If we fall here, all hope will fall with us."

Seraphina felt the weight of leadership press down on her. Evelyn was right, of course. But the thought of abandoning Elyria, of letting the Convergence consume it...

"We will have a contingency plan," she admitted. "But only as a last resort. For now, our focus is on stopping the Convergence here and now."

Evelyn nodded, a hint of pride in her eyes. "Very well. I'll coordinate the evacuation routes with Marcus, quietly. Let's hope we don't need them."

As Evelyn walked away, Seraphina felt a presence at her side. She turned to find Niko, his face a mixture of concern and determination.

"How are you holding up?" he asked quietly.

Allowing herself a moment of vulnerability, Seraphina leaned into his strength. "Scared," she admitted. "But ready. You?"

Niko's hand found hers and squeezed gently. "The same. But we've faced impossible odds before. We'll do it again."

Their moment was interrupted by a commotion at the entrance to the command center. Alira Vex strode in, flanked by a group of former Council soldiers. The room tensed, hands moving to weapons.

"Stand down," Seraphina ordered, stepping forward to face Alira. "What do you want?"

Alira's face was a mask of determination. "To help. We have seen your truth, heard your words. If the Convergence comes, we want to fight alongside you."

A murmur ran through the room. Seraphina studied Alira's face, looking for any sign of deception. She found only determination.

"Do you understand what this means?" Seraphina asked. "Fighting alongside men, treating them as equals?"

Alira's jaw clenched, but she nodded. "Old habits die hard, but we're willing to learn. To change. Elyria's survival is more important than our pride."

Seraphina felt a wave of hope. This was what they had fought for - not just to overthrow the old order, but to build something new, together.

"Welcome aboard," she said, holding out her hand. Alira took it firmly, a pact sealed.

The next hours passed in a blur of activity. The bunker turned into a beehive of preparations. In the labs, Zara and Chen worked feverishly on their anti-convergence virus, their debates punctuated by bursts of inspiration. Alara coordinated with the engineering teams, setting up a city-wide broadcast system for the failsafe signal.

In the armory, Niko and Marcus led a mixed group of rebels and former Council soldiers, training them in the use of the

Founders' advanced weaponry. The awkwardness between the two groups slowly gave way to a grudging respect as they worked toward a common goal.

Seraphina moved between the teams, offering encouragement, making decisions, and keeping everyone focused on the task at hand. But as the hours ticked by, doubt gnawed at her. Would it be enough? Could they really stop a force that had nearly consumed them once before?

She found herself in a quiet corner of the bunker, staring at a holodisplay of Elyria. The city she had grown up in, fought for, dreamed of changing. Now it stood on the brink of destruction.

"Credit for your thoughts?"

Seraphina turned to find Finn approaching, his usual grin tempered by the gravity of their situation.

"I wonder if we're doing the right thing," she admitted. "Staying to fight. Risking everything."

Finn leaned against the wall, his eyes on the holodisplay. "Having second thoughts about your rousing speech?"

Seraphina sighed. "No. Yes. I don't know. We've come this far, Finn. We're on the verge of building the kind of society we've always dreamed of. But if we lose here..."

"We lose everything," Finn finished. He was silent for a moment, then turned to her. "You want to know what I think?"

"Always," Seraphina said, managing a small smile.

"I think you're right to be afraid. We'd be fools not to be. But I also think that is why we have fought so hard to change things. The old Elyria, the one ruled by the Council? It would have crumbled in the face of this threat. But what we've built here? The way we've brought people together, across all the old divisions? That is our strength."

Seraphina felt a warmth rise in her chest at Finn's words. "When did you become so wise?"

Finn grinned. "I have always been wise. You're just learning to appreciate my genius now."

Their moment of levity was interrupted by Alara's voice over the comm. "Seraphina, we have movement. The convergence is accelerating. New ETA... 4 hours."

The bottom fell out of Seraphina's stomach. "Understood. I'm on my way."

She exchanged glances with Finn, seeing her own mixture of fear and determination reflected in his eyes.

"Showtime," he said quietly.

They hurried back to the command center and found it abuzz with activity. Zara and Chen looked up from their work, faces drawn with exhaustion but eyes bright with excitement.

"We did it," Zara announced. "The virus is ready. Combined with the failsafe signal, it should be enough to disrupt the Convergence's network."

"Should be?" Niko asked, his voice tense.

Chen shrugged. "We haven't had a chance to test it yet. But the simulations look promising."

Seraphina nodded, putting aside her doubts. "It'll have to do. Alara, is the transmission system ready?"

"Online and ready," the cyborg confirmed. "We can blanket the entire city and its environs with the signal."

"Good," Seraphina said. She turned to address the room. "This is it, people. Everything we've fought for comes down to the next few hours. I won't lie to you - the odds are stacked against us. The Convergence is unlike anything we've faced before. But look around you."

She paused, meeting the eyes of rebels and former Council members, men and women, humans and cyborgs alike. "We've done the impossible before. We've bridged divides that seemed insurmountable. We've begun to build a society based on equality, mutual respect and understanding. That's what we're fighting for. Not just for our lives, but for our future. A future where everyone has a voice, where everyone has a chance to reach their full potential."

Seraphina's voice grew stronger, filled with conviction. "The Convergence thinks it can assimilate us, erase what makes us unique. But our strength lies in our diversity, in our ability to come together despite our differences. We are Elyria. All of us. And we will not go quietly into the night."

A cheer went up, faces set with determination. Seraphina felt a surge of pride and hope. Whatever came, they would face it together.

"All right," she said, her voice cutting through the din. "To your stations. Niko, get our ground teams in position. Alara, start the countdown for the signal transmission. Everyone else, be ready for anything. The Convergence will not go down without a fight."

As the room erupted into action, Seraphina felt a hand on her arm. She turned to find Evelyn, the First Matriarch's eyes shining with unshed tears.

"You have done well," Evelyn said softly. "Whatever happens next, know that you have made the Founders proud. You've shown us all what Elyria can be."

Seraphina swallowed the lump in her throat and pulled Evelyn into a tight embrace. "Thank you," she whispered. "For everything."

They broke apart as Alara's voice rang out. "Convergence sighted! They've breached the outer defenses!"

Seraphina rushed to the holodisplay, her heart pounding. The sight that greeted her sent shivers down her spine. A wave of silver and blue energy rolled across the landscape, consuming everything in its path. Where it touched, matter was transformed into grotesque amalgams of flesh and machine.

"Mother's grace," someone whispered.

Seraphina steeled herself. "Alara, begin transmission. Niko, engage the ground forces. Keep them occupied while the signal does its work."

The next few minutes were a blur of chaos. Reports poured in from every sector of the city. The Convergence was advancing, unstoppable, but their forces fought valiantly. Men and women who had once been enemies now stood side by side, united against a common threat.

"Signal broadcast initiated," Alara announced. "Virus deployed."

For a heart-stopping moment, nothing seemed to change. The Convergence continued its relentless advance. Then, slowly, almost imperceptibly, it began to falter.

"It's working!" Zara exclaimed, her eyes glued to the read-outs. "The network is destabilizing!"

Hope rushed through the room. But it was short-lived. A new alarm sounded, and Alara's face grew pale as she read the incoming data.

"The Convergence... it's adapting," she said, her voice cracking with fear. "It's evolving to resist the virus. We've slowed it down, but we haven't stopped it."

Seraphina's mind raced. They had thrown everything they had at the Convergence, and it wasn't enough. She looked around the room, at the faces of those who had fought so hard, who had dared to dream of a better Elyria. She couldn't let it end here.

An idea flashed through her mind. A dangerous, perhaps suicidal idea. But it might be her only chance.

"The stasis chambers," she said, her voice cutting through the despair. "The ones with the thousands of sleepers. Could we use them?"

Zara's eyes widened as she realized Seraphina's meaning. "As a power source? Theoretically, yes. The bio-electric field generated by so many sleepers... it could amplify our signal exponentially."

"But the exposure could kill them," Evelyn protested. "We'd be sacrificing thousands to save millions."

Seraphina felt the weight of the decision press down on her. "We have no choice," she said quietly. "If we do nothing, they all die. At least this way we give Elyria a chance."

The room fell silent, the gravity of the moment settling over them all. Finally, Niko spoke.

"Whatever you decide," he said, his eyes meeting Seraphina's, "we are with you. Until the end."

Seraphina took a deep breath and squared her shoulders. This was it. The moment that would define everything they had fought for.

"Do it," she ordered. "Reroute power from the stasis chambers. Give the signal everything we've got."

As the others rushed to carry out her orders, Seraphina turned back to the holodisplay. The Convergence was closing in, a tide of destruction threatening to engulf everything she held dear.

But as she watched her people rally, as she saw the determination in their eyes and the strength in their unity, Seraphina felt a spark of hope ignite in her chest. Whatever came next, they would face it together. As one people. As Elyria reborn.

The final battle for their future was about to begin.

TWENTY-SEVEN
THE PRICE OF FREEDOM

The bunker shook as power surged through the ancient conduits. Alarms blared, warning of system overloads and critical failures. In the heart of the command center, Seraphina gripped the edge of the holographic display, her knuckles white with tension.

"Status report!" she barked, eyes fixed on the advancing tide of the Convergence.

Alara's fingers flew across her console, cybernetic implants pulsing frantically. "Power diversion at 87% and rising. Stasis chambers are... holding, but barely."

Zara's voice cut through the chaos, tight with barely contained panic. "We're losing them. The bioelectric field is destabilizing. If we don't stop soon, we'll kill them all!"

Seraphina's heart clenched. Thousands of lives hung in the balance, her sacrifice possibly dooming her to save millions more. She opened her mouth to speak, but Niko beat her to it.

"We can't stop," he said, his voice firm but tinged with regret. "Not yet. Look!"

All eyes turned to the main display. The amplified signal, amplified by the power of the Sleepers, rippled across the landscape. Where it touched, the convergence faltered. Its relentless advance slowed, then stopped.

"It's working," Chen breathed, wonder and horror mixing in his voice. "The virus is breaking through their adaptations."

For a moment, hope swept through the room. Then a new alarm came to life.

"No!" Alara cried, her organic eye wide with fear. "They're... they're evolving again. Faster this time. The virus can't keep up!"

Seraphina watched in growing fear as the Convergence began to move again. Slower now, but still moving. Still consuming everything in its path.

"We need more power," she said, her mind racing. "Is there anything left that we haven't tapped?"

Marcus shook his head, frustration etched into his face. "We're redlining everything. Push any harder and we'll blow the whole system."

Silence fell over the command center, heavy with the weight of impending doom. They had given everything they had, and it wasn't enough. The Convergence would consume them all, and with it, the last hope for a free Elyria.

In that moment of despair, an unexpected voice spoke.

"There is... one more option."

All eyes turned to Evelyn. The First Matriarch stood tall, her face a mask of grim determination.

"The Founders left one last failsafe," she continued. "A way to channel the full power of the bunker, of all our systems, into one massive burst. It would destroy the facility, but the energy release might be enough to destroy the Convergence once and for all."

"And what's the catch?" Finn asked, his usual sarcasm tempered by the gravity of the situation.

Evelyn's eyes met Seraphina's, filled with sorrow and determination. "It requires a live conduit. Someone to manually trigger the failsafe and channel the energy. They... wouldn't survive the process."

The room erupted into chaos. Voices overlapped, shouting arguments and protests. But Seraphina heard none of it. In her mind, she saw the faces of all those who had fought and died for this moment. All those who had dared to dream of a better Elyria.

"I will do it," she said, her voice cutting through the din like a knife.

Silence fell, broken only by Niko's anguished whisper. "Sera, no."

She turned to face him, her heart breaking at the pain in his eyes. "It has to be me, Niko. I started this. I have to finish it."

"The hell you do," he argued, stepping closer. "I won't let you sacrifice yourself. It should be me."

"No," Evelyn interjected. "It has to be a direct descendant of the Founders. The fail-safe is keyed to our genetic signature. Seraphina is the only one who can do it."

The finality of those words settled over the room like a shroud. Seraphina looked at the faces around her-friends, comrades, people who had become family in the crucible of revolution. She saw the grief, the fear, but also the understanding. They knew, as she did, that this was their only chance.

"How long do we have?" she asked, turning back to Alara.

The cyborg's voice was soft, almost apologetic. "At the current rate of progress... twenty minutes. Maybe less."

Seraphina nodded, squaring her shoulders. "Then we'd better get moving. Evelyn, show me what to do."

As they prepared to leave, Niko caught her arm. "Sera, wait. I... I can't let you do this alone."

She opened her mouth to argue, but the look in his eyes stopped her. It wasn't just love she saw there, but a fierce determination. A refusal to be left behind.

"Okay," she said quietly. "Together."

They made their way through the bunker, now a hive of frantic activity. People rushed to and fro, carrying supplies, weapons, anything that might give them an advantage in the coming battle. Seraphina's heart ached at the sight. These were her people, united in the face of annihilation. She couldn't let them down.

Evelyn led them to a sealed chamber deep in the heart of the facility. As the doors hissed open, Seraphina gasped.

Before them stood a massive device, pulsing with barely contained energy.

"The Founders' last gift," Evelyn said, her voice hushed with awe. "And their greatest burden."

She moved to a control panel, her fingers dancing over ancient keys. A holographic display came to life, showing a complex sequence of symbols.

"This is the activation code," Evelyn explained. "Once initiated, you'll have about three minutes before the energy surge reaches critical levels. You'll need to remain in physical contact with the device until the end."

Seraphina nodded and memorized the sequence. "And then?"

Evelyn's eyes were sad. "And then you channel every ounce of power this facility has to offer into the signal. If we're lucky, it will be enough to shatter the Convergence's hold on our world."

"And if we're not lucky?" Niko asked, though his tone suggested he already knew the answer.

"Then we die knowing we gave everything we had," Seraphina replied, her voice steady despite the fear coursing through her veins.

A tremor shook the bunker, more violent than before. Alara's voice crackled over the comm, tight with urgency.

"The Convergence has breached the outer defenses! We've got five minutes at the most!"

Seraphina's eyes met Niko's, a lifetime of unspoken words passing between them in an instant.

"You should go," she said quietly. "Help the others evacuate. There's no need for both of us to..."

Her words were cut off as Niko pulled her close, his lips crashing against hers in a desperate, passionate kiss. When they finally broke apart, both breathless, his eyes blazed with determination.

"I told you," he said. "Together. Always."

Seraphina's heart swelled as it broke. She turned to Evelyn, who watched them with a mixture of pride and sorrow.

"Go," Seraphina said. "Get everyone out. As many as you can."

Evelyn hesitated, then nodded. She pulled Seraphina into a fierce hug. "You are the best of us," she whispered. "The true heir of the Founders. May the Mother watch over both of you."

As Evelyn left, sealing the chamber behind her, Seraphina and Niko turned to face the device. The air crackled with energy, the walls themselves seemed to pulse with power.

"Ready?" Seraphina asked, her hand hovering over the control panel.

Niko's hand found hers, their fingers intertwined. "Ready."

Together they entered the activation sequence. The device roared to life, tendrils of energy arcing out to envelop them. Pain shot through Seraphina's body, every nerve ending on fire. But she held on, gritting her teeth against the agony.

Through the haze of pain, she heard Alara's voice over the comm. "Convergence breaching inner defenses! Sixty seconds to contact!"

"Hang on," Niko growled, his body shaking with the effort. "We're almost there."

The energy built to a crescendo, the air itself seemed to vibrate with power. Seraphina could feel something vast and ancient stirring within her, the legacy of the Founders awakening in her blood.

"Now, Sera!" Niko shouted. "Do it now!"

With a cry of defiance, Seraphina unleashed the full power of the fail-safe. The power exploded outward, a shockwave of pure energy that shook the very foundations of the earth. The last thing she saw before darkness claimed her was a blinding flash of light and Niko's face, fierce and beautiful in its determination.

Then nothing.

...

CONSCIOUSNESS RETURNED SLOWLY, in fits and starts. Seraphina became aware of a dull pain throughout her body, of cool air on her skin. She opened her eyes, blinking against the harsh light.

"Easy," a familiar voice said. "Take it slow."

As her vision cleared, Seraphina saw Lyra bending over her, a relieved smile on the young medic's face.

"Lyra?" Seraphina croaked, her throat dry and raw. "What... what happened? The Convergence..."

"Gone," Lyra said, her smile widening. "You did it, Sera. You stopped them."

Relief washed over Seraphina, quickly followed by a wave of panic. "Niko? Where's Niko?"

Lyra's smile faltered. "He's... alive. But Sera, you must prepare yourself. The energy surge, it... changed him."

Before Seraphina could demand more answers, the door burst open. Finn burst in, his face aglow with excitement.

"You're not going to believe this," he said, slightly out of breath. "You have to see for yourself."

Despite Lyra's protests, Seraphina struggled to her feet. Leaning heavily on Finn, she made her way out of the medical bay and into the main cavern of the bunker.

The sight that greeted her took her breath away.

The cavern was filled with people - not just the survivors of her group, but hundreds more. Men and women of all ages were milling about, looking dazed but very much alive.

"The sleepers," Seraphina breathed. "How...?"

"We're not sure," Finn admitted. "But when the fail-safe was activated, it didn't just stop the Convergence. It... woke them up. All of them."

Seraphina's mind reeled at the implications. Thousands of people from before the Cataclysm, now awake and ready to help rebuild Elyria. It was more than she had ever hoped for.

But one face was conspicuously absent from the crowd.

"Where's Niko?" she demanded.

Finn's expression sobered. "This way," he said, leading her to a secluded corner of the cave.

As they approached, Seraphina saw a figure hunched over, surrounded by worried onlookers. Her heart stopped as she recognized Niko's broad shoulders and dark hair.

"Niko?" she called, her voice shaking.

He turned and Seraphina gasped. Niko's eyes, once a warm brown, now glowed with an alien blue light. Veins of energy pulsed beneath his skin, giving him an almost ethereal appearance.

"Sera," he said, his voice carrying a strange resonance. "I... I can hear them. All of them. The Convergence, the sleepers, everyone. It's all connected."

Seraphina approached slowly, her hand reaching out to touch his face. Despite his altered appearance, his skin was warm, familiar.

"What happened to you?" she whispered.

Niko leaned into her touch, his bright eyes full of wonder and fear. "I don't know. But I think... I think I might be the key to rebuilding Elyria. To making sure that nothing like the Convergence ever threatens us again."

As Seraphina looked into Niko's transformed face, she felt a mixture of hope and trepidation. They had won the battle against the Convergence, but at what cost? And what new challenges awaited them in the aftermath of their victory?

The future stretched out before them, full of possibility and danger in equal measure. But as Seraphina looked around at the faces of her people - old and new, united in their determination to build a better world - she knew one thing for certain.

Whatever came next, they would face it together. As equals. As Elyrians.

The real work of rebuilding their world was about to begin.

TWENTY-EIGHT
DAWN OF A NEW ERA

The cave hummed with a cacophony of voices, a mixture of excitement, confusion, and fear. Seraphina stood at the center of the storm, her mind reeling as she tried to process the magnitude of what had happened. The Convergence was gone, but in its wake they faced a challenge perhaps even greater - the integration of thousands of people from a world long gone.

Niko's hand found hers, his touch sending a jolt of energy through her body. His eyes, still glowing with that eerie blue light, met hers.

"What do we do now?" he asked, his voice carrying that strange new resonance.

Before Seraphina could answer, Zara pushed her way through the crowd, her face a mixture of awe and scientific curiosity.

"We need to run some tests," she said, her eyes fixed on Niko. "Your connection to the Convergence, to the sleepers-it could be the key to understanding everything."

Niko tensed, his grip on Seraphina's hand tightening. "I'm not a lab rat, Doctor."

"No one's suggesting you are," Seraphina interjected, her voice firm. She turned to the growing crowd. "Everyone, please! I know you're confused and frightened. But we need to stay calm. We've all been through a lot, and we have a lot of work ahead of us."

A murmur went through the crowd. An older man, one of the newly awakened sleepers, stepped forward. "Who are you? What's happened to our world?"

Seraphina took a deep breath, weighing her words carefully. "My name is Seraphina Blackwood. I'm... I was a member of the Council that ruled Elyria. But things have changed. Our world has changed. And now we have a chance to build something new. Something better."

"But what about our families?" a woman shouted. "Our homes? How long have we been asleep?"

The questions came in rapid succession, each more desperate than the last. Seraphina felt the weight of their fear, their confusion. She looked at Niko and saw her own uncertainty reflected in his glowing eyes.

Evelyn's voice cut through the chaos. "Enough!" The First Matriarch stepped forward, her presence instantly commanding respect. "I know you're all frightened and confused. But now is not the time to panic. We are the legacy of the Founders, all of us. And now we have the chance to fulfill their vision. To build the world they dreamed of."

Her words seemed to calm the crowd, at least temporarily. Seraphina seized the opportunity.

"Evelyn is right," she said. "We have an unprecedented opportunity here. But we must approach it methodically. First, we need to assess our resources, our manpower. Then we can begin to plan our next steps."

Marcus stepped forward, his soldier's mind already strategizing. "We should form teams. Medical, engineering, logistics. We need to know what capabilities we have."

Alara nodded, her cybernetic eye whirring as she processed the information. "I can set up a database. Start cataloging everyone's skills and experience."

"Good," Seraphina said. "Zara, I want you and your team to start medical evaluations. Make sure everyone's healthy after their long sleep. Finn, work with Marcus to set up living quarters. We need to make this place habitable for everyone."

As the others moved to complete their tasks, Niko pulled Seraphina aside. "What about me?" he asked, his voice low. "What about... this?" He gestured to his glowing eyes, the veins of energy pulsing beneath his skin.

Seraphina's heart ached at the fear and uncertainty in his voice. She cupped his face in her hands, marveling at the warmth of his skin despite his changed appearance.

"We'll figure this out," she promised. "Together. But right now, I need you. These people need you. Your connection to them... it could be crucial in helping them adjust."

Niko nodded, some of the tension leaving his shoulders.

"Okay. I'll do what I can. But Sera... what about us? After all we've been through..."

Seraphina leaned in, pressing her forehead against his. "We're still us, Niko. No matter what changes, it won't. I love you. We'll face this like we've faced everything else. Together."

Their moment was interrupted by Alara's urgent voice. "Seraphina! We've got a problem. The bunker's systems are failing. Without the Convergence energy to power them, we're running on emergency reserves. We've got maybe 48 hours before life support fails."

Seraphina's blood ran cold. They had survived the Convergence, only to face a new, equally deadly threat. She turned to Niko, seeing the same determination in his eyes that she felt.

"Looks like our plans have just been accelerated," she said. "We need to find a way to power this place, or we need to evacuate. Quickly."

The next few hours passed in a blur of activity. Teams were formed, resources cataloged, plans made and discarded. Seraphina moved from group to group, offering encouragement, making decisions, keeping everyone focused on survival.

In the engineering bay, she found Chen and a group of awakened scientists huddled around a complex array of machinery.

"Talk to me," she said, fighting to keep the exhaustion out of her voice. "What are our options?"

Chen looked up, his face streaked with grease and fatigue. "We might be able to retrofit some of the power cells from the stasis pods to boost our reserves. But that's a stopgap measure at best. We need a more permanent solution."

One of the sleeper scientists, a woman with close-cropped grey hair, spoke up. "What about geothermal energy? If we're underground, we could tap into the earth's heat."

"Possible," Chen nodded. "But risky. Drilling could destabilize the entire cave."

Seraphina's mind raced, weighing the options. "Keep working on the power cell idea. But start preliminary scans for geothermal potential. We need to be ready to move on that if we have to."

As she left the engineering bay, Seraphina nearly collided with Finn. The usually jovial man looked grim.

"We have another problem," he said without preamble. "Food. We've got enough rations for maybe a week, and that's with strict rationing. After that..."

Seraphina's stomach clenched. "Understood. What about the hydroponics bays? Can we get them operational?"

Finn shook his head. "Not without power. It's a catch-22. We need food to survive long enough to solve the power problem, but we need power to produce food."

"There might be another way," a new voice interjected. Seraphina turned to see one of the awakened sleepers, a middle-aged man with kind eyes and calloused hands. "I'm Dr. Elias Chen. I specialized in sustainable agriculture before... well, before all this. If we can gain access to the surface, I may be able to establish some fast-growing crops.

It won't solve our problem completely, but it might buy us some time."

Hope sparked in Seraphina's chest. "The surface...yes. Finn, get a team together. I want a surface reconnaissance as soon as possible. And Dr. Chen, you're with them. If there's any way to start food production up there, I want to know about it."

As Finn and Dr. Chen hurried off, Seraphina felt a familiar presence at her side. She turned to find Niko, his bright eyes filled with concern.

"You need to rest," he said quietly. "You've been walking nonstop for hours."

Seraphina shook her head. "I can't. There's too much to do. If we don't solve this power problem..."

"We will," Niko interrupted, his hand finding hers. "But you're no good to anyone if you collapse from exhaustion. Come on. Even leaders need to sleep sometimes."

Despite her protests, Seraphina found herself being led to a quiet corner of the cave. As she sank onto a makeshift cot, the full weight of her exhaustion hit her. She was asleep almost before her head hit the pillow.

She awoke to the sound of agitated voices. Blinking away the fog of sleep, Seraphina sat up to find Niko and Zara deep in conversation.

"What's going on?" she asked, her voice hoarse with sleep.

Niko turned, his face aglow with excitement. "We may have found a solution to our energy problem. Zara, tell her."

The scientist's eyes sparkled with the thrill of discovery. "It's Niko. His connection to the convergence energy... we think we might be able to use it to power the bunker. Maybe even more."

Seraphina's mind raced with the implications. "How? And what would that do to Niko?"

"We're not sure yet," Zara admitted. "But preliminary tests show that Niko is generating a significant amount of energy. If we can find a way to channel it safely..."

"No," Seraphina said, her voice firm. "It's too risky. We don't know enough about what happened to him. I won't put him in danger."

Niko knelt beside her and took her hands in his. "Sera, it's okay. I want to do this. If there's any chance I can help, I have to try."

Seraphina looked into his glowing eyes and saw the determination there. She knew that look. It was the same one she saw in the mirror every day.

"Okay," she said finally. "But we'll do this carefully. No risks. And at the first sign of danger, we stop. Understand?"

Niko nodded, a small smile playing on his lips. "Understood, boss."

As they made their way to the engineering bay, Alara's voice crackled over the comm. "Seraphina, the surface reconnaissance team is back. You'll want to hear this."

In the command center, Finn and Dr. Chen stood in front of a holographic display of the surface. Seraphina's breath caught at the image. Where she had expected a barren wasteland, she saw rolling hills covered in lush vegetation.

"It's incredible," Dr. Chen said, his voice filled with wonder. "The convergence energy... it didn't destroy. It terraformed. The whole area around the bunker is like a Garden of Eden."

Finn nodded, his usual grin tempered by awe. "And it's not stopping. We've been watching it. Plants growing, evolving in real time. It's like the whole world is waking up."

Seraphina's mind swirled with possibilities. A fertile surface meant food production, expansion, a real chance to rebuild civilization. But it also meant potential danger. Who knew what else might have evolved out there?

"All right," she said, her voice steady despite the turmoil in her mind. "We need to take advantage of this. Dr. Chen, start planning for large-scale agriculture. Finn, I want reconnaissance teams ready to map the area. But be careful. We don't know what else might be out there."

As the others moved to carry out her orders, Seraphina felt a familiar warmth at her side. She turned to find Niko, his glowing eyes fixed on the holographic display.

"It's beautiful," he said softly. "And terrifying. What have we done, Sera?"

Seraphina leaned into him, drawing strength from his presence. "We gave ourselves a chance. A chance to build something new. Something better."

Niko's arm wrapped around her waist, pulling her close. "Together?"

Seraphina smiled, feeling hope blossom in her chest for the first time in what felt like an eternity. "Together."

As they stood there, watching the image of their new world unfold before them, Seraphina knew they had faced challenges beyond anything they could have imagined. But they had done the impossible. They had united a divided people. They had literally changed the face of their world.

Whatever came next, they would face it as one. As equals. As the architects of a new Elyria.

The dawn of a new era had begun. And they were ready to meet it head on.

TWENTY-NINE
ECHOES OF PROGRESS

Sunlight streamed through the newly constructed biodome, casting mottled shadows over rows of lush vegetation. Seraphina walked among the plants, marveling at their rapid growth. Three months had passed since they had emerged from the bunker, and already the landscape was transforming.

"Impressive, isn't it?" Dr. Elias Chen's voice cut through their reverie. The agricultural expert beamed with pride as he gestured to the thriving crops. "The convergence energy has accelerated growth rates beyond anything I've ever seen. We'll have our first harvest within weeks."

Seraphina nodded, a small smile tugging at her lips. "It's a miracle, Elias. But what about the long-term effects? Are we sure this accelerated growth is sustainable?"

Elias's excitement faded slightly. "That's the million credit question. We're monitoring soil composition, nutrient levels, everything. So far, everything looks stable, but..." He trailed off, his brow furrowed.

"But we're in uncharted territory," Seraphina finished for him. She placed a reassuring hand on his shoulder. "Keep up the good work, Elias. Your team's efforts keep us all fed and hopeful."

As she left the biodome, Seraphina's comm unit buzzed. Alara's voice came through, tense with urgency. "Sera, we've got a situation in the residential sector. You'd better get down here."

Seraphina quickened her pace, her mind racing through possibilities. Integrating the awakened sleepers with the survivors of old Elyria had been... challenging, to say the least. Cultural clashes were inevitable, but they couldn't afford any major conflicts, not when their fledgling society was so fragile.

She arrived at the residential sector to find a crowd gathered, voices raised in anger. At the center of the commotion were Marcus and one of the awakened sleepers, a woman Seraphina recognized as Dr. Amelia Roth, a renowned physicist from the pre-Cataclysm era.

"What's going on?" Seraphina demanded, her voice cutting through the noise.

Marcus turned, relief in his eyes. "Seraphina, thank the mother. Dr. Roth here seems to think she can override our security protocols and access restricted areas of the old bunker."

Amelia bristled, her voice sharp with indignation. "Those 'restricted areas' contain technology that could revolutionize our power generation capabilities. Technology that I helped develop! You can't just lock it away because you're afraid of progress!"

Seraphina raised her hands, silencing both parties. "Enough. Dr. Roth, I understand your frustration, but we have protocols in place for a reason. Marcus, perhaps we've been overly cautious in restricting access to some of our resources."

She turned to the assembled crowd. "I know this transition hasn't been easy for any of us. We're trying to build something entirely new, combining the best of the old world with the realities of our current situation. But we can't do that if we're at each other's throats."

A murmur went through the crowd. An older man, one of the former Council members, spoke up. "And who put you in charge, Blackwood? Last time I checked, we didn't vote for this new 'leadership' of yours."

Seraphina felt a familiar twinge of doubt. He had a point. In the chaos of their emergence and the scramble for survival, they had fallen into old patterns. She had taken the lead because someone had to, but was that really the best way forward?

Before she could answer, a new voice cut through the tension. "She's in charge because she's earned it."

Niko stepped forward, his glowing eyes scanning the crowd. The veins of energy pulsing beneath his skin seemed to glow brighter as he spoke. "Seraphina Blackwood risked everything to save us all. She's the reason we're standing here, arguing about the future instead of being assimilated by the Convergence or starving in that bunker."

He turned to Seraphina, his eyes softening. "But he's right. We can't just fall back on the old power structures. If we're going to build a truly equal society, we're going to have to do it together. All of us."

Seraphina nodded, feeling a surge of gratitude and love for Niko. He always knew how to get to the heart of a matter. "You're absolutely right. Both of you." She addressed the crowd again. "I propose that we form a Council. Representatives from all groups - former council members, residents of the outer districts, awakened sleepers. We'll make decisions together, for the good of all Elyria."

The tension in the air eased slightly as people considered her words. Dr. Roth stepped forward, her former anger replaced by cautious interest. "And how would this council work? Who would have the final say?"

"We would have to work that out together," Seraphina replied. "But the basic principle would be equality. Every voice heard, every perspective considered."

Marcus nodded slowly. "It could work. But we'd have to set clear guidelines so that no one group could dominate the others."

As discussion broke out among the crowd, Seraphina felt a hand on her arm. She turned to find Evelyn, the First Matriarch's eyes bright with pride. "Well done," Evelyn said quietly. "This is what the Founders envisioned. A true democracy built on mutual respect and understanding."

Seraphina smiled, but before she could respond, Alara's voice crackled over the comm again. "Seraphina, Niko, you need to get to the lab immediately. Zara has made a breakthrough with the convergence energy, and... well, you need to see for yourself."

After exchanging glances with Niko, Seraphina addressed the crowd once more. "All right, let's take a break. We'll reconvene in two hours to work out the details of this new council. In the meantime, talk to each other. Share your concerns, your ideas. Remember, we're all in this together."

As the crowd dispersed, Seraphina and Niko made their way to the research lab. They found Zara hunched over a complex array of equipment, her eyes wild with excitement.

"You won't believe this," Zara said without preamble. "We've been studying the convergence energy, trying to understand its properties. And we've discovered something... incredible."

She gestured to a swirling vortex of energy contained within a force field. "This is a concentrated form of the energy. We've been able to stabilize it, control it. And watch this."

Zara pressed a button, and a small object - what looked like a piece of scrap metal - was introduced into the vortex. Before their eyes, the metal began to change, its very molecular structure shifting and reforming.

"It's not destroying the metal," Zara explained, her voice filled with awe. "It's... improving it. Making it stronger, more resilient. We think... we think we can use it to improve our technology, our infrastructure. Even our food production."

Niko stepped closer to the vortex, his own energy signature seeming to resonate with it. "I can feel it," he murmured. "It's like... it's alive, somehow. Conscious."

Seraphina's mind raced with the implications. "This could change everything. But Zara, are we sure it's safe? The Convergence almost destroyed us all. If we start playing with its energy..."

Zara nodded, her excitement tempered by caution. "You're right to be concerned. We're taking every precaution. But Seraphina, think of the possibilities. We could solve our energy problems, increase our crop yields, maybe even find ways to heal the damage done to our world by the Cataclysm."

Before Seraphina could respond, an alarm rang through the facility. Alara's voice, tense with panic, came over the comm. "We have a breach in the outer perimeter! Multiple unidentified entities approaching rapidly!"

Seraphina's blood ran cold. They'd known this day might come - that they weren't alone in this new world. But she had hoped for more time.

"Battle stations," she ordered, years of Council training kicking in. "Niko, assemble our defense teams. Zara, secure the lab. We can't allow this technology to fall into unknown hands."

As they rushed to respond to the threat, Seraphina's mind whirled. They had come so far, overcome so much. They were on the verge of building something truly remarkable. She wasn't about to let it be destroyed now.

The command center was a hive of activity when they arrived. Alara's fingers flew over the console, her cybernetic implants pulsing rapidly. "I have a visual," she announced, bringing up a holographic display.

Seraphina's breath caught in her throat. The approaching force was unlike anything she had ever seen. Humanoid figures, but twisted, changed. Not convergence, but... something else. Something that sent a shiver down her spine.

"What are they?" Niko asked, his voice tense.

"I don't know," Seraphina admitted. "But they're coming straight for us, and they don't look friendly."

As they watched, the strange beings began to spread out, encircling their fledgling settlement. Their movements were coordinated, purposeful. This was no random attack. They had been found, and for whatever reason, these creatures wanted what they had.

"Options?" Seraphina demanded, her mind running through scenarios.

Marcus stepped forward, his soldier's instincts kicking in. "We have defenses. Energy shields, weapons. But we've never tested them against a threat like this."

"We can't risk open conflict," Evelyn interjected. "Not if we don't know what we're up against. We should try to communicate, understand their intentions."

Niko's eyes glowed brighter, his connection to the Convergence energy surging. "I... I think I might be able to reach out to them. Mentally. But it's risky. If they're hostile..."

Seraphina felt the weight of leadership pressing down on her. The decision she made now could determine the fate of everything they had built. But as she looked around at the faces of her people - former enemies now united, awakened sleepers and survivors working side by side - she knew what they had to do.

"We try to communicate," she said firmly. "But we are preparing for the worst. Marcus, prepare our defenses. Evelyn, work with Zara to see if we can use the convergence energy to boost our shields. Niko..." She turned to him, her heart clenching with fear and love. "Be careful. If you feel any danger, withdraw immediately."

Niko nodded, his expression a mixture of determination and concern. "I will. And Sera? Whatever happens... I love you."

Seraphina's throat tightened with emotion. "I love you, too. Now let's save our people. Again."

As Niko closed his eyes and reached out with his newfound abilities, Seraphina turned back to the holographic display. The alien beings had halted their advance, forming a perimeter around the settlement. They were waiting.

For what, Seraphina didn't know. But as she watched Niko's face contort with concentration, as she heard the hum of their defenses powering up, as she felt the eyes of her people upon her, she knew one thing for certain.

Whatever these creatures were, whatever they wanted, she would not let them destroy what they had built. They had survived the oppression of the Council, the attack of the Convergence, the challenges of rebuilding. They would survive this, too.

The future of Elyria was once again at stake. And Seraphina was ready to fight for it, with every fiber of her being.

THIRTY
AN UNWRITTEN FUTURE

Tension crackled in the air as Niko stood at the edge of their settlement, his eyes closed in concentration. Seraphina watched, her heart pounding as tendrils of energy pulsed beneath his skin. The strange beings surrounded them, motionless, waiting.

"Anything?" she asked, her voice barely above a whisper.

Niko's brow furrowed. "It's... confusing. Their minds, they're not like ours. But I'm getting something. Images, feelings."

Marcus shifted restlessly beside them, his hand on his weapon. "Are they hostile?"

"No," Niko said slowly. "Not hostile. Curious. Frightened. I think... I think they're survivors, like us. Changed by the Convergence, but not consumed by it."

Seraphina's mind raced. Survivors. Not enemies, but potential allies. She stepped forward, her voice carrying over the tense silence.

"We mean you no harm," she called out. "We're survivors too. Maybe we can help each other."

For a long moment, nothing happened. Then one of the creatures moved. It approached slowly, its form shifting and changing with each step. As it got closer, Seraphina gasped. The creature before her was human - or had once been. Its body was a mixture of flesh and energy, constantly changing, adapting.

"You... speak?" The voice was strange, resonant, as if several voices were speaking at once.

Seraphina nodded, forcing herself to remain calm. "Yes. We're from Elyria. We survived the Convergence. Who are you?"

The form of the being rippled, settling into a more humanoid shape. "We... were. Like you. Before. The change came. Changed us. Lost... so much. But gained... something else."

Understanding dawned on Seraphina. These weren't invaders or monsters. They were victims of the Convergence, changed but not destroyed. Survivors seeking others like themselves.

"You are welcome here," she said, her voice firm. "We are building a new society, one where all are equal. Where we can learn from one another, grow together."

The being tilted her head, a gesture eerily human. "Equal? Even... us? We are... different."

Niko stepped forward, his eyes glowing with empathy. "So am I," he said quietly. "The Convergence has changed me, too. But different doesn't mean less. It means new possibilities."

A ripple went through the assembled creatures. They began to move, their forms shifting and changing. Some became more human-like, others remained in their energy forms. But the tension in the air eased, replaced by a cautious curiosity.

Seraphina turned to Marcus. "Lower the defenses. Let them in."

Marcus hesitated. "Are you sure about this? We don't know what they're capable of."

"We don't know what we're capable of either," Seraphina countered. "But we'll never find out if we let fear control us. This is our chance to build something truly inclusive, truly equal."

As the strange newcomers began to integrate into the settlement, a flurry of activity erupted. Zara and her team rushed to study the newcomers, eager to understand their unique physiology. Elias and the agricultural experts conferred with the beings, who seemed to be able to accelerate plant growth with a touch.

In the midst of the chaos, Evelyn approached Seraphina, her eyes shining with pride and wonder. "You did it," she said quietly. "This is what the founders dreamed of. A society that could adapt, grow, and embrace the unknown."

Seraphina shook her head. "We've all done it. Every person here, human or otherwise, has contributed to this moment."

A commotion near the research lab caught their attention. Alara burst out, her cybernetic implants pulsing with excitement. "Seraphina! You must see this. The energy of the Convergence, combined with the unique abilities of our new friends... it's incredible!"

They rushed to the lab, where a holographic display showed a simulation of Elyria. But not Elyria as it was - Elyria as it could be. Shining spires of living crystal, powered by clean energy. Vast gardens that seemed to defy the laws of nature. And in the midst of it all, humans and changed beings working side by side, their unique abilities complementing one another.

"It's not without risk," Zara warned, her eyes never leaving the display. "The energy is powerful, potentially dangerous if misused. But the potential... it's beyond anything we could have imagined."

Seraphina stared at the image, her mind swirling with possibilities. This was more than reconstruction. This was rebirth. A chance to create a world better than anything that had come before.

But with that potential came responsibility. The power to shape their world, to change the very nature of life itself... it could be a gift or a curse, depending on how they used it.

"We must proceed carefully," she said, her voice steady despite the excitement coursing through her. "This power... it could easily be corrupted. We need checks and balances, ways to make sure it's used for the good of all."

Niko nodded, his hand finding hers. "The Council you proposed. It's more important now than ever. We need different perspectives, voices from all groups, to guide us forward."

"Agreed," Evelyn said. "But it needs to be more than just a governing body. We need to foster a culture of responsibility, of ethical use of power. Education will be key."

As they discussed the implications, Seraphina felt a tug on her sleeve. She looked down and saw Eli, the boy she had saved what seemed like a lifetime ago.

"Miss Seraphina," he said, his eyes wide with wonder. "Is it true? Can we really build all this?" He gestured at the holographic display.

Seraphina knelt to his level, her heart swelling with hope for the future this child represented. "We can," she said quietly. "But it will take hard work and cooperation. From all of us. Are you willing to help?"

Eli nodded eagerly. "I want to learn everything. About the energy, about the new people. I want to help make Elyria amazing!"

Seraphina smiled and ruffled his hair. "That's the spirit we need. Curiosity, enthusiasm, and a willingness to work together. You'll do great things, Eli. You all will." She looked up and addressed the gathered crowd. "This is our chance to build a world where everyone can reach their full potential. Where the barriers that once divided us are bridges that unite us."

A cheer went up, humans and transformed beings alike united in their excitement for the future. But as the crowd dispersed, eager to begin work on their new projects, Seraphina felt a familiar presence at her side.

"Quite a speech," Finn said, his usual smirk tempered by genuine admiration. "You've come a long way from the uptight Councilwoman I first met."

Seraphina chuckled. "We've all come a long way. But we've got even further to go."

Finn's expression grew serious. "You know it won't be easy, don't you? There will be setbacks, conflict. Not everyone will share this vision of unity."

"I know," Seraphina nodded. "But we've already overcome so much. The oppression of the Council, the Convergence, our own fears and prejudices. Whatever comes next, we'll face it together."

As if on cue, an alarm sounded from the communications center. Alara's voice, tense with urgency, came over the comm. "Seraphina, we're receiving transmissions. From other settlements. There are more survivors out there, and they've heard about us. They want to make contact."

Seraphina exchanged glances with Niko, seeing her own mixture of excitement and apprehension reflected in his glowing eyes. This was it-the next step in their journey. The chance to spread their vision of equality and cooperation beyond their own borders.

"Tell them we're ready to talk," Seraphina said. "And prepare a delegation. It's time to reach out to our neighbors and start building a truly global community."

As preparations began for this new phase of diplomacy, Seraphina found a quiet moment alone with Niko. They stood at the edge of the settlement, looking out over the transformed landscape. The sun was setting, painting the sky in shades of purple and gold.

"Are you ready for this?" Niko asked quietly. "It's a great responsibility, shaping the future of not only Elyria, but potentially the entire world."

Seraphina leaned into him, drawing strength from his presence. "I'm scared," she admitted. "But also excited. We have a chance to do something extraordinary here, Niko. To learn from the mistakes of the past and build a better future for everyone."

Niko's arm wrapped around her waist, pulling her close. "Together?" he asked, echoing their longstanding promise.

Seraphina smiled, her heart filled with love and hope for the future. "Together," she agreed. "Always."

As they stood there, watching the sun sink below the horizon, Seraphina reflected on the journey that had brought them to this moment. From the oppressive rule of the Council to the near destruction of the Convergence, from enemies to allies to something more. They had faced impossible odds, made difficult choices, and emerged stronger for it.

The road ahead was uncertain, filled with challenges they couldn't yet imagine. But they had each other, and they had a vision of a world in which all could thrive. A world of true equality, of boundless potential, of hearts united in purpose.

The future of Elyria - of the world - was unwritten. But Seraphina knew with bone-deep certainty that whatever came next, they would face it together. As equals. As partners. As architects of a new age.

As the last light faded from the sky, Seraphina turned back to her growing community. There was work to be done, a future to build. And she was ready to face it, hand in hand with those she loved, heart full of hope for the dawn of a new day.

The end of a chapter, but the beginning of something greater. The true story of Elyria had yet to be written. And they would write it together, one day at a time.

EPILOGUE: SEEDS OF TOMORROW

The crystal spires of New Elyria glistened in the morning sun, their surfaces alive with swirling patterns of energy. Aria Blackwood-Stormwind pressed her hand against the living wall of her family's home, feeling the gentle pulse of power beneath her fingertips. Twelve years old, she still marveled at the way the city seemed to breathe, growing and changing with each passing day.

"Aria! You're going to be late for the Unity Day festivities!"

Her mother's voice snapped Aria out of her reverie. She turned to see Seraphina standing in the doorway, her once dark hair now streaked with silver. The years had etched lines around her eyes and mouth, but they were laugh lines, the marks of a life lived fully and joyfully.

"Coming, Mom!" Aria called back. She took one last look at the cityscape before hurrying inside.

In the kitchen, she found her father, Niko, preparing break-fast. The glow in his eyes had faded over the years, but veins of energy still pulsed beneath his skin, a constant reminder of the changes the Convergence had wrought.

"There's my little revolutionary," Niko said, ruffling Aria's hair as she walked by. "Ready for your big speech?"

Aria's stomach churned with a mixture of excitement and nerves. "I think so. Do you really think people will listen to a child?"

Seraphina joined them, her expression softening. "Of course they will. You represent the future, Aria. The first generation to be born into this new world. Your voice matters."

As they ate breakfast, Aria's mind wandered to the history she'd learned, the stories her parents had told her. Of a time when men and women were not equal, when fear and oppression ruled. It seemed impossible to her, looking at her parents now, so obviously partners in every sense of the word.

"Mom, Dad," she said hesitantly, "do you ever miss the old Elyria? Before all the changes?"

Her parents exchanged a look, one of those silent conversations they seemed to have so often.

"There are things I miss," Seraphina admitted. "The simplicity, sometimes. The certainty of knowing my place in the world, even if that place was flawed."

Niko nodded. "But what we've built here, what we're continuing to build... it's beyond anything we could have imagined back then. It's not perfect, but it's ours. All of ours."

Aria absorbed her words, turning them over in her mind. She thought of her classmates - humans, changed beings, and everything in between, all learning and growing together. It wasn't always easy, but it was beautiful in its complexity.

The commlink on the wall chimed, showing a familiar face. "Seraphina, Niko," Zara's voice came through, tense with urgency. "We need you in the lab. There's been a development with the Harmony Project."

Aria perked up at the mention of the project. She'd heard whispers about it - an attempt to expand their connection to the Convergence energy, to link minds across great distances. It sounded exciting, and a little frightening.

"We'll be right there," Seraphina replied. She turned to Aria, apology written all over her face. "Sorry, sweetheart. Duty calls. Will you be okay getting to the party alone?"

Aria nodded, trying to hide her disappointment. "I'll be fine. Go save the world again."

Niko chuckled and planted a kiss on the top of her head. "That's my girl. We'll be there as soon as we can. Remember, speak from your heart. That's where real change begins."

As her parents rushed off, Aria finished her breakfast in silence. She understood the importance of their work, but sometimes she wished for a simpler life. One where her parents weren't the legendary heroes who had reshaped her world.

The walk to downtown was a riot of color and sound. Beings of all shapes and sizes bustled about, preparing for the celebration of Unity Day. Aria waved to Mr. Chen, the ancient scientist who taught botany at her school, his form now more plant than human. She high-fived Spark, a being of pure energy who had become one of her closest friends.

As she approached the central square, Aria's steps slowed. Doubts crept in, whispering that she wasn't ready for this, wasn't worthy of the legacy she carried.

"Well, if it isn't the little princess herself."

Aria turned to see Finn approaching, his trademark grin firmly in place despite the grey in his hair.

"Uncle Finn!" she cried, throwing her arms around him. "I didn't know you were here!"

Finn chuckled and returned the hug. "And miss my favorite niece's big debut? Not a chance." He studied her face, his expression softening. "What's the matter, kiddo? You look like you're about to face a Convergence swarm."

Aria sighed, the fear she'd been holding back spilling out. "What if I mess up? What if I say the wrong thing and ruin everything Mom and Dad and everyone else has worked for?"

Finn knelt down and met her eyes. "Listen to me, Aria. You're not your parents. You don't have to be. You're you, and that's more than enough. The future of Elyria isn't written in stone. It's what you and your generation make of it."

His words settled something in Aria's chest. She straightened her shoulders, a familiar determination filling her. "You're right. Thank you, Uncle Finn."

As they approached the stage, Aria saw the crowd gathered in the square. Thousands of faces, all turned toward her with anticipation. She took a deep breath and centered herself, as her father had taught her.

The announcer's voice boomed. "And now, to kick off our celebration of Unity Day, please welcome Aria Blackwood-Stormwind!"

Aria stepped onto the stage, her heart pounding. For a moment, she froze, overwhelmed by the sea of faces before her. Then, in the back of the crowd, she saw them. Her parents, slightly out of breath, had made it after all. They smiled encouragingly, and Aria felt a surge of strength.

She began to speak, her voice growing stronger with each word. She spoke of the world she had inherited, of the challenges they still faced, of her dreams for the future. As she spoke, she felt something stir within her. A familiar energy pulsing in time with her heartbeat.

Gasps rippled through the crowd as tendrils of energy began to swirl around Aria, responding to her emotions. She hesitated for a moment, startled, but then embraced it. This was part of her heritage, part of who she was.

As she finished her speech, the energy gathered around her, forming a shimmering aura. The crowd erupted in cheers, beings of all kinds united in their hope for the future.

Aria descended from the stage on wobbly legs, immediately enveloped in the embrace of her parents.

"We are so proud of you," Seraphina whispered, her eyes shining with unshed tears.

Niko nodded, his expression a mixture of pride and something else. Concern, perhaps? "That was quite a performance, little spark. How do you feel?"

Aria looked at her hands, still tingling with residual energy. "Different," she admitted. "But a good different. Like... like I found a part of myself I didn't know was missing."

Her parents exchanged that look again, the one that spoke volumes without a word.

"We'll talk more about that later," Seraphina said. "For now, let's enjoy the festivities. This is your day, after all."

As they moved through the crowd, accepting congratulations and well wishes, Aria's mind swirled with possibilities. The energy she had felt, the connection to something greater than herself... it was exhilarating and a little terrifying.

She looked up at the crystal spires of New Elyria, at the faces of beings from across the spectrum of existence, at the love shining in her parents' eyes. Whatever challenges lay ahead, whatever changes were to come, Aria knew one thing for certain.

The future was unwritten, and she had a pen in her hand. It was time to start writing.